Ben Leech has had a long ‎‎‎‎‎‎‎‎‎ gh the British education system. H ‎‎‎‎‎‎‎‎‎‎ ous to the publication of this, his f ‎‎‎‎‎‎‎‎‎‎ riting as Stephen Bowkett) is la ‎‎‎‎‎‎‎‎‎‎ orror genres. He still writes for teenagers, and is starting to work on ‎‎‎‎‎ ideas also.

He has travelled across the country giving talks and running creative writing workshops.

He is now at work on further adult horror novels.

THE
COMMUNITY

BEN LEECH

PAN BOOKS
LONDON, SYDNEY
AND AUCKLAND

First published 1993 by Pan Books Ltd

a division of Pan Macmillan Publishers Limited
Cavaye Place London SW10 9PG
and Basingstoke

Associated companies throughout the world

ISBN 0 330 32973 1

9 8 7 6 5 4 3 2 1

A CIP catalogue record for this book is available from
the British Library

Typeset by Intype, London
Printed by Cox & Wyman Ltd, Reading, Berkshire

To my agent Sheila Watson
for patience and perspicacity

DIS ALITER VISUM ————————————

HEAVEN THOUGHT OTHERWISE

THE COMMUNITY

All of human life was here. Tracy watched the people pass by and knew that this was true. She looked at them and her mood was double-edged; longing and loneliness that cut and jabbed. She tipped back the remains of her drink, feeling it stale in her mouth and down her throat. Her head throbbed bluntly. She looked across at her partner for the night, her smile as unfocused as her glance.

'Another?'

'Yeah . . .' She nodded and the pain swung more forcibly behind her eyes.

'Gin and . . . ?'

Tracy shrugged. Gin and something, but the something didn't matter. The man retrieved his glass and hers, and stood up to queue at the bar.

Tracy wanted to cry. It wasn't him. It wasn't even where she found herself now, drawn to this wet Friday night in a shitty little town, in a dark anonymous pub thick with smoke and laughter. None of these things. They were the results of life's ebbtide, out of her control. Circumstances . . .

No, it was her. She felt stranded. Had it been only three months since the shrink told her she was cured now, that her therapy was complete? All of those intricate, startling dreams; those wonderful visions of people not like these – her people, calling, yearning for her to belong once again . . .

For a time, she'd thought herself a child of Atlantis, her scraps of ecstasy glints of some deeper, glowing purpose. Down in London she'd gotten into some pretty weird stuff among the oddballs and pseudo-mystics of the New Age. New Age, my ass! They'd been after what everyone was after, and as time went by and the dream went unfulfilled, she'd given it to them. Tracy the Tart, her Soho nickname; slagbag, scrubber. She was all of those things, and gladly, when the emptiness needed assuaging.

She sighed and turned on her smile for her escort.

God, she needed a miracle tonight . . .

'Gin and orange, double. Cheers, my love.'

'Bottoms up, darling.'

They both chuckled at the ambiguity, a low shared sound full of knowing.

A break in the monotonous rap-rhythm of the jukebox caused conversations to pause a moment. Tracy and Walter – Jesus, could this be happening to her? – gazed into the pub's hazy depths. Nearby, a girl was playing pinball. A regular, she was wearing an American baseball cap, a Coke-Is-It T-shirt and tight blue jeans. Her blonde hair hung down in a pert ponytail and her feet, in their stylish Reeboks, tapped even in the musicless lull.

Tracy watched the man staring and wondered if he'd abandon her for this rival before the evening was out. A cold gust of desperation swept through her.

More music started, a megamix staple diet high on bulk, low on nourishment. The pinball girl's backside started to twitch and sway.

'Hey, remember me?' Tracy said, voice husky with sadness, not sex. She slid her hand under the table and along his thigh. He was rock hard there already, but she knew that when they made it, he would not see *her* face in front of him.

2

He gulped his drink in a single tilt and took her hand and led her out.

The rain had just about stopped; fitful specklings that seemed to drop the temperature an extra couple of degrees. Tracy's thin windcheater was no protection: she was shivering two yards out on to the pavement. Walter's breath steamed as he took a double handful of her curls and dragged her close, close, his tongue licking out her mouth. She gasped at him, pushed and grasped and hugged. Cheap gutter beauty bought by the hour, but she didn't care. At least she was near to someone!

'Come on, sweet. I want it now.'

He led her like baggage away from the Talbot's gaudy frontage lights, left, left again to his car parked in puddles around the back. There was a battered Ford Transit keeping it company, and a superb black and chrome Norton bike that glittered seductively with raindrops raised on its wax.

Walter headed for his grey Sierra, de-activating the alarm with a bleep of his keyring gadget. He walked round and opened the passenger door for Tracy, she allowing his hands to feel and fondle as she deliberately took her time climbing in.

He turned on the engine and pushed up the heater-slide all the way, to warm the cab. Meanwhile, Tracy went about her work, hauling off the windcheater, lifting her woollen sweater up and over her head. She heard Walter's harsh breathing, each breath trembling, and then a moan as her bra came off and she showed herself to him. She spent a few seconds planing her hands across her own breasts, faking self-pleasure, then slowly leaned forward and tugged down his zip. He was hot and smelling of arousal; her lips felt cold on his flesh. He began the hip-shimmy and Tracy took it from there, controlling him with ease.

They moved with a kind of first-date clumsiness, awkwardly, urgently undressing; both finding the indignity of the struggle amazingly erotic. Walter pushed Tracy down into the tilted-back passenger seat, angled himself between her upthrust legs and eased into her, his face a snarl. Their movements rhythmed up, almost a choreographed battle; phased, together. Walter started to grunt.

Tracy closed her eyes and reached for the images that burst in such ephemeral moments of passion. She felt the man's wiry chest hair tickling her smoothness, his lips around her face and eyes in gadfly kisses. He increased his pace and weight, his hands pushing her thighs apart further.

'Ah, Wa – Walter. What are you doing there?'

And yes – now! That second of extreme meaning: a clarity of vision beyond anything glimpsed in ordinary mundane life. Her kinsfolk, calling. Come home. Come home. The reason for her being . . .

After a series of ragged, rising cries, Walter roared out, rose up above her and in his twisted passion backhanded her across the face, twice, three times. Her own cries and sobs were wild, pain and pleasure contending. She could not stop coming, even after he had withdrawn.

But then, the melting away: the reason for the universe being here folding back into itself. The cold world returned and Tracy felt herself growing pointless and very tired.

She hauled on her jeans and sweater, her skin prickly in the stuffy confines of the car. Walter was cursing softly, busying himself with tissues on the smart upholstery. Tracy wanted to laugh at him – laugh and laugh. He was a travelling salesman in lightbulbs.

When she mentioned it, he paid her with bad grace, a little extra for hitting her.

'Bye bye, Walter,' she said with no emotion at all, and stepped out of the car leaving the door open.

'Filthy fucking bitch,' he told her, then reached across to slam the door closed.

'I hope your dick drops off, Walter,' Tracy said quietly as the Sierra's back wheels whirled in greasy mud, gained traction after a second and spun away. She watched the tail-lights flare at the alley junction. Then he was gone.

Tracy thought that maybe she'd go back in for another drink, or at least to get warm. Maybe shoot a game of pinball. Maybe wiggle her rear for the punters.

She smiled, feeling desolate.

It was raining again.

He was the tide, and she was the moon he had been chasing. Drawn by the same backwash that had brought her here, the stranger stood in shadows and watched as the liaison ended and the rain-speckled Sierra jounced away over the rutted car park and down the narrow side-lane. He strained to see details of the girl's face in the fleeting bloom of brakelights: it was a roundish face, tending towards plumpness. A nice face. Her body likewise, though a little bulgy in her Levi's. She didn't look like a whore, he thought distantly: but then, who could ever judge from appearances?

The girl gave a kind of sigh and fluffed up her black curls that were threatening to damp down to stringy rats-tails in the drizzle. She was wearing a thin, pale blue showerproof that he thought would be woefully inadequate for these October temperatures.

Ah well, it wouldn't matter for much longer . . .

He was ready, had prepared well; followed her invisibly since her arrival in this town just over a week ago. She was not even a novice at what the two of them shared: his perceptions were vastly more powerful, more precise. He had looked through her eyes at the squalid two-room bedsit she had taken in a poor street not far away; dressed as she dressed, fed as she fed. Her couplings with straining, hoggish punters had disturbed him greatly at first, and excited him ... He chuckled silently to think that he had almost scraped up the money to visit her personally ... But that would have smeared human indignity across what he had to do; made it less than just necessary.

But still, he saw that she was confused and alone, trying so very hard to make sense of a life that would always be senseless to her. She could never understand. Her blood had been thinned too fine during the long course of her ancestry.

She shrugged up the windcheater's hood over her hair, wrapped her arms about herself and began to negotiate the puddle-field back towards the pub.

The stranger bent, unzipped his bag, then stood up and waited for her.

The sight of the man standing there in darkness gave Tracy a quick shock. For an instant she thought that bastard Walter had returned to claim back his money, or perhaps to rough her around a bit more ... but, no. This guy was taller, thinner; almost gangly. She squinted, trying to bring detail out of the gloom: beyond him, the orange light of a sodium streetlamp smeared like veils in the rain, casting false colour across his right side. His eyes looked sunken and tired; his hair long and unkempt. He was wearing a frayed sleeveless denim jacket over a scuffed and worn black leather one, and oily jeans patched at the knee – she wondered if the Norton was his (and did he want a ride?). He was smiling ... Or was it another kind of expression moulding that ragged face so strangely?

This gathering of impressions, and the flow of her thoughts, ended abruptly as he took a single decisive step towards her and swept his arm by, slicing her throat.

'Jeeezussss!' Tracy hissed at the sheer unexpectedness of this act; the second syllable sprayed out in blood.

She wondered whether to run, but the man had his left hand clamped to her chin and was forcing her back against the wall: she felt it hard and cold and wet, braced herself, tried to struggle—

He drew back the knife and plunged it into her abdomen. She heard her stomach puncture, rather than felt it; and was shocked by the steam and the stink, and the hot flow of her own liquids down her legs.

'Please,' she tried to say, but was now beyond all speaking. Their eyes were still locked, though, and in his she saw many wonderful changes of mood, many pictures, many promises.

Please.

Tracy sagged down the wall and sat on her own entrails. Her windcheater crumpled up around her shoulders with a crackling sound. The dark rich glint of her blood in the rain and the splashed puddles amazed her – and that she was still alive.

Now the killer loosed his grip, rummaged unhurriedly in a bag for a change of weapon.

Tracy felt darkness coming closer, but yet, perversely, wanted to stay around to see how this would end . . .

If she had been able to laugh, she would have laughed at that.

He advanced once more carrying – oh, God Almighty – it was a cleaver. Its first swing took off her arm very cleanly. The second, her head.

Tracy watched him complete his business with a detached interest. He was soaked in her, and sobbing. How odd that such barbarism should make her want to mother him, because he was sobbing and looked so lost. No hope of telling him that now, and yet, beneath the pain and beyond it, something was happening. She saw horizons, both in time and space: ages and light-years whirling together, mixed with dreams of home.

I'm home, she thought, struck by the wonder of it. This is where it has all been leading to . . .

The stranger was almost collapsing in his efforts, crawling in the mud to chop and chop. How ridiculous, Tracy mused; he must know I can't do him any harm at this stage. Although her mutilated hand still trembled in supplication, and her torso, she could see, heaved yet as if to right itself and hurry away.

I'm sorry, a voice crept into her mind, soulfully. I'm sorry. And in a whispered background many voices, a million of them, bemoaned her fate and shared a grief at her ending that she, even now, did not feel.

The stranger flung the cleaver back into the bag, where it clinked against other tools. Now he picked up a square metal can and sloshed liquid over the wall and the alley, and her remains. When the petrol leapt at her eyes, she blinked frantically to clear them.

The dropped match called up a wonderful curtain of colour and light. It swept towards her.

I'm sorry, he told her in agony, I'm sorry.

And in her final instant, she forgave him and wept also with a fragment of understanding.

The killer watched the fire do its work. Somebody stepped into the alley to pee, saw what was happening and ran off, trailing screams.

No time now. He had to leave.

But he stayed on and stayed on in desperate indecision,

not wanting to be caught, for his purpose wasn't fulfilled: not daring to leave just yet, until he was sure she could not return later to haunt him.

Pete McAuliffe read about it in the midday edition of the *Clayton Herald*, stood up and dropped his ham and tomato sandwich into the wastebin. The ambience of weary boredom that hung in the air of the staffroom together with wreaths of still cigarette smoke became tainted with a vague disgust, and more than a distant fear that such a gross murder could have happened in Clayton.

'Bloody animal!' he spat out to no one in particular, to the world in general. McAuliffe made himself another coffee and chucked ten pence into the Swindle pot. He returned to his seat, decided for the third time that he bloody well was not going to mark that pile of exercise books in his lunch hour, and picked up the paper again.

The details of Tracy Vines's murder were sparse but spectacular; frightening, because her annihilation had been so brutal and so motiveless. More than that, she had been the second victim slain by fire in nine months. The first was a middle-aged man – McAuliffe thought his name was Johnson – who had been found in his burned-out car on the Colliersby road last February. Then, as now, not much was given away officially but gossip had spread through the town that the guy had been dismembered and badly hacked up before being torched.

McAuliffe took a few seconds that were taut with private horror, thinking about what it would be like to die thus; taken apart, still conscious, then burnt. It was beyond his imagining, he realized.

He rewrapped the rest of his sandwiches in their polythene, pitched them at the condominium of pigeon-holes racked along one wall, and found his own with unerring accuracy.

'Years of practice,' he told Matheson opposite. 'Too many sodding years of practice!'

Matheson stirred himself enough to laugh.

McAuliffe stood up and headed for the door. The stale atmosphere was aggravating his asthmatic condition; but more than that, he felt claustrophobic in the staffroom, and despised himself briefly for letting his life shrink down to musings on the agony and terror of someone else's dying.

Jesus, he thought, as he snatched his coat from the gents' cloakroom, that's what the real world is about: it's about war and madness, fear and disease; it's about compassion and struggle, triumph, love . . . And here I am teaching the niceties of clause analysis to kids who want to be out there engaging with the world – wrestling with the stuff it's made of.

McAuliffe experienced a second's splintering anger that life had led him the cowardly way through.

Then he slipped on his mackintosh and walked towards the nearest exit.

Foggy day, progressively lost in greyness. McAuliffe found himself walking around the battered high chainlink of the tennis courts: a few kids were playing a hit-and-miss game in the murk, but most were inside where, if it was noisy and stuffy, at least it was warm. They called to him – Hello, sir! – with no sarcasm. He lifted his hand, raised a smile and walked on.

Peter McAuliffe was thirty-eight years old and had been teaching for seventeen years. 'Mid-career' everyone else called it, but that implied a career, some kind of upward and onward progression that had not come along in his case. It had been easier simply to sit out the years, dabbling at writing and evening-class work, dreaming big dreams, waiting for that major break to happen. Or even a minor one, now, he admitted to himself; although he was loath to admit any more that in fact he had made one huge balls-up of his life and would die without ever impacting on the world. Comfortably married; nice house; nice car; no kids; no prospects. Only old age – and that's what scared him most. McAuliffe calculated, in his most depressing thought of the day, that he had been young so far in his life, but would spend the rest of it old. 'Life begins at forty', just two years away. He guessed it was a euphemism for 'death begins at forty', so whatever you planned to do, it's too late now, sucker!

His ramble took him to the very edge of the playing fields, and back twenty years to his college days. Then, he'd had hair, plenty of it that he'd worn long and straight in the current style. It had been a kind of trademark, along with his old suede coat with the woollen collar and elaborate embroidery that his incredibly sexy girlfriend had done for him over the first term of their relationship . . . That girlfriend had become his wife Judith, and the coat had at last been consigned to the trash-bin when his 'career' as a professional had started. Now, his head addled with chalk-dusty dreams, he just leered secretly at the girls he would once have pursued, filling his free hours with a bitter mixture of reminiscence and despair—

McAuliffe's foot twisted itself in a ruck in the grass. He stumbled, swore with all the heat he could muster, and decided to stop being a maudlin old fart and get back to the staffroom: it might not be sane there, but at least he could anchor his suicidal impulses in good solid apathy.

A message was waiting upon his return, together with Matheson's bad temper. 'Could you come down to the Head's office after p.m. register, please?' the note said, signed by Doreen the secretary: Matheson was not quite so polite.

'And it's muggins who's been caught to baby-mind your bloody lot this afternoon!'

McAuliffe just shrugged. 'Don't blame me, Dave. I've no idea what this is about.'

'Reckon they must have found out about your black-marketeering in board rubbers,' Matheson said with rough-edged humour. 'Either that, or you've been touching up the Year Tens.'

'I'll leave that to the dirty old men on the staff – young man,' he added, as the other glared at him over the rim of his paper.

The Head – or 'Headess' as she was universally titled – packed the firepower of a Sherman tank and tits like barrage balloons. Out of hearing the staff and kids alike called her Molly French, for reasons that McAuliffe had never yet fully comprehended. Close up, she was known as Mrs Adams.

McAuliffe sat in the outer sanctum a little nervously. He hated not knowing what something was about: loved to have it all planned out. That's what came of living to timetables.

Molly did not keep him waiting for more than ten minutes, after which time Doreen asked him to go through, and would he like coffee or tea?

'Tea,' McAuliffe decided, 'please,' and made a small joke to cover up his awkwardness as he walked into Adams's office. After all these years he was still intimidated by authority . . .

The Headess was seated behind her strategically placed oak desk, finishing a chatty sentence with a guest. McAuliffe glanced and did a double take. The girl was striking: not beautiful, but oddly startling. Dark-haired, pale-complexioned, with eyes so deep they were beyond his fathoming. She was subtly made up, carefully dressed in a smart skirt and jacket. But an echo of memory placed her in some other context ...

'Mr McAuliffe,' said Molly, all smiles and politeness, 'I trust you remember Christine Lamb. Studied in our sixth form a couple of years ago. She's at university now.'

'Of course,' McAuliffe said, shaking hands formally before taking the only empty chair. Molly loved academic achievement and would die happy if any ex-pupil gained a first at Oxbridge. 'Have you come to teach?'

'Actually, no. I've asked Mrs Adams if I can do some counselling work as part of my undergraduate studies. I'm at Lancaster ...'

McAuliffe smiled. He'd forgotten her lilting Scottish Lowland accent but now, as the girl spoke, the jigsaw of memory pieced itself completely: she'd been one of the A Level students he'd leered after, but alas, and of course, never attained.

'Well, you can gladly counsel my lot; there're some real psych – some really interesting cases to be found there. You're training for social work?'

'More likely child psychology in the end: depends on my end-of-year grades.'

'Sure. Well, if I can help ...'

'That's why I summoned you, Mr McAuliffe.' Molly brightly but firmly took control of the situation again. 'Since you do a lot of your teaching at the lower end of the ability range, and since you live locally and know the community, I've suggested to Miss Lamb that she might shadow your classes for the duration of her visit.'

'Certainly.' McAuliffe found himself in a playful mood. 'And while it's true to say that I do teach at the lower end, I'm sure Miss Lamb will confirm that even the cleverest of children might be in need of her skills – the stress of genius, and all that!'

'It goes without saying, Mr McAuliffe.' Molly coloured slightly and swung her eyes towards him.

Well, that's blown out my promotion, McAuliffe thought wryly.

And he didn't give a shit.

Since that crusty old bugger Matheson was covering his lessons, McAuliffe decided that a coffee with Christine Lamb as part of her induction into the school would be a good idea. But he didn't take her to the staffroom: the place was a shameful tip. And anyway, no point in starting gossip prematurely.

He walked her over to the sixth-form block, where there was a vending machine and a quiet, open area for them to sit. Somehow, McAuliffe didn't mind so much if students saw him with this girl: maybe it was because they were old enough to smell the truth, but too young yet to be cynical about it.

'Old stamping ground.' He pushed coins into the machine and pressed for two coffees without asking her.

'Yours or mine, Mr McAuliffe?'

She was smiling at him slightly, had the measure and the better of him straight away. Hell, did university make you grow up so fast and so sharp these days? Couldn't the modern woman in her equality deal with small talk without suspecting ulterior motives (even if they existed)?

'Pete, please. It'll make both our jobs easier . . .'

'OK. And sorry. It's just that this place used to be a leg-watcher's haven—'

'Yours, or mine?' he wanted to know, raising a laugh from her. And the ice, it seemed, was broken.

'Why back to Clayton?' he asked when they were settled. 'Family?'

Her shrug was delicate but, he thought, guarded.

'Um, no. It's just that I know the school. I don't have family here; they're all up in Scotland—'

'But—'

'Some friends looked after me when I was a pupil here.'

'Ah.' But again, why Clayton? McAuliffe held back from pressing for an answer, not wanting to sour any professional or personal relationship with Christine Lamb.

'But you've got digs . . . ?'

She sipped coffee tentatively and almost didn't grimace.

'A house I rent, with a friend.'

'Right.'

'Down on the Western Road.'

McAuliffe knew the street: it was not even half a mile from where the murder had happened. Real slummy area.

'Nice view of the old railway yard.'

'And you can see the gasworks on a clear day.'

She smiled at him, and that smile was lovely. He felt a sense of sudden, shuddering loss that he'd painted himself into this dull corner over the years; a cul-de-sac job in a nowhere town, all ready for the downhill run into his grave. Quite without warning, McAuliffe was aware of his thinning hair and the crowsfeet around his eyes. And did his beergut show? This girl was unselfconsciously powerfully attractive to him, whether she knew it or not. But, he guessed, he was just not in the running.

The conclusion depressed him immensely, and it was he who terminated the conversation by downing his drink and rising.

'Right then, I must get back to the little ba— to the little darlings. When do you start your project here?'

'Monday. And I have to admit, I'm slightly nervous of it. I mean, when you're one of the crowd, one of the kids, you feel kind of safe in your anonymity.'

'Yeah, I know. But don't worry. I'll steer you through until you've found your feet. You'll get used to being on the other side of the desk.' He smiled, and thought, God, how you'll get used to it!

They walked out into the chill fog, which had thinned, like much-washed linen, to show the faint blue of the sky. McAuliffe doubted that the sun would make it through before it set.

'Might be a frost tonight,' he said idly.

'Likely. I'll turn the fire up full.'

'Shall I see you to the gates?'

'No need.' She faced him, and across the yard's distance between them, McAuliffe smelled the shampoo she used. His heart started to tear. 'I used to play truant here, remember.'

'And never got caught.'

'Never,' she agreed. 'See you Monday, Pete.'

'Yep. A lamb to the slaughter, eh?'

She didn't laugh, and he felt a fool.

'Bye,' she called to him, walking away, fading into the fog and out of his sight.

Safe home, Christine, McAuliffe thought, and sod it!

Doctor Marius was fifteen years older than D.I. Scobie,

and had been in the job for that much longer. Over that time he had built up a system of working, and a reputation, that led to his nickname of 'Doctor Dissection'. He didn't mind it, unless it was used openly and in front of the Chief Inspector. In fact, it pleased him to think that his punctilious techniques of analysis were so clearly recognized. If it could be taken apart, it could be understood: that was his private motto, and the source of his success in this, the most unusual of jobs.

Trouble was, what the hell did you do when that motto broke down?

He turned to Scobie standing a discreet yard away.

'Damnedest thing.' His voice was muffled through the mask.

Scobie nodded, his eyes squinting and thin. He hated morgues, always had: they always smelt of liver, even through the drop of olbas oil he put on the gauze of his mask. And the liver smell was strong today, mixed with the stink of char.

'Bitch of a way to die.'

'I wasn't meaning that, but you're right of course.'

Both men looked at the small pile of black remains laid out on the plastic sheet. For all his infractions of the law, the landlord of the Talbot had been quick on this occasion, both in calling the cops and dealing with the situation. No hope for the victim, of course: she – Marius was sure of that much – she would have died in the first few seconds of the axe attack prior to being set alight. But without the landlord's swift action in smothering the flames, not even these few burnt bones would have been left.

Marius now touched at a splintered length with a probe.

'I mean, there are some odd features here. Deformities.'

'What?'

'Well, I think so. You want me to get technical?'

'Will it help?' Scobie sighed. It rarely did, but Marius took a delight in rolling out those Latin tags.

'Here we have what's left of the victim's second cervical vertebra, lateral surface facing us. Notice the unusual elongation of the transverse process, which is paralleled on the corresponding side . . .'

'So?'

Marius paused in his 'lecturette', as Scobie called them, and tried to hide his impatience.

'The purpose of these processes is to act as anchor points for the tendons which support the spine and the slabs of muscle plating the back. Lower down, these areas form articulating surfaces with the ribs. If the elongations were not simply deformities, they would suggest a grotesquely powerful musculature uncharacteristic of the species . . .'

'You mean, not human?'

'Don't get science-fictional, Detective Inspector.' Marius tutted. He paused to let the barb sink in, then probed delicately again and continued.

'Look here, also, at the linked enlargement of the vertebrarterial canal, through which the vertebral artery passes, and the neural canal that acts as a channel for the spinal cord: both spaces bigger than they should be – suggesting once again, either a deformation of the bone, or a huge throughput of blood and nerve tissue.'

'That it?'

Marius let his eyes flash fire. He appreciated Scobie as a good cop, but Christ he was a poor listener!

'One more thing.' The pathologist eased aside another fragment, curved and about six inches long. 'It is a rib, possibly the fifth or sixth to judge from the degree of curvature relative to length. Here's the costal groove ...'

Sounds like a dance, Scobie thought, but said nothing.

'Now, look—'

Marius held the end of the rib with one gloved hand and took a spatula from his labcoat pocket. He pushed its flat, spoonlike end against the specimen.

Instantly, a speckling of black flakes fell away, exposing pinkish bone tissue. More pressure produced a thin oozing of blood.

'So ...' Scobie fought for understanding.

'So the tissue was not utterly destroyed, as it should have been. This is living bone, Detective Inspector. Nineteen hours after the death of the body, this piece of bone lives on.'

'Conclusions, then?'

Marius did not know whether to get angry or sarcastic.

'None. It's a vanishingly rare phenomenon, a fluke of nature. Taken with the oddly formed vertebra, though, it makes a mystery ...' Marius drew a green sheet over the remains and pulled down his facemask. Scobie followed suit.

'I really would have liked to meet that girl,' the pathologist said.

He showed Scobie to the door. They paused there and both turned round to look back at the slab.

'Same m.o. as the Johnson case.'

'Looks like it. Dismemberment followed by incineration ...'

'We'd never have found out the guy's identity if the licence plates of his car hadn't survived.'

'But the two killings are eight months apart,' Marius pointed out. 'Would the murderer hang around for so long?

Or even return to Clayton to repeat the crime? Why?'

'Another mystery, Doctor.' Scobie felt cold, and a certain sickness sloshed in his stomach. What was left of the girl formed such a pathetic scattering. She had been loved by somebody once, and had loved in return. She would have played on roundabouts and swings, yawned her way through school and shivered with delight on Christmas morning. Somebody out there would be missing her.

Scobie almost heaved. The liver smell was back.

'We're just fucking animals,' he proclaimed with a sneer, 'all of us.'

Marius looked at him, deadpan. 'What you choose to do at the weekend, D.I., is entirely your own affair.'

Another nightfall; the sun almost down in the thickening layers of bloodsoaked cloud. Christine Lamb stepped off the bus and waited until the straggle of other passengers had walked out of sight. Colder tonight; more fog coming down. And a frost, as McAuliffe had said. Shoplights and streetlights were on, and rush-hour traffic crawled along the congested main roadways.

She walked a hundred yards from the stop, then turned left into a much quieter road; a dead-end street in more ways than one. On the right were the old railwaymen's cottages that formed a now dilapidated redbrick terrace: no front gardens, but a thin and miserly strip at the back adjoining the gardens of the next row. On the left stood a sagging barrier of prefab-concrete wallslabs, supplemented by corrugated-iron sheeting where the concrete had crumbled. Almost opposite Christine's house, number sixteen, were the old double gates to the railway yard; bolted and barricaded, fringed with barbed-wire coils, they had not been opened in years. No one ever went in there. No one would ever want to.

She fumbled in her pocket for the house key, a tarnished Yale. It was laughable. The door looked to be made of warped hardboard, painted a pale lime green, with a grey letterbox of spotted aluminium. A single strong blow could cave the whole thing in, making the lock redundant. But a burglar would find nothing useful to steal inside, though much, maybe, that he had never bargained for.

She stepped straight off the pavement and into the gloomy hallway. The smell hit her two steps down the passage; a hot, meaty stink of blood, of excrement. Her heart pulsed more strongly as she hurried to the living room and stumbled inside.

'Bruce?'

For a terrible instant, she failed to take in the scene: the light was dim, a rosy-red light from the gas fire, all its radiants glowing full on, the gas hissing quietly in the room's close silences.

He was huddled there, covered in a blanket. Another blanket, a mound of pink shadow, was tossed into a corner.

'Bruce,' she said again, more quietly, less in alarm. She knelt beside him and felt his body, searching, judging. The man was trembling as though in a fever. Sweat gleamed on the paleness of his skin, making his black hair and eyebrows stand out starkly.

'OK, Chris. S-Still here.'

'Thank God for that. Are you cold?'

'Warmer now . . .' but his voice was shivering, close to collapse. She should never have left him, and cursed herself mentally for her absence. At the same time, Christine felt a slowly growing apprehension that the whole plan was coming apart – and it would be her fault, hers and this weakling's!

'Can you hear them? Are they talking to you?'

He nodded without speaking. Together they listened: it was like seashells pressed to the ears, a faraway lambent swishing of tidewaters that unravelled moment by moment into individual voices. The voices of the Kin. And, like the sea, the sound had layers that swirled through all the levels of the mind: bright whitecaps of immediate meaning, darker depths of barely fathomed fears.

She hugged him tight.

'They'll never leave you, Bruce. I won't. But you know that we can't stay in this house indefinitely. We must feed . . . I don't mind going out. You stay in, conserve your energy; keep yourself strong—'

'Strong!' His bark of laughter was almost hysterical, and as he glared at her with wild eyes, his open jaws seemed to stretch and bulge, and pieces of flesh writhed busily within.

Christine slapped his face, following up by drawing him to her as the pain of her blow stung and startled him.

'I'm not strong,' he told her more calmly, on a shuddering sob. His breath was hot on her shoulder. 'I can't do it. They should have picked you.'

He lifted his head, like a dumb animal away from its master's support, and regarded her fearfully.

'I almost lost control earlier.' He giggled. 'After all these years of stability, I nearly blew it.'

'OK, OK, Bruce . . .' she began, but his eyes had swung to look at the corner, at the blanket stirring sluggishly in the hot room.

Christine took a deep breath, rose and went over. She dragged the blanket away. The flesh beneath was shapeless, pointless; not even foetal, not even the beginnings of differentiation. Without direction, it was merely and temporarily alive: muscle, nerves, maybe some rudimentary bone tissue that was probably unarticulated. No senses. No sense.

She felt a profound self-sorrow, then, that original greatness should have come to this – but not just sorrow for herself. Her pain was close to grief for all the lives of her people descended to frantic scuttlings in human towns; hidden, hunted, hoarding up the last wealth and energy to try for a new start. Well, October would see the end of it one way or another.

Bruce looked away, turning back to the fire. Christine busied herself. She quickly stripped; jacket, skirt, blouse; unashamedly and without exciting any interest in her companion. She hauled on a pair of black denim jeans and a purple mohair sweater, then went out to the hall for a quilted jacket, her warmest.

She covered up the slowly moving shape and lifted it in the blanket, struggled with it out of doors to the back garden. It was a wilderness of bramble and long-untended roses frozen and rotted on the stem. At the bottom, beside the fallen-in remains of a shed, was a dustbin with holes hammered in the sides, the site of many old bonfires.

Christine part-filled the bin with sticks and grass, laid down the thing in its shroud; went back inside for newspaper and the bottle of white spirit she remembered seeing under the kitchen sink.

She poured the spirit over the pile and threw in a match. The flames boasted more vigour than the pathetic offspring could ever have managed. She hoped its pain was brief and that nothing had grown within it that would harbour transient hate or blame, or even a knowledge that this was its fate.

The fire burned high and hot for a few minutes before dying down, its pale smoke lifting into the fog coagulating over this part of Clayton, close to the river.

She waited on until the last sparks guttered out, then turned and walked back towards the house. Hurt, fear, the dread of the coming doom all fled through her soul.

But never once did she think to pray.

Melsham was a quiet one-shop village a few miles out of Clayton. McAuliffe regretted that the pinnacle of his achievement thus far took the form of a four-bedroom detached on the main street, and a double garage – for his Nova and her Fiat Panda, both of which he refused ever to wash on a Sunday morning, in contrast to the other residents of the road. For Melsham was a respectable place, at least by outward appearances. There was the Grange on the southern end (the village itself standing on what used to be the Earl of Calvering's land), and nearby the Manor Farm which housed one of the finest collections of rare pig breeds in the country. The pub – the Crown – did not allow in kids wearing motorbike leathers, and closed promptly at eleven p.m., except for those few regulars who were well known to the landlord. And of course, the milkman was deferential and never made passes at Melsham's bored housewives.

At least, McAuliffe assumed he didn't. He wondered if 'Mr Goldtop' had ever tried his luck with Judith: the notion made him grin. Judith was so prim he was amazed she didn't demand McAuliffe take a mistress, to save her the ordeal of making love. But then, maybe he was being unfair. It was as much his fault as hers that their intimacies were so rare and, then, so conventional. He recalled the old joke about a teacher's twelve-pack of condoms – save money, buy a twelve–pack: one johnny for January, one for February, one for March . . .

He swung the Nova up on to the metalled driveway

and cut the engine. As soon as the blower went off, he felt the cab cooling: the first wisps and coils of mist were already curling around the front garden's neatly planted cherry tree. But the house looked warm and welcoming behind its glowing green curtains.

McAuliffe used his key and stepped inside. The hallway smelt of sweet potpourri overlaid with the spice of the casserole Judith had put in the oven in time to be ready by six.

'Home, love!'

'Down in a minute,' came the voice from upstairs. McAuliffe had a moment's wild vision of 'Mr Goldtop' dragging on his trousers and jamming his peaked cap aslant on his head before swinging down the Virginia creeper to his turbo-charged milk-float parked discreetly round the back.

He was still smiling as Judith came through to the lounge and leaned over the sofa back to peck a kiss on his head.

'Had a good day, Pete?'

'TGIF, my love – Thank God It's Friday.' She never remembered the acronym.

'And Saturday tomorrow. What shall we do?'

'Stay in and play Monopoly.' McAuliffe turned round to look at her, hoping his silly wit had not been misplaced. He saw that it had; her smile was faint and ambiguous. These days, it was a smile that often infuriated him; a face that often infuriated him. What did familiarity breed? But it also bred sparse moments of the deepest love he had ever known for another person, made all the more poignant because of the staleness in between. Judith was still very attractive; still thin, almost skinny, with a waist he could encircle with one arm. And her fair hair had not greyed at all: she wore it long and proudly during the casual day, tying it up into elaborate plaits and knots only for the dinner parties McAuliffe was occasionally forced to suffer.

'Have you been working today?' he asked, hoping by this conversational jujitsu to divert the sting of his clumsy humour.

The smile came back more warmly. Judith held out her hand.

'Come on, I'll show you.'

They went along the hall, through the steamy savoury kitchen and into the plant-infested conservatory that was Judith McAuliffe's workplace. Art had been her major subject at college, and McAuliffe still felt she'd been lucky to have both talent and determination and – let's face it – a husband willing to support her while she carved out a career.

It was still not completely a career, he concluded. Even after these long years, her earnings did not match his own. She'd illustrated a few children's books that had sold moderately well, had a few of her finer pictures taken by a gallery shop in London (bigger money there, but rare sales); and she always did a roaring trade at the biannual craft fairs at the Grange, usually with her hand-printed greetings' cards and watercolours. A tantalizing glimpse of success, rather than the full-blown bucks-in-the-pocket achievement she so badly wanted, and quite properly deserved.

The conservatory was cosy and pleasantly warm, its glass surfaces covered by pulldown pastel blinds. A brick ledge ran right the way round, save for the back wall, and on this was scattered a profusion of house palms and ivies, tradescantias and many others that McAuliffe had never bothered to identify. The air smelt of peat and paint: he imagined it would be lovely to sit here alone on a silent sunny afternoon, pondering your place in the scheme of things. Kind of transcendental. Briefly, he envied her.

Judith did not let go of his hand until she had placed him in front of the easel on which was perched her latest work. McAuliffe mentally described it as a 'mistscape', and was immediately impressed. A wash of pearly shades creating depth and mystery, the light gathering and gathering upwards to a splash of abalone brightness near the top left corner, where the sun was hidden behind veils. Through indeterminate distances, McAuliffe could almost see the shadows of trees and hedges, Melsham's church spire, the planing wing of a bird in flight . . .

He lifted the canvas off its pegs and held it up.

'That', he told her, 'is not bad!'

'Only not bad?' Her pout was sexy, but serious. He frowned.

'You know me, Jude – a master of understatement. By "not bad", I mean "bloody brilliant".'

'So when your students get a C-plus for their essays, they ought to feel desperately pleased with themselves?'

'That's about it . . .'

He felt the mood start to change, like ice entering the air. It was a familiar pattern between them. If he wasn't careful, the conversation would get heavy, a minefield of subtexts he couldn't handle right now: didn't want to.

He put the painting gently back and turned to her.

'You have skill and imagination, Jude, and an incredible perseverance that makes me jealous. Me, I get cynical when what I want fails to come along: you get more determined. That's a lot going for you. And anyway, I love you.'

'I love you too, Pete,' she said, and snuggled into his chest.

'I'll make some drinks, then we'll eat. And then—'

'Early night?' she suggested. He'd had TV together in mind.

'I'm randy already . . .'

She did not trouble to confirm that statement. Instead, she became bustle-y and said she'd check on the casserole.

He followed her back, helped set the table, went through to the kitchen where she was flushed and harried-looking as she tried to have everything ready at once. A strand of loose hair floated down in front of her eyes. She stopped to blow it aside.

'G-and-T?' McAuliffe asked gently.

'Yes, if you like,' she said without pausing from her crisis. He bit back his temper and made up the drinks. Two strong ones.

But the meal went well. They chatted easily and for over an hour about this and that, a backwash of gossip that meant nothing much, but which they both took pleasure in. The little dining area partitioned off from the lounge was cosy, like a corner table in a tucked-away bistro. With a touch of splendid romanticism, McAuliffe had placed a lit candle among the condiments. More of Judith's plants arranged in canework hanging baskets nearby completed the picture. There was a bottle of wine, some superb ice-creamy dessert, liqueurs; and then a slow and satisfied silence filled with alcohol-buzz and a warmth between them he wanted to go on forever.

McAuliffe knew he should have been happy.

Later, the bedroom midnight-cool and black, he turned to her again. A while ago, she had guided him in her precise and careful way, but skilfully enough, along their well-trodden path of love.

Now, he wanted more, and he wanted it different. It

was the drink; always made him like this in the early hours. Usually, she shoved him off and told him to go to sleep: and he, being exhausted and half-doped anyway, would do so.

This time, when he pushed her satin nightdress up to her neck and pulled her round, her saw-edged breathing came faster as she struggled under her own drunk-sleep to respond. He liked her like this, too pissed to argue, too numbed to tell him it hurt.

McAuliffe straddled her high up on her chest, took a double handful of hair and pulled Judith to him. He gently rhythmed, grew to a pitch of excitement as her slickwet mouth gasped and gulped; drew away and lay on her, forced himself down on her and cried out in an abandon he so rarely felt.

It was exquisite, the Little Death that made you so electrically aware of being alive.

'Oh, Jesus, ah God – ah – ah!'

He came quickly, letting go, calling and calling, his head wreathed in dreams, his teeth clenched tight on another girl's name.

The big Scania truck backed up slowly towards the loading-bay doors, inch by inch with a wheezy puffing of airbrakes. Positioned offside at the rear, Kevin Steiger watched the gap narrow as he guided the driver with a delicate repertoire of hand movements.

'Come on, come on... bit more... and a bit more...'

The truck driver thought this guy was a dick, standing there in his bloody butcher's overall with his stupid greasy rocker's haircut and gold ring in his ear. He must've got the brains of one of his sheep's heads crammed in his skull...

'Another inch – bit more—'

The driver banged the brakes and the truck stopped with a shudder. He leaned out the window. 'Will you shut your fucking lip and let me do the job!'

'Sorry, pal,' Steiger said, truly shocked to discover he'd not been of help. The driver eased back another few inches and halted finally with a fraction to spare, swung down out of the cab and reached back for his clipboard. One of the warehousemen had a forklift ready to offload the pallets.

The driver broke the lead seal on the meatwagon's double doors and opened up the refrigerated container. Frosty air plumed out. Steiger gazed in and saw the sides of beef and lamb hanging there like rows of strange cold chrysalises, swinging gently on their S-hooks.

'D'you want me to . . .' he offered.

The truck driver bared a fearsome grin of nicotine-stained teeth. 'Just stay out the way till we've finished, or go and wank a sausage or something. OK?'

'I've got to supervise.' Steiger decided to stand on his dignity by quoting Brad's instructions. Brad Goss was the manager of the meat department and had told him to go and oversee the delivery. But now Steiger frowned, realizing it to be a ploy to get him out of Goss's hair for an hour.

'I'll lift the sides down for you,' Steiger added, hard-voiced, 'unless you want to do it with your mouth!'

The driver and the forklift operator laughed together, not really including Steiger; but the kid had suddenly earned the right to be there. The driver nodded.

'Fair enough. Wait till these pallets are out, though.'

Steiger had left school two years earlier, eager for work and a paypacket to squander each week. He'd hated Clay Comp – detested it with such force he could still taste the acid in his mouth sometimes. The last day of that summer term had been brilliant. Steiger and some friends, all leavers, had rampaged; scattering books and papers, making bright, obscene graffiti with spray-cans everywhere. They'd gotten hold of Miss Benfield, a junior French mistress, and whipped her skirt off before the second scream – used it as a banner throughout their triumphal tour of the campus.

Mr de Vleig was next: physics teacher with about as much soul as the wooden bench he leaned across to shout at them each and every lesson. First off, they'd taken his false teeth and done ventriloquist's impressions to one another, just for some fun. Then, with a lit and slowly licking Bunsen Burner, they'd singed off the man's goatee beard until he'd roared in pain and humiliation.

Then they'd smashed up the lab.

The police had been called, naturally. Even Mrs Adams, the Clay Comp dreadnought, wouldn't dare confront the mob in this mood. But before the cops arrived, each wild and transient member of the gang had helped empty some of the rooms in the English block, piling up the furniture – desks, chairs, all at fractured angles – outside the main gates. If it takes two pigs ten seconds to move one desk, then how long would it take . . .

Steiger remembered the soaring exhilaration of that day, that crazy hot July afternoon when the world was theirs, with no one strong enough to touch them. When the police Rovers came screeching around by the gym and pool, the crowd scattered, each yelling, swearing, giving the finger regardless, unafraid and howling in their moment of glory.

There had been ripples through the town for weeks, but precious few reprisals. Over a hundred kids had taken part in the riot, causing twenty-thousand pounds worth of damage all told. No one had positively identified Steiger; he'd got away with it all scot free, and chuckled behind his hand right through the vacation.

'WHAT THE HELL IS CLAYTON COMING TO?' the paper demanded to know. Nothing the frigging slum hasn't been all along, Steiger remembered thinking.

The madness in him died down quickly from hot flames, to the slow simmering rage that was always in his heart, some days worse than others. He remembered fondly his weeks of freedom, before his mum badgered him out of the house to look for work. He'd worn a tie to his interview with Goss and the supermarket manager, together with an Oxfam blazer bought especially for the occasion. Steiger was convinced Goss had sniggered at him to the manager. But he'd landed the job and was told there was always the chance of training up to become a department manager himself, if he worked hard and showed loyalty.

Steiger had called both men 'sir' and felt hugely grateful to them for allowing him this chance, in a town whose industrial infrastructure had collapsed and where unemployment was running at twenty per cent. Despondency, Steiger reflected, was running rather higher than that.

Still, you never knew what was round the next bend, he told himself with a smile, hefting the iron-hard sides of meat like dancing partners up on to the rails. Once, when the frozen carcass started sliding out of Steiger's gloved hands, he roared like a bull and flung it bodily to the back of the loading bay. Felt better for it.

The forkliftman stared at the truck driver and shrugged.

'Mad as a fucking fruitcake,' he said pleasantly. 'Where do I sign the chit?'

An hour later, it was Steiger whom McAuliffe asked about

a particular cut of meat he was looking for – Judith's explicit instructions for something called 'noisettes à la jardinière'. Personally, he would have preferred a good curry or, even better, a Sunday supper down at the Crown.

The kid looked at him stupidly, as mutual recognition dawned in that moment. The boy, bigger than McAuliffe now and much bulkier, reddened. McAuliffe felt awkward too: he'd never liked this boy – damned if he could think of his name – recalling him as a slovenly troublemaker with a foul mouth and not much up top; two strawberries short of a punnet, as they said in the staffroom.

He felt compelled to ask, though: 'So, how're things these days?'

'Fine, s—' Steiger bit off the title that even now came like a reflex. He didn't have to call this bastard 'sir' any longer, so no way was he going to. McAuliffe recognized the situation. They both smiled, each warily.

'Well, you've got yourself a job; pretty good for round here.'

'Yeah.'

'A lot of kids have to move away.'

'Guess I was just lucky.' With heavy irony.

McAuliffe swept a cursory glance at the meat cooler, wrapped redness on white enamel.

'Loin of lamb is what I'm after.'

Steiger's eyes followed. He pointed a much-washed pink finger; McAuliffe noted the blood under the nails.

'Lamb's at the top end.'

'Ah. I don't need the whole loin: can you do a special cut for me?'

'I can ask.'

'I'd be grateful,' McAuliffe said, seeing some of the sullenness drop from the kid's eyes. A teacher being grate-

ful to a kid was a turn up. McAuliffe said what he
wanted.

'Back in a minute, sir—'

It was said before he could stop it. Steiger turned away
before his face darkened: McAuliffe turned away before he
could grin.

He guessed the boy would take some minutes articulating his request, and in any case could find him wherever
he was in the store. He carried on with his shopping; a
special treat on his part for Judith, allowing her a few extra
hours at her work. She had arranged a dinner party at the
end of the month for some dealers, a few friends – even
her editor was coming along. She was already nervous, but
very excited that this could be a breakthrough in her career.
The 'mistscape' had been painted just for that occasion,
and she wanted to complete a couple of other pieces also.
This would be as well as planning the food, arranging
where in the house to display the pictures, etc., etc., et-
bloody-cetera . . . McAuliffe sighed at the imminent hassle,
mentally preparing himself at this early stage for the
reserves of patience he would need to call upon, knowing
she'd get worse as the time approached. He regarded the
whole thing not so much as a challenge, but a test – a test
of them together; a sort of crisis in the middle of a long
and dragging term.

I can do without it, he thought heavily; rounded a corner
and stopped.

Christine Lamb stood not five yards ahead, half turned
away from him. She was stooping to talk to a little blonde
girl – Vicki Bell, one of his pupils – who was listening very
seriously, it seemed. McAuliffe's pulse raced up. He studied
carefully Christine's lean elegance, her rough beauty. He
noted that her mouth was quite thin, her lips down-turned

slightly when expression had faded from them. It might be a cruel look, or some ingrained unhappiness she was no longer aware of. Her hair dazzled him; tangled and dark, it was almost blue-black under the diffused fluorescents of the store. She looked – not so much beautiful – but exciting in a way he could not quite pinpoint. She wore jeans and a purple sweater, no jewellery; and if there was makeup, it was applied so subtly that he couldn't spot it. Her nails, he saw, were unvarnished and cut short. Then he laughed at himself at the way these details seemed important. When the hell did he ever notice Judith like that?

Someone came up behind McAuliffe, startling him. The butcher boy back, holding out his pound of cellophaned flesh.

'Your noisy lamb, Mr McAuliffe.' It was a gruff kind of friendliness. The kid looked silly with his black straggles of hair dribbling out from under his hygienic paper hat; his big shovel hand offering the meat.

'Thanks, uh . . . ?'

The boy wasn't going to give anything, but then his name came back to McAuliffe with a little break of memory, as he turned away.

'Good luck to you, Steiger,' he said to the broad, retreating back.

The small encounter had caught Christine's attention. When McAuliffe looked round, the little girl was walking away, leaving Christine standing there alone.

'She's a bright button.' It was a way in, at least; a clumsy opener.

'Vicki. Yes I, uh, know the family.'

McAuliffe caught the lie, knew it as such from his years of sifting what kids said to him for truths not spoken, for untruth masked as gospel. He ignored it outwardly, but it shot to the back of his mind as a niggling piece of the jigsaw puzzle. He lifted his eyebrows at the huge trolley-load of groceries parked beside her.

'All for you?'

'Um, and my housemate. He eats like a horse!' Her laughter was quick, but brittle. McAuliffe's heart sank at the 'he'. But what was she hiding other than that?

'How will you get it all home?' The opportunity bloomed in his mind, even as he recognized the danger of it. The girl was smiling back at him guiltily.

'I was going to push the whole lot back, trolley and all!'

'And then return the empty trolley, of course . . .'

'Of course.'

'Well, look,' McAuliffe said, trying to play it subtly – but she would know; young girls always suspected the approaches of middle-aged men, whatever the motive, and laughed at them – 'Why don't I run you and your mountain of tins round to your house – I mean, it must be over a mile. Stupid to wear yourself out . . .' His attempt at being casual seemed like cheap stage scenery to McAuliffe; amateurish, with all the strings showing.

'Why not,' she agreed, to his amazement. And there was more: 'But I owe you a drink for this favour. How about now? The pubs'll just be opening.'

'Well, if you insist,' McAuliffe said, after a moment's faked hesitation.

She was relying on McAuliffe to make up his own reasons for her distractedness: nervousness about the Monday start to her counselling work; some uncertainty about being seen out with an older man, her ex-English teacher; maybe boyfriend problems or money worries. Anything. It didn't matter. While he went to the bar (he insisted on paying), Christine closed her eyes and listened to the voices.

They were cautioning her; full of fear and underlying sadness that this was to be the end of things. Committed now to this place, this forgotten town, the Kin were sacrificing the last of their vigour in a final attempt to continue. Should it fail, then the life fields would wash over the clay of ignorant humanity unsensed and unheeded. An ancestry here of thirty-thousand years would be lost . . .

Not that she would allow it to happen while her heart still beat and her lungs breathed on. She had dire apprehensions about Bruce: the boy was scared and, perhaps, ultimately incapable of controlling the change. The tides were so very strong, and the process depended upon an equally powerful guiding mentality. Christine swallowed back her worry. Maybe, after all, she should have been chosen, instead of him and the others. But then, however carefully the selection was made, all opportunity could be wiped out by the one who stalked their shadows and burned away their heritage in a blaze of petrol-flame. The insane hybrid. The Kin Slayer.

'Scotch with water, half and half. Sorry it's just Glenfiddich. You were lucky to get a malt here.'

McAuliffe offered her the glass and saw how the liquid rippled in her hand as she took it from him. Her broken smile unnerved him.

'Nothing wrong with Glenfiddich. I'm not a whisky snob, um . . .'

'Pete.'

She sipped gratefully and nodded. 'I needed that.'

'Supermarket shopping has a high stress factor,' McAuliffe pointed out. 'I've been reading up on it. You must not accumulate more than one hundred points in a year. Bad for your health – like, moving house is fifty points, getting married is seventy-five or thereabouts. Losing someone close to you—'

'Don't, McAuliffe.'

'Sorry.' It was a reflex apology. Shit, McAuliffe thought, I've just blown all my chances. He leaned forward to her. 'Look, I really am sorry. Someone in your family? If I can help—'

'Someone in my family,' Christine answered quietly, not meeting his eyes. She took a slug at the Scotch and steadied herself.

'A parent?'

'I have no father, McAuliffe. I have no mother . . .'

Suddenly she looked strange to him, veiled. He did not understand her. Christ, he thought, and she's the one doing the counselling course!

McAuliffe put out his hand across the no-man's-land of the table between them. Any other intentions he had were moved aside by the sight of her grief. She was, for the moment, just a young kid who was in trouble and needed a little support. He remembered the black agony of losing his own parents, within a year of each other; one soul purposeless without its mate, his father had wasted away by the Christmas after his mother's fatal summer stroke.

Christine's hand felt cool and small in his own. How rarely he comforted another like this! And she did not pull away, accepting his gift of sympathy.

'Really, Pete, there's no need to worry. I'm OK.'

'Like hell,' he told her gently. 'You're away from home, not exactly living in a penthouse paradise, trying out new skills in a school you won't ever have loved to pieces—'

'Put like that, I suppose you're right.' She finished the last of her drink and pointed to his beer glass. 'Can you drive on two? My round I think.'

'I can. Thanks.'

He walked with her to the bar and stood there beside her, the closest he'd ever been.

'Listen, Christine. My shoulder is vacant. Cry upon it all you like. And' – he could've kicked himself for saying so – 'and no strings, all right? I mean, I'm not after—'

She smiled and kissed his cheek.

'I understand you. And thanks: it looks like a friendly shoulder.'

Anyway, Christine thought with deep weariness, in a world of such slaughter and betrayal, I might need some human help.

God had wrapped up the moon in blue lace and flung it there to hang above the hill. It was motionless amidst the purple haze of twilight, yet as his eyes drifted back to it minute by minute, the pattern of thin cloud in which it was embedded was always changing; and by and by it grew brighter, and lights came on in greater profusion down in the town, and the temperature dropped towards freezing.

The kid shivered, flicked up the collar of his denim jacket, wrapped his arms about his body and swore softly into the darkness. He'd known it would be tough – to the point, perhaps, where he might not survive; but to die of exposure rather than in the glory of ambition could not be countenanced. He had to survive, and saw now that the old powers of the Kin lying latent in his blood would be needed for this.

He cast a last glance at the moon, then hunkered down on the grass and faced Clayton. It looked like a join-the-dots puzzle done in diamonds, each jewel glinting due to air inversions. Traffic moved easily now the rush-hour was over. Streets and avenues looked like necklaces of warmth and comfort.

He closed his eyes and searched for the landscape existing within this one; a panorama of impressions that were voices and pictures, odours, scraps of thought and bright pulses of emotion; a lattice more delicate and telling than the gross valley of lights below.

Yes, it soon came to him. He heard the undercurrents of the Kin, all of them calling soulfully in their despair. Genuine fear – the fear of extinction and oblivion – shot through his body like needles. But he would not be threaded on their need! That need was corrupt and selfish; parasitic as it had always been upon the rightful claimants to this world. He would ignore them, wipe out all chances of their continuance!

He focused in, moved like a ghost along the avenues and terraces; sweeping through minds, never lingering although he might have done so a hundred times. He embodied a mixture of bloods, and through the genetic route of his forefathers had come to appreciate the particular qualities comprising humanity. People were such confusions! They dwelt among contradiction and conflict, moved in circles, lived and died and never seemed to find a way through. What they were made him laugh! Yet how he loved them for what they were not . . .

Quite without effort, his drifting mentality chanced upon his goal: one of the Kin, living in an outer suburb. His questing mind's eye saw trees and a fine big house; a warm kitchen and a table laden with food. A family gathered there . . . He walked among them, sifting human from Kin – and soon found her out. Oh, how clever they had become! This artifice would fool anyone not as single-minded as himself. She was beautiful, tiny, unknowing. No terror throbbed and sparked in her bones. She had only the vaguest and most innocent of notions that she was a princess with a marvellous gift to lay before the world – when the time was right, of course. When she was told.

He hated himself, then, for deciding that she would be the next.

An hour wore by. The moon drew higher over the turning world beneath. The boy was a still and silent mound among the grass.

Nearby, a rustling started; reticent paws shifting carefully. A rabbit sniffed at the air with a fragile quivering of whiskers. It could smell the fruit not far away, close to where the patch of dead bracken started. A rare and exotic morsel – but set against what dangers?

The animal maintained its questioning pose: body lifted, head staring in the direction of the meal, front paws delicately poised; temptation balanced against risk.

Finally, a decision having been reached, it moved four-legged towards the source of the scent – apple slices, it saw, rich with juice and nourishment. It hopped warily over a thin membranous surface on which the fruit rested, dipped its nose to the apple . . .

. . . and the ground snapped up and engulfed it in grey skin ribbed with a trap of hooks.

It struggled for its life, screaming thinly.

The boy scrambled to his feet, half opened the huge bat-like hand and pierced the thrashing creature with a stiletto-blade of a fingernail. The rabbit convulsed and died, twitching as the boy's lengthening jaws reached down to suck out the flesh that still lay warmly in its bag of fur.

Moments later, the boy flung away the skin-and-bones, barely satisfied. He knew that the hunger was upon him; and more than the hunger for food. It had been many months since he'd last made use of these abilities: to break beyond the boundary of this one form was an ecstasy. And there was still the cold to consider, his own survival through the night.

His eyes, bright and questing, scanned skylines. He smiled a wide and ancient smile. Then he made off up the hill at an easy lope, arms as long as his body held out in front.

The horse stood like a monolith, its breath feathering weakly in the frost-laden air. It knew that something was wrong; felt the strange ropy saddle flung across its back, and knew that a man's weight hung from its belly. There was no pain, but a kind of numbness was growing in its chest, and a darkness was blurring the distant stars. It stamped a little nervously, tried to turn . . .

A bag of fluids burst deep within. The horse whinnied, frightened in its last instant. Something was busy at its underside. Slicing.

The beast's entrails gushed out, dropping to the ground. Slowly the horse settled down upon them and rested its nose to the turf, heedless now of the occupant inside.

Parties before this had never held such strange electric magic; an excitement of almost understanding. Andrew's parents had actually gone up to the study – or somewhere – to let the kids get on with their fun. This time they hadn't hovered around, fussing with food; hadn't complained about the music being too loud or too weird; hadn't insisted that festivities wind up at around nine . . .

It was ten o'clock now, and Vicki knew that things couldn't go on like this much longer. Parents were bound to start arriving, the wonderful spell breaking with a doorbell chime.

She cuddled up to Andrew Wilkinson on the sofa in the

lounge, and kissed him. But he was grinning so she caught his teeth instead. They both giggled, tried again. His lips were cool, and he shifted beneath her as though she was too heavy on him.

'Are you OK?'

'I'm OK,' he told her. 'Vicki, this is a brilliant party.'

'I've loved it too . . . But, Andy, won't they all talk at school? About this?'

''Bout what?'

'Us.'

'Let them talk,' he said with defiance. She noticed he had put cologne on, or aftershave or something – though he didn't shave of course – and the scent, plus his blond hair which gleamed in the low light, and his fresh, handsome face, all contributed to the enchantment. Thirteen years old, and she not far behind him. A whole lifetime opening out ahead . . .

'Oh, Andy.'

Vicki kissed him again, more deeply this time, like her friend Sarah had told her to do. This time Andy groaned and tried to speak. He put his hand on Vicki's chest, a chest that was as flat as his own for the time being, but it felt good all the same.

He was working out his next move, when the front door bell sounded and there was a collective moan from kids huddled in various corners of the room.

Andy's father knocked on the door before entering, and his son appreciated that small gesture of courtesy and understanding. He struggled out from under Vicki Bell, straightening himself just in time.

'Uh, hiya, Dad . . .'

Mr Wilkinson grinned at his boy's flushed face. Jesus, they started young these days: he hadn't tried anything with a girl until he was fifteen – although admittedly that was from want of opportunity, as much as anything else.

'It's Mr Parks at the door, son. He's come for Robert and a couple of others who live along the way: Connie, Todd and, um, Vicki. Sorry, Andy.'

Andy shrugged. Vicki, all demure and coy, was standing nearby. She was wearing pink tracksuit bottoms and a Tigger sweatshirt, real casual. No one wore party clothes these days.

'I'll get your coat,' Andy told her, a gentleman to the end. People began to stir around the room.

'Hope you enjoyed yourself,' Mr Wilkinson said to the little group of kids assembled in the hallway, but he was smiling at Vicki as he did so. She blushed, not quite knowing what he meant.

Andy came along, helped her on with her Chinese-style padded jacket, and let his hands linger on her shoulders for a second. He whispered: 'See you Monday, Vicks. Love you lots.' Nobody else heard. Vicki went out beaming, not letting anyone else see or know the secret of her happiness.

Mr Parks was a tall, thin man; the tallest she'd ever met, but gruff and glum with a son soaked in the same bad humour. Robert Parks had spent the whole evening reading Andy's football magazines in the kitchen, yet he told his dad he'd had a great time. That must say something about him.

Father and son sat in the front of Mr Parks's big Volvo estate, which meant that Connie Fry, Todd Stonely and Vicki were packed in the back together. Well, not packed, but any distance from Todd was too close. Vicki's friend Sarah said that he suffered from WHS – Wandering Hands Syndrome. Vicki hunched herself up as close to the passenger door as she could get. If he tried anything with her, she'd hammer him right in the nuts. Sarah said that always worked, and Vicki had always wanted to ask how she knew, but had never dared . . .

But tonight, Todd was subdued and neither Robert nor his father seemed inclined to talk either. Mr Parks had the radio on low, some talk programme, and that and the blow-heater formed a comfortable background sound, preventing the silence from growing awkward.

Vicki wiped away the window mist with her jacket sleeve and stared up into the sky. Streetlights slid by like hazy orange galaxies. Between them and beyond, in the pools of autumn darkness, shone the stars, very faintly. Once, she caught sight of the moon, a little past full, its eastern limb nibbled. Then it moved behind a building and she lost it.

Tonight she was in a mood to appreciate these sights and what, maybe, they meant. The moon, the stars, seemed important to her; though she couldn't say why. She hadn't always felt like this – only in the past couple of years, since she'd started at the Comp, had she sensed herself growing up and been ready to contemplate what the world was about. If there was any moment marking the beginning of her new thoughts, her deeper, adult thoughts, then it must have been the day she started at the big school . . .

She had been so scared: the kids seemed huge, and much louder and rougher than those at Abbey Junior. That first breaktime, Vicki had stood shivering on the forecourt while boys zoomed by like thundering giants, heedless of her terror. Once, a teacher came out of the building and yelled at them, and her, to get round the back of the school and on to the fields. Vicki moved off, in tears, turned the corner by the gym and was sent flying by a kid running full tilt in the opposite direction.

The impact slammed her down to the ground, her hands

skimming the macadam surface to break her fall. After a
stark second's shock, the pain came like a tide; the throb
and ache of the collision, the fiery sting of hands and knees
skinned by stone chippings. She'd sobbed and sobbed, not
only because she was hurt, but because of what she'd lost
and what could never be the same for her again.

Later – seconds that seemed like minutes – someone
eased her up and whispered comfortingly in her ear. Not
a teacher, but a prefect.

'OK, sweet, you're all right. All right now. I've got
you.'

Vicki's sobbing subsided, partly due to the girl's beautiful soft accent; round and fluid like water over stones. And
she was pretty – grown-up pretty with a lovely shape and
long tangles of dark hair, a bright and honest smile: I'm
your friend, it said: I'll take care of you, Vicki . . .

But how did the smile know her name? And why did
it sound like a voice in her head at the same time?

Questions, questions that blew through her brain like a
soft wind. Vicki's eyes widened for a second in fear, but
were soothed again by the prefect's easy, sincere manner
and the sensation that lots of friends were around her now
– not her old Abbey Junior pals, but family going way
back: uncles, aunts, fathers and mothers and relatives for
whom no names existed – the Old Ones, the ones who
knew everything.

'My name's Christine,' the prefect told Vicki.

'I'm Vicki Bell.'

'I know, honey . . . Let me help you here . . .'

Christine rubbed Vicki's grazed and bleeding hands
between her own, wiping away the dirt and bits of stone.

'Ugh, don't do that—' Vicki protested as Christine lowered her head and licked at her wounds. But the protests

died away under the balm of her tongue and the swift diminishing of pain ...

And that, Vicki concluded, was when the magic had started.

A duty teacher hurried along moments later to find Vicki Bell standing up, smiling tearfully, with Christine Lamb's arm around her shoulder. Amazingly, the little kid had not cut herself up on the road gravel; just reddened palms and kneecaps. It was a relief.

'You all right, girl? No damage?'

'I'm OK. Christine helped me. She's my friend.'

'That's just fine, then.' The teacher gave a tentative thanks-for-that smile in Christine's direction: it would save having to fill out an accident form if all present agreed the girl had not been harmed.

'Who's he?' Vicki wanted to know, watching the man's tweed-jacketed back dwindle into the distance.

'That's Mr de Vleig, Vicki. He'll teach you Physics.'

'Don't like Fizzix ...' Christine smiled as the mind-word shone in Vicki's head. She hugged the girl close.

'Don't worry. Listen, hen: as long as you're here, you'll have me to help you. We'll talk lots. And I'll tell you things that are much more interesting than Physics: things about life and the future, and all about how you can help me, when the time comes. Me, and all my family.'

'When will that be?'

'Not yet. But soon.'

But soon.

Vicki came out of her reminiscence like waking from light sleep. They were almost home. Christine Lamb, true to her word, had stayed her friend until she'd left and gone back to Scotland. But it was as though no distance separated them at all, for the two still talked in the deep of the night, or in quiet sunlit seconds with a teacher's droning monotone as a backdrop.

And then, Christine was home. Vicki had been so pleased to see her in the supermarket yesterday; although she was no more vivid than she'd been all the while in Vicki's mind. And she was just the same – almost – yet filled now with a new urgency that she tried to keep hidden. But Vicki knew. She was growing up too and understood much more about the fact that people wore two faces; one was the real face, and the other they showed to the world.

Christine's true face was not smiling. And nearby, Vicki knew, crouched the monster that was making her frightened.

'Don't worry, Christine. As long as you're here, you'll have me to help you . . .'

Christine laughed at that, but it was sad laughter as though, maybe, something could happen to break what they shared.

'Home, Vicki,' Mr Parks said. He swung the Volvo round into Shelley Drive and cruised to a halt under the shadow of the old lime tree that grew at the end of the front garden. Mr Parks's skull was long and thin, carved into an odd smile, of jealousy perhaps, that his life was more than half gone, while those of his passengers were just beginning.

Vicki pushed open the car's heavy door and loved the feel of the cold night air pouring over her.

'Thanks, Mr Parks, Robert. Todd. Connie. See ya.'

'S'long,' Robert said, the only words he'd spoken to her all evening.

Vicki watched the big square car drive off into the gloom, waiting until its last engine sounds trailed away to silennce before turning and walking up the front path.

The Bells owned a large house in a salubrious part of the town. Vicki's father was an accountant, a man who had earned his money honestly by hard work. They'd bought the place ten years ago, mainly to be on the fringe of Clayton, but partly because the house was set in generous grounds filled with trees. Vicki used to play among them all day long, knew each by a name she'd invented, and looked back fondly on the warm dry hiding places she'd made and kept secret in the undergrowth . . .

She was casting back across those lost years when a sound froze her to the spot: a stirring in the bushes; a shifting of weight; a low growl.

She started to move – whether to run or to see what it was, she didn't know herself – when something came at her, seemingly from all directions at once. A hand smashed her sideways with a soft thunder: a bodyweight dropped down on her ribs, crushing her scream before she could voice it.

She opened her mouth anyway – the horror of what she was seeing just had to escape!

This was it, then, the monster of the dark; her friend's fears personified. Vicki gave up struggling and wished with all of her heart that Christine was here at her death, helping her through it.

The killer, in the heat of the deed, was melting like wax. He used a blade first, drove it powerfully into the open, soundless mouth, and through into the grass beneath, pinning the head to the ground: his own jaws stretching grotesquely.

There was no time for much else. Someone had heard the car's departure, curtains were moving aside in one of the front rooms.

The boy went quickly to work with the petrol, sloshing

the stuff over the girl's thin body. And he cried as he did it, a wrenching sorrow, but set light to the spirit-soaked clothing anyway, before he ran.

He sought shadows and distance; knew he could outrun pursuers, but never this agonizing remorse. They were torturing his human half by forcing him to kill a child; making him question his motives, then doubt them. Even now, their voices wailed like a choir in his head. Closer in, not a mile away, the other Kin watched his sacrilege and despised him for it – called him Betrayer in a thousand tongues.

He heard the police sirens soon after, but by that time was lost among side-streets. He passed a scrap yard and squeezed through its sagging, broken gates, hammered his way into a wrecked auto and lay there, shuddering.

No one witnessed the penalty he paid for acting against his own kind. He lost control, gave himself up to it as he watched his own limbs extrude like soft rubber, the eyes enabling this vision to multiply by the minute. The beat-up car filled with his flesh, which almost burst the wreck asunder before his mind reaffirmed his purpose.

The life-tides ebbed, the madness faded like an echo. He lay still.

'I am not wrong in this,' he said aloud to which ever god might be listening, and knew he had never acted on impulse or through insanity. No one should aspire to geno-cide without very careful consideration.

The night felt bad. It had nothing to do with Steiger's consumption of twelve pints of beer, though this did not ease the nausea that swilled like a heavy oil in his guts.

Word was around that another murder had been com-mitted in the town, this time out in the posh southern suburbs Melsham way. It wasn't that Steiger himself was frightened by this close approach of violent death – he was pretty sure his bulk and fierce appearance would deter most would-be attackers. No, not that. But the news cooled his heart another degree, nailed down his conviction a little more firmly that life was a bitch and then you died. He laughed thickly, upturning his brutish face to the sky. Pretty slick thought, that, after so much ale. Not fucking bad for a drunkard; best thing to be done, Steiger told himself, on an evil night like this.

He had been wandering around Clayton centre since opening time, three hours ago. On a Sunday night, the pubs shut early, so there was time for just one more in the nearest hostelry to hand. Or maybe two . . .

He staggered down an alley that stank of cats and rotten fruit; broken bottle glass crackled under his boots. And when he put out his hand to support his dizzy weight, the wall ran slick and slimy from a leaky overflow above.

Beyond was the shopping centre, a strange split-level architecture of galleries and squares designed in the boom-time of the sixties. Steiger found himself on a wide flag-stoned space, its emptiness relieved by large low tubs made of brick, which once had held flowers and dwarf hedges, but now, dog shit and abandoned lager cans. In his alcoholic haze, Steiger wanted to weep or rage for the death of the town, its pathetic decline to this state. Weep or rage. Neither would help.

He unzipped and emptied his bladder into one of the ex-ornamental troughs, then stumbled on through the cold quietness. No one normal came down here late at night. Steiger remembered his mother telling him that, years ago. Place was full of drunks and queers; weirdos. He recalled being scared as he walked through the busy shopping centre, hand in hand with Mum, imagining the galleries and frontages draped over with darkness, home to a hundred breeds of danger. Now he grinned, then moaned low in his throat to think that he could be counted among them.

Not far away stood the Malt Shovel Inn, a townie pub famous for its fights. Not that Steiger was interested in violence this night; his reactions were as slurred as his speech. Although, as he decided this, he felt again the slow anger burning up inside him. Someone had done all this to Clayton: someone had done this to him. Both it and he were, now, near derelict, left to come to nothing.

So someone had to pay.

He walked by a boarded-up shopfront crazily wall-papered with advertisements, handbills, rock posters; Axeman Cometh, Charnel House, Deathwish, Thrash – bands he loved, and had seen play: some of his best ever nights and moments of meaning had happened to the sound of their guitars . . .

Steiger played an imaginary instrument for a few seconds, headbanging until he stumbled and dropped to one knee. His head buzzed. He felt a little sick now . . . And there was a noise coming from somewhere: a deep, keening wail or moan that sent a chill to his soul and sobered him up more quickly than anything else could have done.

Holy Mother, it was coming from inside the empty shop! He snatched his hand away from the wall, all the old childhood terrors scattering through him like insects caught in a sudden light.

Eyes wild, Steiger turned to flee.

And ran straight into a fist that floored him with a single blow.

He woke to candlelight and many eyes, watching; he

struggled to rise but was pressed back gently by a cool hand on his forehead; it was a girl's hand, long nailed, slim. Steiger thought, correctly as it turned out, that he was inside the closed-up shop.

'Uh ... Whu ... Oh shit ... Feel ...'

Steiger rolled on to his side and dribbled vomit on to the ground. He felt ridiculous in the presence of these strangers who had, obviously, rescued him from the pre-dations of some passing mugger. He spat, wiping his mouth with his hand.

'Uh – look – uh, thanks.'

The girl moved forward into the sphere of candleglow. Steiger was stunned by her beauty. Her hair was white-blonde, her smile seductive and gentle. He saw that she was wearing tight blue jeans and a leather jacket over a Belladonnna Tour black T-shirt.

'My favourite fucking band, that,' he told her grinnning. 'At least it is now.' He loved the way the band's motif – little purple flowers twining through a skeleton hand – contoured the curve of her breasts. She was lovely, the most gorgeous girl he'd ever seen.

'I'm Steiger,' he added, almost sheepishly.

'I—' The girl caught herself, reconsidered. 'I'm glad to know you, Steiger. What happened here?'

He gave her his theory. She nodded and her hair swung silkily. He wanted to know her name, but you never pushed a girl like this: you always waited for her to decide the action.

'Ozzie here saw a couple of guys running off ...' The girl indicated one of the group, a big, friendly looking kid with a frazzled mass of reddish hair and round-rim wire glasses. 'Have you lost any money?'

Steiger patted his pockets, dug in and dragged out some change and a crumpled note.

'How about that – I haven't! Enough here to buy you folks a drink.' He squinted at his scratched-up Timex. 'And I will too, if we get a move on to the Malt Shovel . . .'

They helped him up, Ozzie and another kid called Johan. The girl – she told him her name was Anna – walked beside Ozzie, not linking arms with him. Steiger wondered if she was going out with any of these dudes.

As they walked, Steiger realized that something had been troubling him. For a minute or more he struggled towards it, then it came in a gush of memory: before he was floored he'd heard the noise of – of lost souls singing. That's what it sounded like to him. A choir of the dead.

So he mentioned it. Ozzie, Johan, the other two lads, stopped walking.

Anna came up close to him. She ran her fingers along his lapels.

'What you must understand, Kevin, is that we're into some heavy stuff—'

'*You* were singing!'

'Chanting,' Ozzie corrected. Anna quelled him with a glance.

'It's like this: when you want to dance with the devil, you gotta sing his song . . .'

Steiger could barely believe this. Yes, the bands he listened to were full of this kind of thing, laughing at the gates of hell to blitzing guitar riffs. But in reality it was all – well – crap.

'You into black magic, then?' He tried to keep his voice steady. Anna shook her head.

'No way, Kevin. We're against it, man. But to be against it, you must understand it, follow it, get near it.'

'We're into life,' Ozzie continued. 'We're into rebirth, man – the New Age.'

'Earth magic?'

'Earth magic.' Anna settled it with a smile. She pointed back towards the deserted shopping centre. 'In there, it's dead. It's the cold, dead heart of Clayton. And the town has a maggot, Kevin, that wants to eat out the rest of its life. A killer.'

'Those murders . . .'

'They're obscene, right? What you heard was like a prayer to the forces that can help us, strengthen us . . .'

'Yeah. Right.'

The little group continued walking, out on to a main street. The doors of the Malt Shovel were still open, and suddenly Steiger was thirsty again.

He thought about it all, very hard. Earth magic? Why not? The papers were full of stranger things. Anyway, the little angel must have some kind of phoneline to beyond: how the hell did she know his name was Kevin, for one thing?

It seemed to Scobie that he never saw Dr Marius these days except in the presence of filthy death. The pathologist, bearded face palely gleaming under the portable floods, picked through the blackened remains in the garden on Shelley Drive; he, they, and the Detective Inspector enclosed by a double barrier of plastic partitions and red-and-white boundary tape. The tree canopy flickered in the lights of the assembled ambulance and police vehicles. A thin crystal frost covered the lawns.

'Same pattern,' Scobie remarked, the capacity for speech all but beyond him right now. Marius stood up stiffly with a grunt.

'No time to use his axe on this occasion: just this awful wound to the face and then the burning.'

'But why? What's the bloody point in any of it?'

Marius looked seriously at his friend. Scobie was forty-eight now and, on days like this, could be ten years older. He was a good detective, the pathologist knew: but being good meant being thorough, meant caring about cases. Just at this moment, Scobie would be trying to think through the logic of the killing and, perhaps, concluding it was patternless, would try to understand the perpetrator's mind. It all took energy and effort, and now it was past eleven on a freezing October night. Tomorrow, Monday morning, would start with paperwork and grief.

'Could be some kind of ritual killing,' Marius offered. His ideas, not caught up with chains of circumstance and reason, were sometimes useful.

'Maybe so, John. God knows the motive is beyond me. The sales rep Johnson, Tracy Vines, now this little girl – this lit-tle . . .' Scobie felt his voice going, so shut up. It was no time to come apart. He clenched his fists hard inside the baggy pockets of his big winter coat as the police photographer, a man called Simmons, lifted a corner of the partition and stuck his head through.

'Shall I start the next batch, sir?' he wondered, meaning the ground beneath and around the body once it had been moved. The body. Scobie felt crazy laughter bubble in his throat. Why not just shovel the ash into the flowerbeds; do the plants a power of good!

'Give me a minute, will you?' Scobie said with unnatural calm and politeness. This new murder had pushed him further than he'd ever been before – to a new brink where the whole edifice of sanity and justice trembled in his mind. It was as if the entire world had rotted out from under him and he and the rest of civilized life were slipping through the fractured crust into some dreadful mayhem . . .

Then he checked himself. It was bullshit! This was a murder inquiry and he was a cop, one who had the wit to solve it if anybody could. Vandalism, theft, fraud, drugs: they all existed on his patch, and maybe he'd beat them and maybe not . . .

Scobie stared down at the barely human outline of blackened flakes and fragments.

But he'd get this bastard for sure.

'I'll go on up to the house,' he told Marius. His man, Carter, was already up there, trying to deal with the girl's parents and the enormity of their pain. There was no more he could do on site; and Marius would clue him in soon enough if anything came to light.

The pathologist nodded and stooped once more to his work as the D.I. vanished behind the partitions. Marius himself would be just a few more seconds finishing up his—

Something caught his eye, then; the merest glint of white where the grass ended and the dry soil beneath the bushes began. He carefully placed his wellington-booted feet astride the body and used a ruler to lift aside the leaves. His heart beat in a single deep pulse of – not excitement, not shock. Maybe it was wonder.

He had spotted a little cluster of wristbones, burned on one surface, but otherwise undamaged. They lay like an untidy toss of dice; scaphoid, triquetral, lunate . . . all there. And the fingers beyond, partly covered over with skin.

Marius eased the twigs higher out of the way . . . Metacarpals in position. And beyond, the fingerbones . . . My God . . . My God . . . The bones were many inches long, thin and brittle as bird's claws . . .

Judith was busy with her pre-dinner-party painting already, at this early hour. McAuliffe felt slighted and hurt. He wolfed down more cereal, finished it, and flung his spoon aggressively into the bowl. He poured coffee for himself and stared moodily out through the kitchen window. Cloud cover had come over during the night from the southwest, lifting the temperature but bringing dismal rain that he really could have done without. What he could see of the garden looked like a wilderness of greys. He thought ahead to those steamed-up noisy classrooms, and his depression slipped another notch downwards. BHIM – Bloody Hell, It's Monday . . .

He tightened his tie, put on his jacket and coat, scooped his keys from the hallway table, then went back through to the conservatory.

Judith was busy, lost in a world of pastel perspectives; a spring or early-summer scene where leaves in bright sprays of green burst through a pink dawn haze. Nothing to do with reality at all, McAuliffe decided. He bent to kiss his wife's neck.

'See you, Jude. Have a good day.'

'I will.' She turned to regard him with abstracted eyes. 'I really enjoyed – you know – the weekend . . .'

'Sure. Me too.' It was the closest she ever got to passion, and then had not remembered the peak of it that stood out in his mind. 'I like the new scene . . .'

'Mmm. It'll be the last one I'll do before next weekend. I'd better get on.'

McAuliffe left her to it, reckoning that maybe this was the way she coped with the world – by painting it as she would like it to be. Me, McAuliffe concluded, I'll settle for a big Pools win and a mansion in the Channel Isles!

He backed out of the drive, cruised to the end of the road in low gear, then turned left and accelerated quickly up to speed along the dual-carriageway towards the town.

He turned down the heating from Friday's high, flipped on the radio and settled back to the routine of his journey.

The local newscaster was reporting another murder in Clayton, uptown on the Wordsworth estate. McAuliffe's eyebrows lifted. Pretty costly property out that way: in fact, he passed by the fringe of the development on his way to the school. He'd always mildly envied those folks with their big secluded houses, their Jags and Mercs . . . Police were baffled (of course), and were asking the public to be alert for anyone suspicious they might see hanging around . . .

How the hell do you decide who's suspicious-looking? Could be a cop undercover loitering on the street corner . . . Sorry officer, I thought you was a pervert or maybe even a serial-killer . . .

McAuliffe took his foot off the accelerator pedal and let the car slow as he came up behind a school coach; its square back end almost lost in fine spray. He was still doing over fifty, but tended to cruise a little faster than that and now wondered whether to chance overtaking.

He pulled back a few yards and saw a row of faces grinning down into the car through smeared windows and a screen of upflung drizzle. One of the kids poked her tongue at him cheekily, another lifted the finger . . .

Little sods. Wait'll I get into sch—

' . . . named the victim as Vicki Bell, twelve-year-old daughter of Gareth and Victoria Bell, both long-time residents of the town. Mr Bell works as . . .'

McAuliffe startled, knowing the girl's name; seeing her face in its usual place in his classroom. Oh, please no, she can't have—

He had a flashing image of blood, a fantasy of her scream.

And so death was on his mind as it started to happen in front of him.

The coach, for no reason that he could see or ever worked out, started to slew round from the rear. It was like the slow motion slide of some metal brontosaurus – almost graceful. Headlights flashed from the opposite direction. Horns blared in panick shrieks. McAuliffe experienced that exquisite moment of white shock as adrenalin flooded his system from a single pulse of it somewhere down in his guts.

He slammed on the brakes.

That brought time spinning up faster than life. Out of nowhere, out of the curtains of grey rain, a biker erupted at eighty-five or above, oncoming with no chance to stop as he bypassed the slower vehicles. McAuliffe caught a glimpse of the machine hurling into the coach's nearside: the biker, doll-like, flailing through the air on his final journey: the big red Suzuki spinning on wet macadam, spurting sparks.

It might not have been so bad, but then the petrol tank went up, rupturing with a liquid gush of yellow flame. The coach swung right round and swayed on its springs. Kids' mouths were wide open, filled with terror and bubblegum.

McAuliffe's body was working by itself; his right foot pumping the brakes, his left on the clutch pedal as he went down through the gears, slowing, slowing . . .

Behind him, that awful squeal of tyre-rubber on wet stone. A car shunted him violently. His Nova ploughed forward and hit the front grille of the coach with a bang producing a cloud of glass fragments like outsize crystals of sugar.

McAuliffe felt their spraying agony and saw his own

blood spatter the grey plastic dash ... Disgusting. He had a moment to think it. But he was alive, and there was no deep pain yet. He was going to be OK ...

Then the asthma took him off-guard, a severe and sudden attack. It lay like a weight of glue in his lungs, pulling drapes of suffocating desperation over his popping eyes ... Somewhere close an engine was revving itself to destruction. He heard kids crying. A man yelled. The rain hammered tinnily on the car roof ...

McAuliffe tried to lurch forward in his seatbelt, but the inertia mechanism gripped him tight. In his panic he struggled with it, and it got him nowhere ...

He used two different kinds of inhalers – and by Christ he needed them now – but both were lost in the alien land beyond his hand's reach. He fell back, breath bellowing, each lungful drawn with a shudder.

Now, McAuliffe thought, I will die. And he believed it too. If only it hadn't been like this ... Just a few more years dear God ... He felt briefly sorry for himself, and was still waiting for the Dark Angel to pass by when the ambulance came like a banshee to his side.

A young woman paramedic gave him a shot of hydrocortisone straight into the quadriceps muscle of his right leg; then she held an oxygen mask over McAuliffe's face: he was half drowned and only muzzily aware of what was going on. In a dream, he stood on a flat, empty beach with a cold wind streaming in off the sea. The prevailing breeze chilled him, drenched him – and yet he could not seem to breathe it in. All this fresh air, and his damned lungs were not working!

Meanwhile, a second paramedic was unstrapping him and easing him out of the car, leaning him over with his head low above his knees. 'Bronchodilator?' he suggested. His partner agreed.

McAuliffe was fed more inhalants while they walked and carried him to the ambulance—

He was running down the beach, his track parallel with the waves folding and folding over the shore. Something was there up ahead – could he see it? Breathing was easier: he felt the atmosphere again, smelt its cold and salt. And distantly, in the headland haze, he saw a swirl and a shadow; a vastness, an elation . . .

McAuliffe increased his pace, experiencing now a small but growing desperation. It was such a wonderful day! A day of utter freedom. Here he was in this landscape of light and space, cleansed by the sun, chasing what was most important to him . . . It was . . . It was . . .

It was the secret of all life, the purpose of being. The future. The reason.

All at once he stopped, glanced down.

The ocean had cast up a stone, which lay half embedded in the flat gold sand. McAuliffe prised it up with cold fingers and walked to the sea's edge to clean it.

Never had he seen such a perfect shape; its colour, its texture and weight. Here, symbolized, was the answer to every question he might ask. But there was no need even to ask. McAuliffe knew that all he had to do was stare at this stone and he could enter it, tease out its every wonder.

I wish, he thought.

A hand came out of nowhere, from the air, and laid itself warmly over his shoulder.

McAuliffe gasped, felt his heart race. The stone fell from his fingers . . .

He never saw it land . . . Woke instead to a smiling Asian face, middle-aged, full of understanding. But she would never, ever understand what he had just lost. Despair echoed through him.

'Cup of tea, my dear? Milk? Sugar?'

McAuliffe closed his eyes.

He slept for three hours and woke with the tissue of his lungs feeling tender. There was also an ache in his thigh, down to the bone; and he had a big bass drum of a headache. But otherwise, he felt great.

Judith was sitting on a tubular steel chair beside him, reading a women's magazine. Her face wore an expression of mild disgust at the sound of a man in the next bed seemingly trying to cough himself inside out. McAuliffe wanted to giggle madly at her turned-down mouth and turned-up nose, as though she had just caught scent of the father of all farts.

Instead, he reached out and touched her leg; he was surprised to see a drip-feed going into the back of his hand.

'You're awake . . .' Judith put down the magazine.

'I'm alive,' McAuliffe said, revelling in it. It was the worst attack he'd suffered – one that in a man of his age, who did precious little exercise and worried more than he should, could put a dangerous strain on the heart.

'Your face is a mess,' she told him.

'Windscreen went . . .' He searched her features for concern. 'I guess we've got to rely on your Panda now . . . Shit, no wonder they're nearly extinct!'

McAuliffe thought that was pretty good off-the-cuff. But Judith's face had hardened, her moistening eyes filled with anger.

'It isn't funny, Pete. None of this is funny!'

The man in the next bed gave a great crackling cough and hawked up a golfball of phlegm into a cup.

McAuliffe thought the entire scenario was incredibly funny. He might have died, and she was angry that they were down to one car, that her careful dinner-party plans had been disrupted!

That was the nub of it. She did not want to shelve her chance to impress . . . McAuliffe cast back over the years of their marriage to see if he alone had created this moment but he came up with empty nets. No, they had both made this gap that now lay between them. Each had bustled about making a career, busily shooting at the moon. And a decade-and-a-half later, the real world was just as close, they saw. There was nothing at the end of the rainbow. And they had not even enjoyed the walk along its curve together.

'Listen, Jude. Don't worry about it. I can hire a car – or grab a lift with Jeff North if it comes to the pinch. I won't be in work for a day or so, anyway; I won't cramp your freedom.'

She looked at him sharply, her mouth disapproving.

'The ward sister said they're going to keep you in overnight for observation, to be on the safe side.'

The safe side. He wanted to cry.

Judith stayed on another half-hour and they chatted about nothing much. She'd brought fruit and a bottle of glucose drink in a carrier bag, and a sci-fi book she thought he might enjoy. McAuliffe had read it before, but didn't tell her.

The tea trolley coming round again gave them the opportunity to break off. Judith stood up and leaned to kiss her husband. One time, McAuliffe would've taken the chance for a good feel, and that would have led . . . Well, happy days, he thought, and accepted her careful kiss with a tired smile.

He watched her walk down the ward . . . She still had

good legs, but a certain haughty aloofness that he hated.

He took tea this time and was effusively pleasant to the Asian lady to make up for his coolness with Judith. It pained him that he had ducked the Grim Reaper's scythe winging over, only to find himself back in a minefield of double-meaning and pettiness. Was that what he wanted; more years of grumble and grind? Didn't his future amount to anything more than that? Was that it until the real Goodbye – being on the safe side?

McAuliffe was still smouldering quietly as Christine Lamb arrived and sat with her hands in her lap, wondering what to say . . .

It was worse for McAuliffe. Her appearance triggered off a vivid replay of both of them in the supermarket, he catching sight of Christine talking with Vicki Bell. She had not been as lucky as he: he was not stretched out on the slab, what was left of a murderer's madness . . .

He recalled that Vicki's eyes had been blue – as blue as the sky above the dream-beach he'd walked in his head. And her hair as yellow as the sand. So pretty. Dead now. Dead.

A pressure built up in McAuliffe very quickly, and overwhelmed him. He was amazed to find himself crying, a release he could not have allowed in Judith's presence. The sobbing would not stop, like a huge hand shaking him with grief.

Christine seemed embarrassed at first, but then sat on the bed and hugged him, pressing his trapped hand between them, his fingers moulded to her breast. Even in his pain he was aroused, acutely aware of her: enfolded by her hair, her perfume, he needed her so badly.

'She's not really lost to us,' Christine told him quietly. She

hadn't returned to the bedside chair, but sat midway up
the bed, at ease at last. Something had broken in McAuliffe
this day; a tension was gone. He seemed to be ten years
younger and three stone lighter. Now, instead of shooting
the moon, he could hurdle it.

But what was the girl talking about?

His face registered his confusion.

'I mean, not until all the lives that Vicki touched have
ended, will she end also. She lives in us, Pete: we live in her.'

McAuliffe wondered if Christine had 'got God', been
bitten by the Jesus bug. Somehow he hadn't imagined her
following a religion, but then, why shouldn't she? His
impression maybe was caused by an unconscious patroniz-
ing attitude towards her, because she was young and
attractive . . . Not that she wasn't intelligent. He remembered from her sixth form days that Christine had a sharp
mind – yet an erratic one. She knew everything about some
things, nothing about plenty: an odd, imbalanced kind of
education.

'You're going to make a good kid-counsellor,' he said,
smiling. She shrugged off the compliment.

'Well, I've blown out my first day coming to see you.
I'm sure Mrs Adams would not approve.'

'She doesn't know?' He was mildly surprised: pleased
too that Christine was not here through official channels,
but by her own choosing.

'She would not deem it proper for an ex-pupil to catch
sight of her teacher in his pyjamas . . .'

'Hardly black silk,' McAuliffe muttered. They were blue
polyester, in fact. He grinned to think that half of his
fantasy was assembled – himself, Christine Lamb and a
bed. Shame about the Lucozade on the side table and the
clatter of bedpans, and the years' accumulated smell of
disinfectant.

'Anyway,' he went on, 'how do you know *I* approve? All sorts of people could misconstrue this.'

He never intended to sound serious, or to be taken so. Christine's eyes understood him, and now it was her turn to play.

'Let them misconstrue . . .'

She was kissing him, and not for show. Her tongue was busy, her breath poured liquidly into his mouth, sweet, scented. And when he responded, she twitched away, returning to lick at his ear, kiss the tender places where his face had been cut.

'McAuliffe, you mean a lot to me . . .'

'I think—' he gasped. 'I think I need intensive care . . .'

'Don't joke, it isn't funny,' Christine told him, echoing his wife. She pulled away and pushed back her tumble of hair. Her realness was overwhelming, though McAuliffe doubted again that this could be happening to him . . .

Christine looked back at the man in the bed and knew she had calculated well. Circumstances had limited her choice, but this was a good man, reliable: and he appreciated now the piquancy of life, the dark terror of dying. She knew he would help her with all of his strength.

'What's wrong?'

'We need to talk, Pete—'

'You're telling me! Do you understand what's going on here?'

'Completely.'

'And you're happy with it? I mean, with us?'

Her gaze was frank. 'I'm afraid you'll suspect all kinds of ulterior motives when I explain about myself . . .'

As she said it, a dozen possibilities raced through his head, all of them unpleasant. He still decided he wanted her.

'If it's money, Christine—'

'Heck no, I'm not that poor! Anyhow, I wouldn't take advantage of you, Pete. I'm just – in a bit of trouble – that is, my family is in trouble. I need some help.'

'Tell me,' he offered.

'Not now. Get well first. Will you be at the school tomorrow – this week?'

'I'm in here for tonight. But I'll take a couple of days just to recover. Are you working?'

'We'll meet tomorrow then,' she decided for them both. 'Come to my house – Western Road—'

'Number sixteen,' he said, 'I remember.'

She returned his smile and leaned to kiss him once more.

'Thanks, Pete.'

'Wait until I've solved your problem for you, OK? Take care.'

She walked away and did not look back.

'Wow,' said the man in the next bed. He was grey and ravaged by phthisis and sounded like he was breathing through canvas. McAuliffe warmed to him for his good cheer.

'Yeah, wow, and I haven't brought my knee up, it's just a hard-on.'

The old guy wheezed out a last laugh and eased himself back on to his pillow.

That night, McAuliffe ran a slight fever. The night nurse gave him methaqualone, checked his blood pressure and pulse, listened to his chest for a while, then left him alone. He seemed to be half asleep during her check. But he was not.

It was no dream that McAuliffe was witnessing. At first he was merely intrigued by the spinning lights and the unusual tingling on his face, coincidentally where Christine had touched him with her tongue. Occasionally in the past, ideas had come to him 'out of the blue' as though offered into his head by some outside source. He'd put it down to the fact that his consciousness had no idea what the rest of his mind was up to. Now the phenomenon was happening again, with a vengeance.

He imagined that a dark door to the cosmos had been hauled open, and he made to stand at the brink and look out. And suddenly horizons did not exist beyond himself, at some vast distance, but inside, and thus were illusory. He knew, in an orgasmic moment of realization, that he could be anything. No gate stood on the public road, so he might walk freely throughout the universe. This was the nature of what he saw, and of what the voices sang to him . . .

McAuliffe listened to them for much of the night. Their rising and falling lambency reminded him of a tidal flow of waters over the land, oceanic in their breadth and depth. And even while he attended to the choir and its millions of mouths, individual whispers came to his ears as delicately as breeze-borne pollen.

I need you, McAuliffe, Christine told him many times. No one is ever lost to us – that was Vicki Bell's voice: McAuliffe wept again as he heard it, and laughed also to see that what she said was true, her floating hair tangling a passing star . . .

Yet there were other voices, horrors to him because they were beyond his experience. He shrank from them, screaming; but felt drawn to them also, since they belonged to him now and he to them, his fathers and mothers.

At the last, wreaths of cobweb decayed in front of his eyes and it was morning.

McAuliffe woke fully and saw that screens had been pulled around the old guy's bed, and that doctors were bustling there. The duty nurse said he'd died in his sleep, round about half an hour ago – at the height of McAuliffe's theophany.

A little later, McAuliffe was seen by a consultant and pronounced fit.

'You're looking much brighter today,' the doctor said with an easy, professional grin.

'Yeah, I know. I slept well. I feel like a new man.'

John Marius had a trim and tidy beard and always wore a spotless labcoat. Scobie noted that point. Literally spotless. Any stain, any spilled spot of chemical was enough to prompt the pathologist to reach into the cupboard for a clean one. Scobie reckoned he must drive his wife nuts at home, unless they were two of a kind, of course. And what a picture that would make!

Certainly Marius demanded the highest standards of cleanliness from Davies, his mortuary assistant. The poor kid was busy now, scrubbing worktops that were already sterile and sparkling: every tool gleamed, each glass and metal surface reflected the ceiling fluorescents beautifully. It was all part of Marius's ordered picture of the universe and his existence within it: neatly arranged, punctiliously planned, precisely defined . . .

Which made the thing on the table all the more difficult to deal with.

'OK, Doctor, give it to me again. It's a human hand—'

'It's Vicki Bell's hand, unburned because the killer was in a hurry and did not have time to tend the flames while they completed their work. I explained where I found it . . .'

'Yeah, you explained all that.' Scobie held up his hands

to calm the man down, finding himself in sympathy with Marius's state of mind. The pathologist was as neat and tidy as ever; only his eyes looked a little crazy this morning.

'But—' Scobie asked the question a second time. 'But how can it be? These bones are grossly deformed.'

'Now that's where we must begin – by defining our terms.'

'Is this going to be philosophy, Doc?' Scobie sighed, hating this kind of bull.

'If it gets us to the answer, who the hell cares? Actually, no it's not. But let's be clear: by "deformed", we mean "not formed according to what's normal". In other words, outside the bounds of what we consider to be usual.'

'OK, with you so far . . .'

'If you patronize me, Paul,' Marius said, quietly, 'you can solve it yourself . . .'

'I'm sorry. Go on.'

'But what if this hand is not deformed, but formed according to some other definition of normal? In its own terms, it might be perfectly formed.'

'But it's a *human* hand, Doctor—'

'Evidently not. Or at least, human with the capability to go beyond what's human.'

'I feel like I'm vanishing up my own asshole.' Scobie grinned wanly.

'What's the weather like?' A smile came and went, briefly, then Marius grew serious again.

'Really, I'm as puzzled as you. This is all pure speculation. Nothing's on record . . .'

'Don't worry, Doc, we're not going to publish this in *The Lancet* to further your career . . .'

'More likely to see print in *Weirdos Weekly* . . . However, I've taken some sections of bone tissue from the metacarpus – that's the skeleton of the hand between the wrist and the fingers – and from the terminal phalanx, the very end of the finger.'

'OK.'

'Here it gets interesting. The metacarpal section shows normally formed bone tissue: Haversian canals, lacunae – ordinary human structures. Now the finger-end is really strange. Ossification is not complete, and the structures are vague. It's as though the substance located at this point has not been finished. My guess, Paul, is that some trigger caused the bones to extend in this fashion, probably the intense trauma of the attack. And the girl's death halted the process prematurely . . .'

'OK,' Scobie said again, not quite knowing what else to say. 'But how? Why?'

'Let's leave the easy parts till the end,' Marius replied drily. 'If you've stayed on the bus so far, try this . . . The bone tissue from Tracy Vines displays the same incomplete formation zones. It is as though, *in articulo mortis* – at the moment of death, or during the period of the attack – the bodies of these girls underwent some incredible change that was never finished. Possibly that transformation was triggered by the shock of dying, or maybe as a kind of defence mechanism that we've never seen before.'

'This all hangs together,' Scobie said quietly. Marius lifted his hands in a 'maybe' gesture.

'How it works remains a mystery. You know as well as I do that individuals develop according to genetic information passed on from their parents, and that species evolve over geological epochs in response to environmental balances, or due to the incorporation of some sudden change to the genes. I will say, though, that there are other theories about life-fields and quantum leaps in evolution, but let's leave those alone for now.'

'Let's,' agreed Scobie. 'So if we can pull this tighter, Doctor, we have here girls that are different: outwardly human and normal, but capable of stunning transformations. Could it possibly be that the killer has somehow identified these individuals, and others, and intends to wipe them all out?'

'If we've gone so far in our thinking, then your idea makes sense.'

'I was forgetting Johnson – same m.o. Could he have been one of these abnormals?'

'Not enough left of him to test. But I'd guess, yes. He was one of them.'

Scobie stared hard at the thin, clawlike hand. 'OK, so what's living among us, Marius? And why are they dying in Clayton? Do they exist elsewhere? How do we find the next victim before the killer does?'

'Well, when you've finished your paperwork, you can start on those problems.'

The pathologist was not being ironic, and both men laughed tiredly. It was two on Tuesday morning and Scobie had not slept for nineteen hours. His brain was buzzing now, a whirl of marvels and horrors that refused to come together.

Marius recognized the signs of exhaustion. He put his hand on Scobie's shoulder.

'I am going to recommend you go home, drink a double Scotch and then climb into bed – if you make it that far up the stairs. But first, Paul, one more thing.'

Marius took a probe and indicated the terminal phalanges of the hand.

'This is where the tissue's unfinished, remember. Well, Paul, it's still growing—'

'Wha—'

'The phalanx of the thumb, for instance, has grown by

73

two millimetres over the past five hours . . .'

He walked the D.I. over to a bank of stainless steel body-drawers and hauled one out by the handle.

'Tracy Vines. Look at the rib I showed you before . . .'

Scobie looked. The smooth grey curve was knobbed and twisted with bubbles of bone, outgrown randomly. And attached to that bone, where there had been none before, were now shreds of living flesh.

'Holy Father.' Scobie crossed himself, the first time in years. He could not drag his eyes from the spectacle, until he realized that Marius was still talking to him in tones subdued by awe.

' . . . as though it was still trying to carry out its instructions – but with no soul to guide it, had no clue how to proceed . . .'

Steiger had stopped believing in Santa Claus when he was five; not down to anything he'd been told, but simply because, with no profit margin, what guy would be stupid enough to run a rooftop delivery service on only one night of the year? And never, ever, had miracles held credence in his mind: there was no God, and if Satan existed at all he was probably an AIDS-riddled wino by now living in cardboard city. No, the philosophy was simple, one he heard screamed daily to axework accompaniment – live fast, die fast, and get out of my fucking way 'coz I'm just passing through . . .

There was a certain revelation, he admitted woozily, in the sight of Anna Fuller's backside as she leaned at the bar ordering her round of drinks. She drank pints, like the lads, and always paid up when it was her turn. Nor did she meekly demur when the fourth jar came along, or the fifth . . . she was a bloody miracle in denim!

Steiger downed what was left in his glass and waited for the next. He was feeling good (though tomorrow the world, as the saying went, would drop out of his bottom). Something strange had happened tonight: he'd made friends. Not that he knew anything about this odd group of mystical rockers, nor did they know of him: but already he could feel the camaraderie of belonging to the band; an easy acceptance, a shared understanding that the world out there was pretty cold and pretty uncaring, and giving a communal V-sign back to it . . .

Ozzie finished a joke he'd been telling. Steiger caught only a meaningless punchline, but laughed anyway with the rest, wondering if they'd spot his façade.

Anna returned with the drinks. Steiger shook his head in quiet amazement. He had personally witnessed her sink four strong ales, and this was her fifth. Yet she looked as though she'd just come in off the street to take her first sip. Her hair hung down tantalizingly as she passed round the glasses: a buckle on her jacket touched Steiger's hand and a bolt of desire shot through him. I think I'm in love, he told himself. I'd do anything for her . . .

Midnight crept up. One of the barstaff locked the front doors and the lights were dimmed and the jukebox shut off. But the landlord continued to serve and no one showed much of an inclination to leave just yet.

The conversation got heavy.

It was Johan who started it. He showed Steiger the palm of his left hand, the skin cross-hatched with scars.

'Someone tried to glass me, it was outside a night club, and I stuck my hand in the way – I mean, anything to protect the face, right?'

Johan was a handsome boy, slick James Dean looks; but Ozzie guffawed like a bull.

'That's right, Yo, you can't afford to let the face get any worse, man!'

They all chuckled at Johan's expense, then fell quiet, knowing the outcome of this story.

'OK, so the guy got me in my hand instead, shredded it. And my wrist—' He pulled his cuff away to let Steiger see. Johan smiled. 'I can't remember it hurting, but I was plenty scared. There was so much blood, man. Enough to scare the other dudes away . . . I ran after them, don't know why – to retaliate or, well, dunno. But I didn't get too far. Fell flat on my back and watched myself bleeding to death. The stuff spurted out, like on the videos . . .'

'Then?' Steiger asked, caught in the tale, though he could guess the outcome, and his heart lifted.

'Then' – Johan looked across – 'Anna came along and was real concerned. I was half out of it by then; I mean, I couldn't see properly, everything had a grey halo that glowed, and the centres were red, man. Red.

'She told me not to worry. She wrapped a kind of dressing around my wrist – like – I dunno – like a tight rubber bandage, to stop the bleeding.'

'And did it?'

'You bet it did. She held on to my arm for a few minutes, then the bandage was gone. I lifted my hand to see, and it was a mess. The skin and flesh, just hanging in tatters. I thought, Jesus, that won't be no use to me now—'

'It was his jacking-off hand,' Ozzie interjected. No one laughed.

'So I looked again at Anna, thinking, like: who the hell is she and why's she troubling over me? "Don't worry," she told me again, "you'll be all right". And then, well, she just healed my hand.'

'How?' Steiger had to ask, believing it automatically,

but the rational part of his mind could not work it out.

Astoundingly, Johan blushed and stared at the table. Steiger saw that the others, too, were sharing his reticence.

'Come on, I ain't gonna laugh.'

'Steiger, I swear. She just kissed it better.'

If he'd not met her, Steiger would have had hysterics. Now he sat in the little sphere of reverent silence, the story's afterglow, and pondered this wonderful mystery. Slowly his eyes shifted to Anna. She was ordinary enough – a cracker, but ordinary enough. Steiger wondered what energy operated through her to cause these impossibilities.

'She's helped all of us, one way or another. Billy here came off his bike one night, bashed his head so hard he cracked open his crash-hat...' Johan indicated the kid beside him, a scrawny red-haired boy with a street-urchin grin. 'She patched up his skull, but we guessed his brains had leaked out by then...'

'Swivel on this,' Billy said, twizzling his middle finger at Johan.

'And Carl' – that was the fourth member of the gang, a tall, silent boy – 'he got beat-up and Anna fixed him.'

'I broke both my arms,' Carl explained. 'But inside of ten minutes, Anna had me up and walking.' His eyes were dark with emotions that Steiger could barely appreciate. 'We all love her for it, Steiger...'

'How about you, Oz?' Steiger asked. The kid pushed his glasses further up the bridge of his nose. He was grinning sheepishly, but there were deeper layers to his expression. Something told Steiger that none of the others really knew about Ozzie.

'Well, it was like this: I caught my dick in some elevator

doors, and Anna made it grow back twice the size—'

'She does that to all the guys, man,' Johan chipped in. 'It's twenty-two inches long now—'

'Get out of it, Oz!' Billy flipped beer-froth in Ozzie's direction. They were all laughing like crazy, but underneath it Steiger was wondering again what Anna's relationship was with these boys. Queen witch and her acolytes, maybe?

Someone rattled the front doors violently, and the pub went quiet inside. Steiger saw the landlord mouth something, probably obscene; he was certainly frightened as he hurried to unbolt them. It was way past supping-up-and-sodding-off time: Steiger checked his watch and it gave him twelve-forty-five. But why was there a problem? The cops knew all about this place, and the other dubious public houses in Clayton, and let things be. At least the problems were contained in a few known locations, and not running wild in the streets.

The doors were pushed open and four police officers came in, three men and a w.p.c.

'Check it out,' Oz whispered. 'Four of the bastards.'

The pub was totally silent now, all eyes on the uniforms. Something big had gone down tonight. With a sick lurching to his stomach, Steiger guessed what it would be.

One of the police officers, a sergeant, took the landlord aside and spoke to him privately. The landlord half turned back to indicate certain tables.

'Another killing,' Billy ventured. 'I'll lay money on it.'

'I was in all evening playing my Barry Manilow tapes.' Ozzie's eyes were hard and hostile.

A policeman came over.

'Evenin' all,' spat Oz. Anna glanced at him sharply.

'Stow it. How can we help?'

'There's been another murder, yeah?' Steiger asked. He hated the police and feared them, but still looked to them to solve horrors like this when they happened.

The cop looked back stonily.

'Landlord says you came in late – late even for this place.'

'So?'

'I need to know names, addresses: I need some I.D.: I need to know what you did all evening.'

'Can I buy you a Campari and soda, Nigel?' Ozzie asked in his friendliest tone. The cop's face coloured.

'Listen, smart boy,' he said nastily, 'if you get clever, you get busted, OK? It was a little girl this time, on the Wordsworth Estate. Now we are not letting go – not until it's solved. So, I want names, addresses and identification. . . .'

Ozzie sighed and pulled out a wallet that was falling apart, pulled from that a library card, a cheque card. The other members of the group followed. Except Anna. She sat still. Steiger picked up her uncertainty and began to worry with her.

The young officer checked each item he was offered carefully, because the instructions that had come down the line were very detailed and very clear. Take nothing on trust. Be alert for everything.

He handed back the scraps of cardboard and plastic and stood over Anna. She was near enough his own age, and so impossibly pretty she made him nervous. Under any other circumstances he would have let her be – no, he would have taken her name and number anyway, 'in the line of duty', then used it as a chat-up line. It had worked plenty of times before, and surely she wasn't making it with any of these morons? But orders were orders . . .

'Miss. Some identification, please?' He tried a smile, tried to switch from hardline cop to the soft approach.

'I don't have any,' Anna said. 'Look, I'm down from Scotland . . . I ran away, OK. I mean, my parents and all they – they just didn't understand me . . .'

'Fair enough, but where are you living in Clayton?'

'I'm living rough. I'm not anywhere permanently.'

The policeman was undecided. What she said sounded plausible he supposed; God knows there were enough runaways around these days. But—

'Your parents' address then . . .'

'You can't think I did these killings—'

'It's not the point. All you and your friends can do is corroborate each other's stories. Do you have any independent proof of where you were earlier this evening?'

'I guess not,' Anna said. She shrugged and gave him an address in Galloway; place called Leadmoor. 'It's a little village high in the heather. My mum and dad know the local constable. They'll tell you about me. In fact, they'll be glad to know I'm all right.'

'We might well not need to follow up on this,' the cop said, appraising her again with interested eyes. If she recognized that, she gave no reciprocal sign. 'But I will need a contact address here in the town, just in case.'

'Use mine,' Steiger offered straight away, with a flash-vision of her standing in his drab hallway, staring wistfully up the stairs. 'I mean, if you like . . .' They would have to meet again if she did. And shit, what the guys at work would say if they saw the two of them together.

'We are very close,' Steiger went on, his heart full of bravado, tantalizing the disgruntled cop. 'I can vouch for her.'

'And who can vouch for you, macho man?'

'I'm a tax payer.' Steiger gave his most irritating smile. 'That's enough in this country.'

The police officer put away his notepad. He gazed down at Steiger with a look of utter contempt.

'If you cross me once, I'll have you. Understand?'

'You been watchin' too many Clint Eastwood movies,' Ozzie told him.

The cop walked away.

Despite their air of tough rebellion, the group breathed a collective sigh of relief as the police left. The landlord almost sagged against his bar.

'It's a point, though,' Johan said, then. They were all staring at Anna. 'Where *do* you go at the end of the day?'

Anna smiled and finished her drink. Struck with a sudden conscience, the landlord was hustling punters out of the door.

'Now wouldn't that just completely spoil the mystery?' she asked them. And not one of them followed when she walked out.

The killer woke from a trembling sleep, shaking his head to clear it of dream-fragments. It was as though a great bag of coloured oils had burst in his brain; a formless fluid of visions and latencies that his human side could neither comprehend nor tolerate. They would, if they carried on, drive him to insanity.

His human side. He smiled. How meaningless that was becoming now, and how ironic, given his self-proclaimed mission.

He was growing easy in his changes, accustomed to them. Indeed, if he was true to himself, he was enjoying each metamorphosis aside from its necessity; exalting in the swell of flesh and bone to his will.

A lorry thundered over the bridge from which he hung. He looked down fifty feet of darkness to the river that swirled beneath, high and fast with October rain. He, too, was black and enigmatic, had an armspan of twenty feet and was swathed in membranes. He was a little cold, hungry again after his previous feast of rabbit and horseflesh . . .

But personal provision must wait. The voices had woken him, and it was of them that he must now take heed. Even at such a late hour they could block him in his aim; make him mad before they died away to silence . . .

He listened with his full concentration. Yes, he could sense death among them. Not just the passing of individuals, but the Great Ending that all Kin must face, unless their seed could be re-established in some new place and the accumulations of centuries be handed on.

The voices reminded him of this in their sad and pathetic choiring. They sang pictures to him, panoramas of the greatness they had seen all down the ages. Hadn't they helped humanity when the two breeds had touched? They had never willingly interfered to mankind's detriment . . .

But the temptation was always there: he was the living proof of it. In coming to hide among them, the Kin had learned to love in human ways – and hate too – patterning themselves so closely on the template of mankind that offspring could result which were neither human nor Kin, but a flawed melding of both imperfections. He was that unnatural product of natural processes, and so had grown powerful through his years, and increasingly torn by the conflicting tides of the two species that had sired him.

The killer shivered, a rippling in the moon-cast shadow of a greater blackness.

His weakness was also his strength, he thought. The ones who had left the nest and come here to establish the new growth proved the rightness of his actions. Already they had corrupted the purely human to their ways, to serve their purpose. His last victim (how her eyes had tried to understand as the blade went in) had been a mortal child, a human girl who had been tainted simply to aid the birth of the new generation. Although her abilities were limited, they were in her blood; her flesh held the entire potential of the Kin. He could not have let her live.

But there were others, pure Kin, living in this town and preparing the way. His mind picked up humans too, a growing number of them were used as vessels to aid that preparation. His work was far from complete, and time was running short.

Beneath the bridge arch, he stirred, shaking out the huge sails of his wings, letting his face slide into new configurations.

Yes, the flesh was still vigorous in Clayton, even though at home it was dwindling down through its last winter. The Community there was exhausted, like an old matriarch sick of life, whose fading hopes lived on only for her sons and daughters.

Well, they would never see the spring. This world had been defiled enough by the parasitic ways of the Kin, who could not forever tolerate a passive existence of hiding and running. Soon they would reach the stage of wanting to direct the evolution of life on the planet. And, not content with a blending of incompatibles, they would assume predominance, and humanity would cease being true to its name.

He could not let that happen.

Closing the voices out of his mind, the killer scanned the rough, grassy ground high upon the nearer bank; there, he spotted the movement of some animal, itself searching for prey.

He slithered over the stone, heedless of gravity, until his body was positioned to give him the best chance of success.

It was a cat, he saw, threadbare from skirmishings; one-eyed with torn and ragged ears. A fighter whose blood understood the ways of nature in all their violence and cruelty. The old tom was poised, listening to scufflings in the grass, mouse-movements nearby. His whole concentration was focused upon a few square inches of ground.

So the creature dropped, vast and silent, emitting only at the end a thin piping cry as it swept up the cat and carried it back to the underhang. There, a newly grown blueblack razor claw disembowelled the animal; and jaws that moments ago had been fantasy chewed and swallowed in two awesome bites.

Looking at Judith was like staring through a sheet of plate glass; like gazing into a TV at a TV housewife going about her business. Although she was rather quiet with him as she made a late breakfast, the change he perceived was not her fault. This odd sense of dissociation was in him. Humdrum life seemed a little flat because he had seen beyond it. The trouble with routines was that you got to feel, in the end, that they were the only reality, the one kind of existence possible. How many times when he had been driving to work had he wondered what it would be like to turn left here, instead of right to the school, and then to keep on going? What would life bring him if he consciously walked away from all it had brought him so far?

McAuliffe smiled. Dozens of times. Hundreds. Yet each time he'd turned right, knowing the impossibility of any other course of action.

Judith caught his expression but did not return it.

'What are your plans today?' she asked him, which McAuliffe took to mean, 'To what extent are you going to interfere with my routine?'

'I think I'll go for a drive, just potter around the countryside for a while. Maybe I'll drop by at school, to let them know I'll be back tomorrow—'

'Can't you ring?'

'I'd rather go in person. All of my colleagues will be so concerned about me, so glad to see me up and walking . . .'

The irony did not help matters. McAuliffe saw the cold impatience in his wife's face, which fuelled his own heat.

'For God's sake, Jude – isn't that why you went ahead and hired a car, to get me out from under your feet!'

'If that's what you choose to think, fine.'

'It's not a question of choosing to think anything! It's just—'

'Go on.'

'It's just your attitude, like I'm some kind of inconvenience . . .'

'I need solitude to work,' she said quietly.

McAuliffe threw up his arms. 'And that's my point. I'm in your way here, so I'll bugger off out. OK?'

Judith looked at the familiar cast of McAuliffe's face as his temper burned, and sighed wearily. It was becoming too frequent: he was often snappy, usually unsmiling, occasionally unbearable due to a deep anger he carried around inside. Maybe he didn't even realize it himself, but she guessed she knew what it was. After seventeen years of working, his achievements were modest: he'd gone nowhere, done nothing. OK, the house was nice and they lived comfortably – but the blandness of it all was a slow torture to both of them. And she couldn't help thinking, now and then in a hidden corner of her heart, that if she'd married someone with drive and a little influence, then her own ambitions might well have flowered early. As it was, she was a bored middle-class childless housewife who painted pretty pictures that people fawned over at village fêtes, but didn't buy: her work had no core of greatness to recommend it. And neither, Judith concluded, had she.

Now, as her husband drank the last of his coffee, Judith McAuliffe could not prevent tears springing to her eyes. They were tears of frustration and anger, yes; but also of a terrible disappointment that after such wonderful beginnings, their lives should come to this.

'Go if you want to, Pete. I don't mind.'

He took it with a surly grunt, thinking it was acquiescence to his plan of pottering about that day. It was more. She had sensed the presence of some other woman in her husband's life; just knew by ways she could not even have articulated . . . Maybe the distant look in his eye as his mind lay elsewhere; perhaps that he was more attentive to small details of personal appearance . . . Maybe that, maybe not. But she knew it; could smell the bitch.

She remembered reading somewhere that an affair can often revitalize a flagging marriage, but Judith was still old-fashioned enough to put betrayal and pain at the top of the spin-offs list. Yet she couldn't blame him. Sexually she was not at all demanding or adventurous – Pete wanted much more from her than she could ever give. In fact, she admitted, satisfaction was more frequently found with her own fingers than by her husband's love-making: self-stimulation being somehow cleaner, more convenient. Less – painful. She wondered if he understood that, or ever could.

Judith watched him now as he pulled on a plain blue jumper over his white shirt, slipped his wallet off the side table and went out for his jacket and keys. Then he came back to kiss her. He always did that.

'Well, I'm off. Have a good day, love . . . Sorry it started on a low note.'

She gave her best shot at feigning a carefree smile.

'Look, you've been through a lot – that awful hospital – that man dying—'

'Poor old sod.'

'Yes, but now forget him. Look, the sun's out; you've got some hours to spare . . . Drive out in the hills. I'll have a dinner ready for you when you get back. Let's eat at seven.'

'I've time for a pint beforehand, then . . .'

'OK, and I'll chill some wine also, for the meal.'

He kissed her lightly, and despite the cooling years between them, this kiss almost broke her heart: sweet, sincere, filled with a sense of ending.

She followed him to the door and watched him start up the hire car; laughed a little as he ground the unfamiliar gears. He drove off and she turned and went back to her paintings.

It was time. The intuitive understanding of that was like a cord between them. But it was all so fast and hurried, made the more urgent by the speed with which the Kin Slayer had found out his victims and slaughtered them. And after all her preparations, Christine Lamb felt completely unable to carry out her duties, to her partner or her breed.

She knelt to turn up the heat of the portable gasfire in the corner of the bedroom: the device burned with a flutter of flames over crumbling radiants, a wet heat that sent condensation streaming down the grimy windows. Christine herself was sweating freely, but Bruce needed the warmth. It helped, he'd told her, to cope with the pain of his unbeing.

The word terrified her. Unbeing. She was not even sure what it meant. The Elders back home had tried to explain that the only way to establish a new and vigorous seed was for one of their kind to give up all trace of identity; to become, as it were, a blank sheet on which the accumulated meanings of the Community could be written afresh. Everything learned by the previous generations was now engraved on the new and latent flesh, including a knowledge of how to ride the life-fields of the resident planet, manipulating its forms and their functions to the will of the rebirthed Kin.

To win, Christine was told, you first have to lose. To find yourself, you first have to give up everything . . .

It remained a tantalizing puzzle of the most frustrating kind, a paradox. Its solution sounded so simple, but the depth of its implications always defeated her.

She worried also about her individual identity. At home, on the moors, the old generation was dying: it had lived out its span. She was one of its progeny, brought to being fully formed, armed with a picture of this world and a purpose within it. She could not remember her arrival; failed always to recall that moment when the wet and bloodstreaked flesh of the fathers parted to let her leave. Her first recollection was of the tiny modest living room of her 'parents'' house – a mother and a father that had never coupled to create her. They had been made to keep up the sham of human ordinariness; no more a part of her, and no less, than the thing on the bed before her. But she smiled fondly to remember them, and wondered what they were doing now, and if they were still together in that little house in Leadmoor.

So, when the old flesh died – whether Bruce succeeded here or not – did she perish also, or was she permitted to live independently with her new freedom?

It was all so unclear! She knew only that the Community had a few chances to live on, and that the others sent here for that purpose were being systematically destroyed.

Frightened, trying not to panic, she hurried across the room to the bed and stared at the thing lying upon it.

He looked awful, a seething twist of stuff that was shaped like a human body, but had nothing of humanity about it. Bruce had lost the capacity for speech hours ago, in the darkest stretch of the night: he was now in close communication with all Kin, including Christine, given up to the mental tide of their voices as they willed and guided him through the change. Her job now was to see him safe, to create the best possible circumstances for it to happen.

Working through the checklist in her mind, Christine ran down the stairs and made sure for the tenth time that the doors and windows were locked and the house gave every appearance of being empty, a minor but perhaps important piece of deception. She had noticed the increased police activity in the town, and reflected bitterly on the irony of them knocking at her door at a critical moment, in their search for the killer of her brethren.

Satisfied that the house was secure, and that the street outside was quiet, she returned upstairs.

He was decaying in front of her eyes, changing even as she watched. The call of the Kin in her head was an ecstasy and a terror, a thing beyond her experience as it reached this new height.

Christine leaned and wiped the boy's forehead, kissing

him in a touchingly human but utterly inappropriate gesture of good luck.

Even as she stood there his lips parted and tore around the bursting balloon of his skull. His arms flailed wildly, then straightened, shooting out and slamming into opposite walls. Something else – no earthly structure – erupted upwards and broke through the flimsy ceiling into the roofspace, bracing the anchored body in preparation for what was to come. His eyes opened, entirely, gushing fluids. The substance of his body melted out over the surface of the bed. A mouth appeared, and snarled. Wiry hair squirmed over the creature's skin, which folded and unfolded upon itself, exuding forms and fragments in a wild uncontrolled transformation.

She could see in these first moments that the transfiguration was not sane, speeding grotesquely out of control. Some dreadful ineptitude was fouling the ungovernable machinery of its body. Visions poured into her head; the curdled magic of dreams gone awry.

It was heart-wrenching to know that most of the Kin were witness to this, linked by the one Mind watching part of itself fail and unravel into chaos . . .

What lived on and around the bed now, a raw and bloody mess, heaved and surged uselessly. The weight of meat ran on like a mad engine, spitting life, most of it malformed, some of it tortured horribly by the degree of its deformation.

'Help me – please – end – this . . .'

Her appeal was agonized, and not asked of God. She knew that although the Community was with her, she being the only physical member present made the decision hers.

But what?

Could she possibly salvage this obscenity? Its first incredible momentum over, it now lay torpid and huge, its energies dwindling. Many hearts pulsed weakly on the surface of the monstrosity; eyes by the score gazed out with more expressions in them than she could name. Mouths stretched in a mad multitude of smiles.

She could not bear to look at it. The thing needed to be burnt, to be put out of its own misery, and hers. That would be the right thing to do . . .

But the sudden darkening of the room as wings swept over the window, and the face that glared in at her, drove all such considerations out of her head.

McAuliffe needed Christine now to help him to make up his mind. That much was clear. Beyond that one thing, he had no clue what to do for the best.

One possibility of course was that he could finish his café lunch, drop by the school as he'd said; accept his colleagues' platitudinous good wishes, and then be home by seven for dinner. The natural extension to that was another, say, fifteen years of work; then retirement, decrepitude and death.

OK, strike it.

What he really wanted to do – what flared like lightning through his imagination – was to track down Christine Lamb and tell her how he felt. He loved her. Or would, at least, if she gave him the chance. Why didn't they go away together – sod the complications! Just go. Just be with one another, enjoying each moment they were allowed. Hell, they both had brains, they didn't mind working . . . It wasn't as though they needed to give up all hopes of a decent life. And he had some savings in a bank account that wasn't shared with Judith – and Judith would make out OK: no need even to sell the house. Judith's parents had plenty, they could buy McAuliffe out . . .

His thoughts idled on in this fashion for minutes, as he sipped at his coffee and scanned the local paper with half his mind.

The killing of Vicki Bell was featured prominently on the front page, with further coverage inside, the usual stuff; background on the family, the shocked reaction of neighbours, veiled police statements about 'the enquiry proceeding satisfactorily'; that guy Scobie sounded like a right berk: he had no fucking clue who did it, but couldn't bring himself to say so . . .

McAuliffe ranted mentally at the ineptitude of the law, until his eye caught a paragraph that made him stop and read more carfully.

D.I. Scobie was speculating that Vicki's murder could be linked to that of the prostitute killed days before – the same dreadful method had been used in both cases – and also to the slaying of a travelling salesman last winter: he too had been repeatedly hacked and then set alight. One other tenuous thread of evidence was that both the call girl – Tracy Vines – and Johnson the salesman had been born in the little Galloway village of Leadmoor . . .

That was it, the thorn in the side of McAuliffe's memory. Where the hell had he heard of that place before? Had he and Judith holidayed there? Quite possibly they'd passed by, since the Southern Lowlands was a favourite touring area of theirs . . .

But somehow, McAuliffe knew that wasn't the connection.

With a mild but unpleasant little shock, he wondered if Christine hailed from Leadmoor. It was the right part of the country – and yet she hadn't named her hometown.

Besides, McAuliffe knew he had seen the word written down; it had not been told him by anyone.

He finished his coffee, left what remained of his lunch and walked out to his car. It was still a glorious afternoon, but now he had to waste it.

He over-revved the engine as he manoeuvred out of the town's only short-stay car park, then took the road out towards Clayton Comprehensive school.

Their apathy at his return was overwhelming. One person, when he walked into the staffroom, asked after him. The others kept their heads down in their marking or scanning the job advertisements in the *Times Educational Supplement*.

McAuliffe didn't make a meal of it; said nothing in fact. He checked his pigeonhole for messages (there were none), binned the small sheaf of circulars that had already accumulated there, then walked quickly down the corridor to the Admin. block and the secretaries' office.

They, at least, seemed pleased to see him back. Maybe it was their professional façade of interest that they displayed, but McAuliffe chose to think not. He was nice in return, and when he got round to asking if he could check out some past pupils on the computer, they readily agreed.

He worked quickly, scrolling through previous years and forms, until he found Christine Lamb's admission number. Using that, he could easily get access to her address and background information; there, he found the address of the folks she'd stayed with in Clayton a couple of years back, and her family address: Leadmoor, Dumfries and Galloway District . . .

McAuliffe realized he must have checked out her details

before, as he had secretly done with all the girls he'd found attractive. Totally unprofessional, of course; but just a little game he'd played in his head.

It still meant nothing, of course. That two murder victims came from the same village as Christine could be sheer coincidence – and obviously the pattern broke down with poor Vicki Bell, who had been Clayton born and bred. Yet it was a link, one that maybe the cops had not yet made . . . McAuliffe could not really ask if the police had run a computer check at the Comp., but he did wonder after Christine Lamb.

'I just hope she's doing OK, with me not around . . . ?'

Doreen paused in her typing and thought a moment.

'Actually Pete, I don't think she's in today. No, that's right. Phoned through to say she was minding a sick friend . . .'

McAuliffe thanked the women and left.

He had enough now to justify calling the cops and talking with this Detective Inspector. That would be the sensible thing to do.

He ran out of the front entrance of the school, jumped in the car and sped crazily away.

Since when, he thought wryly, have I ever been sensible?

If she stayed, she'd die. By running, she had a chance of life, even though it meant leaving the appalling remains of her friend to suffer . . . Christine laughed aloud, a shrill and brittle sound – as if he hadn't suffered enough!

The killer needed to take time gathering himself to human form before entering. Even so, he smashed the glass and window-frame with hands that were twice the normal size and the colour of old pewter, and reached through with an arm still swathed in batskin.

Christine was not intimidated by the sight of him as such – she had seen wonders aplenty at home. But his eyes held such a fearful promise that she could not bear to face him.

She ran, slamming the door behind her, relying for escape on the delay caused by the setting of Bruce's cremation. Maybe neighbours would have heard the noise of his entry – someone might already have phoned the police! And was it possible that some flicker of sense and reason remained in her companion, that he might defend, not himself, but her against the Slayer?

These thoughts fled like blown cloud through Christine's head as she clattered dangerously down the stairs and along the dingy hallway to the front door. She looked back once with curiosity that was an agony in her chest. No sign of him yet. Perhaps she was safe.

The killer regarded what shared the room with him passionlessly. In their haste to perpetuate the Community, the Kin had forced this creature into the process too early, causing a deluge of change instead of a careful engineering. In human terms, this Kin had been all things – had lived many lives – in a single moment: even in its tragedy, it must have felt sublime.

He could hear the girl, hurrying away. No matter. He'd return later to destroy this abortion and concentrate now on following her and putting an end to her threat.

The door slammed. She ran out into the street.

He smiled. There was plenty of time.

McAuliffe slewed the car around into Western Road. His panic had grown during the journey across town. Unaccountably, since the evidence was still slight that she was in danger, and normally he was the most rational of men. Strange, but it was as though he was feeling what she was feeling; a kind of emotional telepathy. He grinned at the stupidity of it.

He raced the car along the terrace of grimy houses and braked hard at number sixteen. The front door was closed: the place looked empty.

He glanced across the road, in time to see Christine jump from the top of the wirelink fencing down on to BR wasteground.

McAuliffe blared the horn and waved, then realized she was unlikely to recognize him in the hire car.

Next second, from out of a side alley, a boy came running. He wore filthy blue jeans and a black leather jacket, scuffed almost to destruction. He was carrying a workbag, which he hurled over the fence and then climbed after it. He stooped to drag out what McAuliffe could see was a hammer.

His impulse then was to aim the car right at the fence and try a manoeuvre that common sense told him was futile. Nor was he fit or fast enough to climb in pursuit. Christine was out of sight now behind abandoned repair sheds; the killer – Jesus wept! *the killer* – was haring after her, and gaining.

McAuliffe accelerated to the end of the street, turned left, turned again in looking for a way on to the wasteground . . .

The girl was trying to feign panic, that was clear. The killer realized that he was being led away – but from what? The creature on the bed was going nowhere . . .

He concentrated on the undersong of the Kin swirling faintly through his mind. She was masking it, and he recognized and appreciated the force of will it took to accomplish that feat. Maybe one like her – an attendant to the seed-bearer – was in another house not far away; perhaps another of those in the squalid little terrace! It angered him to think that the nobility of his kind had been reduced to such undignified existence. Like rats forced to breed in the sewers, living on the shit of humanity.

His anger rekindled his determination and drove him faster on. At one point he lost her, and stood in a wilderness of rust-puddles listening to the silence. Then his mind found her again and he stalked, quietly changing, hammer upraised.

He turned a corner and she was there: he had her boxed in a brick canyon, crouched in a corner and shaking. Her female shape was very pleasing, so that his half-breed self was still able to lust for her: the more so, given the way she had struggled against the inevitable.

Ah well, it was nearly over now. He would wipe her from the world, and with it a fragment more of the Community's vision of its own future . . . Even at the last he could sense her pleas and terror. He advanced with the hammer . . .

Then paused at the sudden exultant look on her face. He spun as the car came at him.

McAuliffe could barely believe what he was doing. This act was part of another world. He just had time to think: in killing a killer, am I utterly damned myself?

The body went under the wheels with a bang, rather than flailing away: McAuliffe felt the axles crunching matter beneath them. He backed off, rode over the boy again; backed off . . .

Christine scrambled up and hurried past him: to the telephone, McAuliffe thought; and then: no, I'd better leave enough for the cops to identify . . . He was terribly scared, but some dark part of him was enjoying this.

He saw the kid's remains laid in a red swathe over the concrete. An arm, horribly twisted, held with a twirl of leather; a black and bloody tuft of hair . . .

McAuliffe reversed another few inches, easing away.

With a roar and a clang, a sabre sheared up through the bonnet and the whole car rocked. The kid was alive – and kicking!

A second later, one of the tyres blew out in a thunder of echoes reverberating from the canyon walls.

McAuliffe screamed and jerked forward, reversed, jerked forward; grinding the thing down, his hand slick with sweat on the gearstick. He felt something tearing at the underside of the chassis; metal was giving with a squeal . . .

Madness broke like a vessel in his head, a nightmare of murder gone wrong. Why wouldn't the bastard lie still and die! He laughed as he rocked the car backwards-forwards, backwards-forwards: then misjudged the juice pedal and drove straight into the wall.

The crash was not much: McAuliffe snapped against the belts, but then swung sideways and struck the side window hard.

He saw the glass smeared with his own blood and spittle, and the sky beyond getting brighter, brighter into a dazzle he could not bear. It hurt until a cool dark blanket was pulled, by someone, over the pain of his consciousness.

He woke grudgingly. The angles of the light had changed. The canyon was hung in blue shadow. McAuliffe shivered in the twilight cold.

All that had happened returned like a toothache, its reality built into his bones. Beneath him lay the kid he'd killed – and killed viciously . . . But why weren't the cops here already, swarming with their questions? Certainly they'd never believe he'd done this unpremeditated and attempting to protect ...

He had to find Christine. She'd vouch for him.

McAuliffe abandoned the vehicle, resisting the morbid temptation to gaze underneath. He retraced his steps back to Western Road and found Christine's house dark in the shadow of the old railway buildings. Dusk was the colour of roofslates: the first of the streetlights blinked on, strawberry red, quickly brightening.

He knocked on the door. Years ago, someone had painted it a pale lime green, but much of this had flaked away to show drab brown beneath. And the door's outer panel had warped through many drenching winters, bulging outward slightly and so enhancing the general air of decrepitude.

There was no answer to his knock. Neither could McAuliffe hear any sounds from inside; and all the front room windows – living-room and bedroom – were dark.

He felt caught by the magnet of indecision, held to the freezing street while he debated whether to break in, look for the girl elsewhere or, as he should do, go straight to the police.

It did not take long to choose this forlorn-looking unknown.

McAuliffe twisted at the corroded aluminium handle of the door; found it unlocked, and stepped inside.

The dark passage beyond stank of vomit, of meat gone bad. The air was rich with it and McAuliffe gagged automatically, dragging out a handkerchief to hold to his mouth and nose. As his stomach-heaving subsided, he searched for a lightswitch, his palm sweeping over mould-spotted paper that damp had half pulled from the plaster. There was no power in the house, he discovered, finding the switch and snapping it on and off several times.

He felt his way along the hall and into the single front room. It was full of cheap chipboard furniture and half-rotted carpets whose colours were turned muddy with grime and sodium light from the street. Even so, the room held signs of Christine's presence and personality, and McAuliffe's heart lifted.

There was piped gas here, to a three-radiant heater that stood in a gaudily tiled fireplace. Against the wall opposite was a sofa sagging with broken springs, and crumpled blankets just left in a messy heap: this is where she must have slept. In the corner were some clip-on shelving, holding a few books, a downmarket stereo, a bowl of nic-nacs, – and there was a torch. McAuliffe reached for it and turned it on. During months of disuse, its batteries had all but lost their charge: the bulb glowed a feeble amber-yellow. Hardly ideal, but sufficient to make the shadows step away, enabling him to complete his examination of the house, which he imagined would be cursory and fruit-less. Quite evidently she had gone.

She had left him.

The kitchen was medieval, with bare whitewashed brick and a few cracked white tiles around the cooker to act as a splashback. There was no fridge, and all the cupboard doors were hanging off or jammed shut.

The floor was surfaced with dirty brown linoleum, he saw as he swept the torchbeam by. Then his hand froze. A rat with eyes as bright as sparks was peering out from the gap between a cupboard and the stove. It was sensing beyond the light; finally decided there was no threat there, and scurried across to a hole in the corner from which it had originally emerged.

McAuliffe tracked it with a dry nausea in his guts: he saw that the floor in the corner was speckled with droppings, and with something larger that lay, black and motionless, close to the hole. It was unidentifiable at this distance. But he did not investigate.

Hurriedly now, to be done with it, McAuliffe climbed the stairs to finish his work. The front bedroom was a shell, containing a few packing cases, an ironing board and some heaps of junk on bare boards. He took a single step into the icy bathroom, smelt the damp, and withdrew.

Christine, he thought with no small bitterness, let me take you away from all this ...

One room left, a small back bedroom; a cramped tucka-way that would overlook the jungle of the back garden, and beyond that the bleak run of streets towards Clayton centre.

McAuliffe's torchbulb faded to a dull red filament as he pushed open the door. He gave the torch a firm bang against the heel of his hand.

He looked into the room.

The eruption of bile from his mouth happened before he could stop it. He leaned forward, to save soiling his clothes. He was instantly disgusted, right to his soul ...

Butchery had been done here with a violence – with a purposelessness – more profound than he could have imagined.

The walls were dappled with blood, the carpets turned to mush from being soaked in it. McAuliffe guessed that if he'd shone the light upwards while exploring the kitchen, he would have seen a topography of gore on the ceiling.

But worse than this, worse even than the vision of this violence, was the sheer quantity of hacked flesh laid out before him. It would surely fill a small meat wagon ... And yet none of it was immediately recognizable ... Merely reasonless masses of muscle threaded with artery and vein, the bluish-white curvatures of joints and bones protruding... Here were jaws, animal jaws, opened back on themselves, tongues purple and torn. Something like a crab's claw was angling out from great clots of a liverlike substance heaped up close to the window, and – Holy God! – what were these things, like bones ten feet long, jammed between opposite walls? Screens of membrane hung down from them, pink and finely capillaried, ripped in many places.

McAuliffe's horror changed then, its emphasis shifting. This was not slaughter. It was something more, something beyond simple death...

Here was a chaos of flesh. Totally foul. Yet McAuliffe now took a step forward. Christine had been here; she knew of this, and perhaps knew, too, the answer to its mystery...

There were tantalizing clues. McAuliffe almost lost his balance as his heel slid on a tangled muck of piping. His torch swung round...

Here was a crow's head perched on the malformed body of a pig, its hooves splayed out like chinese fans. There, a headless length of snake was exploded at one end to deliver a cascade of perfectly formed, utterly dead bees across the stained carpet.

The marvel of it surged and surged again through McAuliffe's mind. What in hell had he stumbled on here? Or what in heaven? This was happening to him now: he was standing amongst it, surrounded by this evil – no, not evil. The room held no sense of demons... No sense at all, in fact. It felt empty, as though this grotesque hulk of flesh had been deserted by its every inhabitant.

It was all so bizarre. McAuliffe imagined he'd walked

through a door to the Twilight Zone and here he was in a painting by Bosch.

He tilted the torch upward, and the extremity of his emotion changed again.

Directly above him gaped a hole, fringed with strings of matter and snapped lathwork that resembled a set of burst and broken ribs. He watched, almost entranced, as a tiny nugget of soft plaster twirled on a thread, spinning one way, slowing, pausing, then reversing its meaningless motion. Aircurrents gave it momentum to turn, surely. But McAuliffe's imagination could not help but speculate that some creature waited up there, claws perhaps hooked in the roof rafters; spreadeagled above the hole, glaring down and judging its moment to drop.

The thought brought a soft laugh from McAuliffe's throat, a twisted laugh husky with dread. For the thing to fall now would make the nightmare complete; a last blood-splashed sentence in the story of his dreams of Christine Lamb.

Ridiculous, of course. But here, anything was possible.

It was not courage but its opposite that caused McAuliffe to wait on another second or two. Nothing emerged from the gap in the ceiling. But something, groping gently like a blind worm on the deep sea bottom, found his foot and and slid over it.

By the faltering light of his torch he glimpsed what was alive and gazing up at him: kicked it and felt the red jawbones dislocate with a crack.

Then he ran, blundering down the stairs, keeping a grip on himself by concentrating on the one plan he could think of – other than bringing the monstrous face of this house out into the public eye which would, naturally, disbelieve what it saw.

McAuliffe recalled seeing candles on a shelf in the kitchen, and leaped at the thought that Christine had needed them to cook by, once the electricity had been disconnected. That meant the cooker worked on gas – please, he begged silently. It has to.

He turned at the bottom of the stairs and startled himself with the shadows that jumped as he aimed the torch along the hallway. His memory had been accurate. He lit the candles from the box of matches beside them: spent a frozen second scanning the ceiling and found proof of his earlier conviction – the crudely applied artex surface was a shocking Rorschach of bloodstains. And all that weight of meat above it, straining the boards to their limit . . .

It was too much for him. This place had stretched his mind, perhaps too far. He needed the company of his own kind again, to be away from this filth.

McAuliffe turned all of the stove's gasrings up to full, and by the hiss of their unending exhalation, and in mortal fear now for his life, he walked back down the passage and out into the street.

After the blue day, the night's stars were frozen on to the sky. Their familiarity made tears prick at McAuliffe's eyes.

He closed the lime green hardboard door, shutting in the gas smell. He shivered, then walked quickly away along the worn flagstone pavement towards town.

He was half a mile away when sixteen Western Road went up with a dull 'thump' of explosion and a bloom of light to the east.

By the time he heard the mad clanging of firetrucks through Clayton, he was standing on a cold platform at the station, waiting for a train to take him north.

To Leadmoor.

Paul Scobie's laugh was that of an exhausted man; low,

quiet, filled with as much bitterness as mirth. He felt like the cliché cop of the movies: ragged and almost too tired to think as he ran through the motions of detection. His In-tray sagged beneath a pile of unattended papers and his ash-tray sported a smiliar hill of dog-ends. To the left of his desk was a grey metal wastebin filled with sandwich wrappers and waxed milk cartons. The half-empty bottle of Scotch was discreetly tucked away in the bottom drawer.

It was an impossible situation: a psycho-killer wielding his mayhem within a mile of where Scobie sat; a pathologist talking in subdued and serious tones about non-human beings walking around – and being murdered – in Clayton; and a police force whose resources were stretched so thinly by Government cutbacks that they couldn't cope with normal crime, for Godsake!

And a man at a desk knowing he had to bring it all together, because that's what he was here to do.

Scobie sat back and sighed. Well, OK, his imagination could accommodate Marius's theories – but he'd be damned if he was going to breathe a word to the Chief Inspector about them! Though maybe they'd prove to be the key that unlocked this whole thing. Fine. Let them lie for now.

Scobie was more interested in the mundane links. Why Clayton, for a start? What was it about this particular town that made it the madman's killing ground? And then there was the slim but tantalizing Leadmoor connection. Scobie had checked the place out in the library. There wasn't much, of course, because the village was three-hundred miles away and these days was a forgotten emptiness on the road to nowhere.

After an hour's research, Scobie had at last found a few paragraphs in a book on the industrial development of Scotland in the nineteenth century. In its heyday, Leadmoor had been a thriving centre for the mining of galena; one of the biggest, and definitely the highest, lead mine in the country. With lead selling for £35 per ton in the 1820s, the area prospered and continued to do so – with ups and downs that followed the tonnage price for the metal – right through until the 1930s. This was a time of drastic closure, mainly due to the increasing cost of mining at greater and greater depth, and because of drainage problems in the galleries. Sustained competition from foreign imports of the metal sealed the fate of Leadmoor as late as 1948; but by this time only a fraction of the original workings were still in use.

Now, over four decades on, Leadmoor was a straggle of cottages amidst a landscape of spoil heaps. Fewer and fewer people lived there, it seemed, and all indications were that the place could be abandoned entirely by the end of the century.

It made sense, then, that younger people should leave to seek work and opportunity elsewhere. Johnson had moved to the more prosperous south to ply his trade – though why he lived in Clayton was a mystery. And then there was Tracy Vines. Scobie wondered if the girl made more per trick here than elsewhere. He doubted it. Prostitutes busted locally always complained that it wasn't worth the trouble of shaving their beavers for the money they could demand.

So, again, why Clayton?

As far as Scobie could see, the most important link was the depressed nature of the place. Leadmoor and Clayton, in their own ways, were both dying. You only had to drive beyond the centre of the town to see the areas of wasteground, the empty buildings and abandoned sites, the half-completed projects left to rot back to rubble by a bankrupt council. And folks were leaving this town too, when they could . . .

Could it be, then, that the killer had once lived in Leadmoor, and had suffered there somehow? Now, he was taking his revenge against those who had tried to leave? Or against the town itself, another cul-de-sac of failed opportunity?

That didn't account for the abnormal nature of the victims, though (one of them being Vicki Bell, who upset the pattern).

Scobie recalled the deformities of bone he had seen. Some kind of plague, perhaps – some hitherto unknown genetic plague that arose in the people of Leadmoor, and was carried south by those that had moved, for whatever reason, to Clayton.

It fitted the facts, Scobie admitted. And as a much-admired fictional predecessor had said: once you have eliminated the possible, whatever remains, however improbable, must be the truth . . .

It might also be, of course, Scobie admitted, that I'm pissing in the wind.

On impulse, he took out his Scotch and poured a generous slug into his coffee mug. Also on impulse, he put through a call to his opposite number in Dumfries, which was the nearest town to Leadmoor boasting a Divisional Office, asking if he could please speak with D.I. Ralph Peterson.

Peterson came on the line a minute later, by which time Scobie had decided not to air his own ideas to someone who might be led to doubt their sanity. He asked simply if any murders were on file for Leadmoor and the district that mirrored the m.o. of the Clayton killer.

Peterson said he'd check and call back.

While Scobie was waiting, a call came through on his other line. It was Carter, Scobie's Detective Sergeant, who communicated for the first ten seconds more by the tone of his voice than by its content.

Scobie shut him up and asked him what he was ranting about. The man sounded more than excited – scared shitless actually.

'Sorry, sir. There's been a gas explosion down near the railway yards. Western Road. Number sixteen—'

'So what does—'

'Doctor Marius says you should be down here, sir. He says it's like nothing we've ever seen before . . .'

Christ Almighty, Scobie thought. It's happened again. He said he'd be right along, and instructed his secretary to contact him on the car-phone with the results of Peterson's check.

He had one of the drivers take him down to the scene: Scobie felt too weak and weary to be safe. During the journey, his secretary called to pass on Peterson's information that no murders of any kind had been committed at Leadmoor for as far back as the records went. That was an anomaly in itself, but at this stage Scobie was looking for killers, not their unusual absence.

By the time he arrived at Western Road, it was full night. Three fire engines and two Gas Board vans had brought the crisis under control; not that the fire had seriously threatened surrounding homes. The explosion itself had collapsed the top floors down to ground level and smashed out the back walls of number sixteen: the house looked like a broken tooth in a crumbling redbrick jaw.

Scobie buttoned up his coat and made his way through danger barriers and ranks of fire officers until he found

Carter and Marius. Both men were standing by the steaming, smoking shell of the house, barely containing their impatience. It looks like the skull of a beast with its eyes put out, Scobie thought, wondering if he was letting his imagination run away with him. Or not.

Carter, tall and blond and still young enough to be enthusiastic, rushed up to his boss and all but dragged him by the elbow.

'This is unbelievable, sir! It's like, right out a horror film!'

'You been taking vitamin supplements again, Carter?' Scobie said drily, his stock response to the sergeant's verve. 'Just calm down and let's see what's what.'

'Who knows what's what?' Carter came back, but by then Marius had his attention, and the pathologist's face looked strained.

'So, this time we've got The Thing From Outer Space cornered and willing to negotiate, right?' Scobie said, but was put off from further sarcasm by the way Marius looked at him.

'Come through,' the pathologist said.

The two men, with Carter hovering on the threshold, went into the shattered gloom of the house, picking carefully over lath and plaster brought down by the blast, or pulled down by firecrews for safety. The sour smell of burnt, wet wood made Scobie wrinkle up his nose; but under that, viscous and foul, was something else.

'Bloody hell . . .'

'Disgusting, isn't it?'

'What died in here?'

'Your guess', Marius told him, 'is as good as mine.'

They came upon the sheep's head first: or something that was like a sheep's head. It emerged from a glossy stretch of scaled skin, like crocodile skin, which in turn grew a thick mat of fur, before subsiding into raw flesh.

Scobie felt his stomach turn, sluggishly, like a reluctant engine on a cold morning. He took out a pencil torch and flipped on the beam. The organic wreckage was astonishing.

'Look at that . . . !'

Huge half-barrel ribs stuck up toward the roof, like the hull beams of a scuttled galleon. Lying in that cupped bone was a mass of tissue, some of it recognizable, most of it just dead flesh, without structure or meaning.

'Noah's Ark', Scobie said quietly, 'painted by Dali . . .'

'You realize that this is part of your case?'

'What?'

Scobie aimed his torch. The pathologist's face leaped out white and stark against a red background of steaming meat.

'This – creature – displays the same proclivity for rapid growth and transformation that the rib and the little girl's hand did . . .'

'But this mess is nothing like—'

'It *is* like,' Marius insisted. 'It is like, Paul. I am telling you that the rib, the hand, this flesh, have all been influenced by the same force. The rib in my lab is growing, still alive: bone is emerging from bone because its instructions stop there. It can only become bone, but randomly. The hand seems to have stopped growing: as though it was given the command to transform into another hand that was less than human – or more. Its job is done. The cells are quiescent.'

'But this—'

'This', Marius said, hazarding guesses, 'is the result of a data overload; a program gone wrong. Just look at it, Paul.

Whatever this being originally was, it has since tried to change into *everything*. Obviously, even with its amazing powers of transformation, it could not accommodate the climax of change that flooded through it . . .'

Scobie suddenly felt the blood drain out of his face.

'It's not still alive, is it?'

'No.' Marius almost sounded sorry. 'Thinking in computer terms again, I'd say that the whole system crashed pretty rapidly. The cells diversified and proliferated in the first moments, a wild and wonderful burst of life, but they had nowhere to go. No end product – or one that was too difficult to sustain. So they shut down. It's dead, all right.'

Scobie offered a sick smile.

'You realize that we could both be starting our first day of early retirement by tomorrow morning, should we repeat any of this.'

The pathologist lifted his hands. 'Here's proof of it. Although it won't be long before the decay forms a health hazard. Let's make a decision, Paul.'

'When in doubt, pass the buck up the line. I'll talk to Haskins. Although personally I'd like to see the gas turned back on: I'd be happy to toss in the lighted match.'

Scobie coughed, hawked, spat.

'The stench is getting to me . . . You take your samples, John, and video what's here. I'll get on the telephone.'

'Fair enough—'

'And remember,' Scobie added wickedly, 'in Western Road, no one can hear you scream . . .'

Outside, he spent a few moments quizzing the fire guys about their impressions. He was told that half of the houses in the street were empty, and that the occupants of those lived in had been evacuated.

'I saw one old lady talking to your man – tall, fair-haired guy,' the Chief Fire Officer said.

'Carter. Thanks. Oh, by the way—' Scobie looked hard at the man, wondering how much to say. 'Did you see anything unusual in that house? I mean—'

'I know what you mean, sir. And I'll tell you, if you strap me down and rig up my bollocks to mains electricity, I still won't breathe a word of what I saw in there. Not ever. Same for my men.'

'Good enough', Scobie said. Probably better that way.

He looked around for Carter, but the sergeant found him. Carter came hurrying up with a uniformed officer that Scobie vaguely recognized.

'Sir—'

'Is it good news, Carter, or bad news?' Scobie had seen too much this night; had too many crazy thoughts. Flippancy seemed the only way to deal with the world.

'Bad, sir.'

'Oh, shit.' Scobie looked at the policeman. 'Holroyd, isn't it?'

'That's right, sir.' The cop was pleased that the D.I. had remembered him. 'I was at the briefing you gave after the Bell killing.'

'Yeah. Turn anything up?'

'Plenty of odd characters in the town's pubs, sir.'

'Clayton is an odd kind of town, Holroyd.'

'Yes, sir.'

'Give me your bad news.'

The brief moment of informality ended as Holroyd's face changed, assuming an expression of professional seriousness.

'We were searching over on the wasteground, sir, at Sergeant Carter's request. Standard procedure in the event—'

'Get on with it.'

'Sir. A body, sir.' Holroyd pointed into the darkness. 'Run over by a car. Repeatedly. Badly mangled.'

'Is it dead?' Scobie asked. A moment's pause.

'I beg your pardon?'

'Is it dead? Is it normal?'

'It's spread over half the—'

'But is it—'

'It's dead, sir.' Holroyd almost laughed. 'Some poor kid has been mashed. He's dead.'

Scobie seemed to relax visibly. He breathed in slowly, deeply. Then smiled.

'Not such bad news after all. OK, let's do the business.'

Judith McAuliffe was not very good at sexual fantasies. Her imagination could accommodate a world-picture of the way she'd like things to be, but when it came to eroticism, it failed her. Not that Pete had protested much, even when she objected to being a part of *his* sex-dreams ... She simply was not interested in the esoteric fripperies of the procreative act. That's how she viewed it, and that was her unassailable position on the matter.

Some years ago, Pete had gone out and bought her 'the kit'; a black basque, stockings, high-heels ... She'd worn it once and felt uncomfortable and cheap. Pete's erection had lasted all day.

Judith smiled to herself. So like a little boy, as all men were, pleased by such silly things. And utterly brain-washed, of course, by the media stereotypes of what constituted desirability and beauty.

She sighed, picked up her glass and swung it unsteadily towards her mouth. She was, as Pete said, 'well ginned': on her third now, and the stuff was tasting stale. She wasn't even enjoying the buzz. But she supposed it was the thing to do when doubt over your husband's fidelity became a conviction of his betrayal.

The casserole was ruined. Her carefully planned mood was ruined. And now, unbidden tears were ruining the mascara she'd put on as part of her condescension to Pete's sexual preferences. Or so she supposed. It had been clear that he'd met someone else: probably right now he was screwing the bitch in the back of the hire car, or in some grubby little hotel room . . .

Judity tried to imagine the scene and the act. She finished her gin, let her head relax against the chairback, closed her eyes . . .

How young would she be? And how pretty? Did she wear 'the kit' for Pete, or just strip off and do the whole thing clinically, without romance or preamble? Just let him lie on her, face to face, flesh to flesh . . .

She imagined their bodies slapping together, their rutting smell, their twisted faces and eyes dark with lust . . .

Judith's fingers slid over her stomach and down, to tease at the playing places there; to rub and rub. Even as she cried, to rub and rub—

'Oh!'

There was a ring on the doorbell and she snatched her hand away guiltily. It wasn't Pete; he had keys.

Apprehensively, and with a flushed face, she hurried to answer the call.

The two men at the porch looked unkempt and tired, one – the older one – much more so. He was holding out an I.D. card.

'Mrs McAuliffe?'

'Yes, but—'

'Police. C.I.D. Can we come in?'

The question, perhaps, was a formality. Both men were already stepping past her into the hallway. Judith followed, and a moment before the misgiving dropped through her heart, she experienced a second of insane desire herself, that perhaps these two were not police at all, and any minute now would rip away her dressing gown and nightdress, and she in her nakedness would fall back before them . . .

'Is it serious?' she asked, stupidly; because that's what everyone asked, and of course it was bloody serious. C.I.D. didn't call for a parking offence . . .

'Could be,' the older one said. 'I'm D.I. Scobie, by the way. This is Sergeant Carter.'

They did not shake hands. Judith McAuliffe started to tremble, ever so slightly.

'Is it P-Peter . . . ?'

'Please,' Scobie told her. 'Don't alarm yourself. We don't know that anything's happened to your husband. It's just that we've found his car, under rather unpleasant circumstances.'

The woman gave a little gasp, the first frayed thread before hysteria unravelled inside her. Scobie thought she looked wrecked; cried out, half-canned, a mess. He felt sorry for her without knowing why.

'How about some tea, Mrs McAuliffe? Then we'll talk.'

'I could murder a cuppa,' Carter chipped in cheerfully, then could've bitten his tongue out.

Judith saw Scobie's withering glare and the younger man's look of guilty apology. It was a pantomime; some soap-opera scene and she an unwilling participant.

'Tea, yes. Good idea.' Or something stronger – her mind ran on – No thank you, madam, not when we're on duty . . .

They helped break the tension together with the ritual of offering milk and sugar, passing cups.

Then Scobie began to talk.

He did not say much, other than that a serious crime had been committed and the hire car was found on the scene.

'Actually, it's booked out to you, Mrs McAuliffe . . .'

'But I haven't driven it, except home . . .' She explained about Pete's accident and then, after a slight hesitation, the reasons for hiring it – all of them. Scobie read the signs of an outwardly normal marriage breaking up from within. It was another straw heaped on the camel's back.

'So you really don't know where Mr McAuliffe went today?'

Judith replayed their conversation of that morning, adding; 'There's plenty of casserole if you're hungry, gentlemen. Could you murder a stew, Sergeant Carter? . . . I'm sorry, that was cruel.'

'Not to worry,' Carter came back. 'I'm the flat-footed bobby who put his foot in it. All my fault . . .'

Scobie tried another angle. 'Does your husband know anybody who lives on Western Road – little terrace down by the old British Rail shunting yards?'

'Down there?' Puzzlement as she thought. 'I don't think so . . . I don't think any of the staff at the school live that way.'

'That's the comprehensive in town, I take it?'

Judith paused before answering. She was thinking that would be where Peter's slag-bitch girlfriend must live. A whore wallowing in squalor. Well, good. They deserved each other!

'Mrs McAuliffe?'

'Um, yes. Clayton Comp. He said he'd be dropping by this afternoon, prior to going back to work.'

'Fine. That'll be our next port of call – Oh, I don't suppose you have the Head's number, do you? If so, perhaps we could ring from here? Saves time.'

Judith dug out the number. Scobie made his call.

'If your husband does turn up tonight, maybe you'd let us know?'

'Of course, Detective Inspector. After I've sliced his balls off, naturally,' she said, stone cold sober by now.

Mrs Adams did not appreciate being woken at this time of night and told to drive out to a cold and empty school. She made that much quite clear in the first ninety seconds of their meeting.

For his part, Scobie explained that this was a serious crime enquiry and that time was of the essence.

They sat in the secretaries' office; a single small room brightly lit, within a maze of darkened spaces. Mrs Adams had her stockinged legs tightly crossed, and her arms folded under her impressive bosom. She looked angry and domineering: not at all my type, Scobie reflected.

He did not go into details, but gently probed about Pete McAuliffe and Adams' impression of him.

'Competent teacher. A little stale in his approach, I'd say: been here too long. Not ambitious. Stable . . .'

'Not likely to fly off the handle or suffer a breakdown, you think?'

'Who can say, Mr Scobie—'

'Detective Inspector.'

'Quite. But his accident must have shaken him up, so one never knows. Why do you ask?'

'You have your personnel files on computer, I take it?'

'Staff and pupils, yes.'

'I'm interested in anyone who has moved to this area from Scotland.'

'I'll check.'

'No need, Mrs Adams. Carter can do that. Any chance

of some coffee? My sergeant and I could do grievous bodily harm to a cup of coffee, right Carter?'

'Absolutely,' Carter said, grinning.

Mrs Adams switched on the office machine and called up the database Scobie wanted. It was a straight alphabetical listing of staff and pupils; biogs and histories, but with no cross-referencing program to enable an alphabetical list of previous addresses to be accessed. Sheer legwork for Carter, but he was used to it . . .

Coffee was duly made. Scobie sat staring at the notices on the walls, and Mrs Adams read a paperback (*Lolita*, Scobie noted with amusement), and over half an hour passed before he thought to ask:

'Mrs Adams, is this a complete listing of people in your school?'

The woman frowned. 'Well, yes, of permanent staff and students.'

'You mean that visitors or temporary staff are not here?'

'There would not be much point, Mr Scobie. Valuable time would be wasted forever updating the files.'

Scobie controlled his impatience. 'Yes. But you do have files of temporary personnel?'

'We have a card file . . . Actually, now you mention it, one of our new students has a Scottish accent. Christine Lamb. Lovely girl, and a past pupil of ours, actually—'

'Could you check her address, please? Carter, access Christine Lamb on your machine . . .'

'And she was under Mr McAuliffe's care. She's doing a counselling course, you know . . .'

Mrs Adams searched through the filebox for the card, and passed it to Scobie.

Fucking bullseye: Christine Lamb, 16, Western Road, Clayton—

'Sir!' Carter's yell made them all jump.

Scobie looked at the screen, then sat down slowly to gather the implications together.

The girl had been born in the village of Leadmoor.

That revelation acted like some kind of sluicegate to the tensions built up in Scobie's body. Outside the school he focused his eyes with an effort and checked his watch, finding the time not far off midnight. Much too late for good little boys and girls to be out on the streets. Carter was cracking his jaw, too, in a mighty yawn, his breath forming clouds in the air.

'Well, Sergeant, a good day's work. Time now, I think, for a good night's sleep. Are you up to taking me home?'

'I'll drop you off on the way to my flat, sir.'

'Good lad.'

They walked across the empty, wind-swept car park towards Carter's Golf GTI: an ostentatious little motor, Scobie always thought, but it couldn't half bloody move.

Carter unlocked his D.I.'s door first.

'Sir—'

'Tomorrow, please . . .'

'I was just wondering about the – animal – down on Western Road . . .'

'If you mean Doctor Marius . . .'

Carter's smile was perfunctory. 'You know.'

'Marius will decide, but I guess he'll have it incinerated.'

'I wonder – where it came from. Why it's here.'

'The largest and most profound questions a man can ask, Sergeant. If I had more than two brain cells awake just now, I'd have a deep discussion with you about it.'

'Do you think they've been here long? These beings?'

That was it, then. Scobie, in listening to the words of his subordinate, who was a very ordinary guy, had come to realize that the universe had been opened up by the simple cut of a claw. The Outsiders were here – and they had not arrived in a storm of blazing comets or a ship the size of New York shaped like a lens of steel. No, they had come in secret and hiding, and now emerged as corpses oozing blood and miracles.

'I think', Scobie said quietly, 'that they've been here a long, long time, Dennis.'

'So it's not an invasion?'

The glass of Carter's windscreen and the side-windows had steamed up. He fired up the engine and flicked the blower on full.

Scobie wiped the passenger window with his sleeve and stared out at the stars. He didn't reply to his sergeant's question, but thought that, no, it wasn't an invasion. Armageddon maybe, but not an invasion.

Carter pulled away and drove with unusual care towards the suburbs.

Kevin Steiger woke with the sun spilling weakly off his windowsill. Another lovely October morning. He couldn't recall going to sleep: couldn't recall, in fact, arriving home ... He remembered the pub, though – another great night with Anna and the boys! And this time it wasn't spoilt by nosey cops or murders ... Some kind of fire, maybe. Fire engines had screamed by right outside, and he and a few of the punters had wandered outside for a look. But there was nothing to see. And anyway, even a minute away from Anna Fuller was much too long.

It was tempting to go back to sleep, since Steiger had a midweek day off in lieu of the Saturday he'd worked. He lifted his head to stare at the alarm clock. Eight-thirty. Shit, what an obscene hour when you don't have to work!

Steiger closed his eyes and felt the waves of sleep lap around him at once. He fixed a picture of Anna in his mind's eye . . . Oh Kevin, you're so handsome, so virile. Ooo, just looking at you makes me want to – want to—

Steiger's hand was between his legs, working. Less than a minute later it flopped limply to the sheet, and he began to snore.

A clatter downstairs woke him a second time; a familiar sound in an unfamiliar context. His mind was alert while his body was still unresponsive clay, inert with sleep . . .

Crockery in the kitchen; someone washing up, tidying, putting away . . .

Steiger let his thoughts run along the problem. Did it matter that much? But yes, it was a Wednesday – his mother would be out, stacking shelves in a local shop – therefore . . . Therefore no one should be downstairs at all!

A little thrill of lightning shot through him. For all his bravado, he admitted to himself, he was deeply scared of the unknown. He kept a French Opinel hunting knife and half a broomshank under his bed in case of burglars, dreading the day when he might have to use them. His father, who had walked out on Kevin and his mother long since, had once said; 'If you catch one of the thieving bastards on your property, don't argue, don't ask any questions – just cripple the fucker! Cripple him and then scream self-defence when the pigs arrive . . .'

Steiger had always remembered that piece of folk wisdom, though perhaps had never taken it entirely to heart.

Now, fully awake but wishing he wasn't, Steiger

retrieved his knife – the folding-blade already open and ready – and his sawn-off length of broomstick, and swung himself carefully out of bed. He halted at the top of the stairs, listening. The radio was on low, playing charts music; the intruder was moving around, it seemed, quite openly, seeing to the washing up that had accumulated over the past couple of days.

It didn't sound like a break-in, Steiger told himself.

He hitched up his pyjama trousers and crept down, identifying his guest before he fully believed it.

'Anna?'

The girl turned, looking a little guilty at being caught. She was every bit as wonderful as Steiger had pictured her in his dreams; tall, well-built, blonde: and her reality hit him again, powerfully. She was here, in his house, at home in his kitchen . . . Now she was walking towards him, her hips swaying fluidly, her smile turned-up and teasing.

'I don't suppose you remember, eh, Kevin?'

'Well—'

'I thought not,' Anna said, but she did not look disappointed or upset. 'You put plenty away last night. Ozzie was amazed at the amount you could drink . . .'

I only had a few quid in my pocket, Steiger reminded himself, but Anna was talking on, almost as though she could hear him thinking.

'But we're your friends now, Kevin; Ozzie, Johan, Billy, Carl . . . Look, when you're spent up, that shouldn't stop you from having a good time, right? We paid for your drinks. And when you're flush again, you can treat us.'

'Sounds fine to me.' Steiger realized he had no headache, no hollow stomach; no after-effects at all. He felt bloody great, in fact.

'That's OK, then . . . Oh, you're wondering why I'm

here? Well, someone had to bring you home. And your mum – she's so sweet – she couldn't bear to see me wandering through Clayton at that time of night, with nowhere to go.'

Anna beamed.

'So she let me stay, in your front bedroom. Hope you don't mind?'

Steiger nearly burst into hysterical gigglings. She had been within five yards of him all night, and he sunk in a stupor and never knew it.

'No, I don't mind . . .' He grinned, stupidly; doubly so when he remembered what he was carrying. 'Uh, no. You stay as long as you like, Anna . . .' Although he wondered what had come over his mother, to be so magnanimous to a girl such as this, 'on the suck', as she called Anna's type, meaning it in all senses of the word.

'But my mum – she doesn't usually – I mean—'

Anna shrugged lightly. 'I guess she just had a change of heart, Kevin. Anyway, what are you doing with that stick of yours?'

He glanced down in a panic. Then laughed. 'Oh, you mean—' And looked up again to find her stepping up to him, bringing her mouth close to his.

'Kevin, you've been so kind to me. I really don't know how to repay you . . .'

Steiger thought of a few ways immediately, all of them obscene. Although he did like her for her personality, of course: he respected her mind.

He had also developed a huge hard-on at her proximity, which stuck out nakedly through his pyjama trousers.

She kissed him: and like on the movies, music started up quietly, but a strange kind of music, sprinkled with whispers. And she knew how to kiss! Felt like her tongue was halfway down his throat – Jesus, what was she doing to him down there – but how could she be when they were kissing – and both hands were wrapped around his neck?

Steiger struggled once, momentarily: but she held him and drew him to herself even more closely.

It felt— Wha – what – is this – I can't believe how wonderful— It felt as though she was surrounding him with her presence. It felt to Steiger like he was in her – a lover – but protected under her wing – a child. All was darkness now, a midnight swirled with colours rising, exploding . . .

He came with a cry; the two of them together. How could he feel so close to her? And then, the untwining; that sad release when life sinks down to its day-by-day mediocrity and heaven recedes to dreams.

The dark. The warm and comforting dark. He was going to go back to sleep again. Why not? No need even to close his eyes . . . Although Steiger realized, then, that throughout his close encounter, he had kept his eyes wide open.

Anna carried Steiger back up to his bedroom without effort. She stripped off the torn scraps of his pyjamas and licked the sweat from his body with what might be mistaken for tenderness. Her tongue, as he had surmised, was remarkably long.

She pulled the sheets up around him and drew the curtains fully closed. He would sleep now until he was needed again.

Anna walked out on to the landing. It was no difficulty for her to reach up and push open the flimsy trapdoor to the roofspace, then ease her head and upper body through . . .

It was hot in here: the slates soaked up any heat from the sun, but the heat from the attic's occupants added to the stuffiness.

Shirley Steiger, Kevin's mother, hung from a grey hammock of skin that was carefully slung from the beams. Her eyes were open, but she was not conscious. She looked very pale. A number of thin, proboscis-like pipes ran from her body into Ozzie's open mouth. When Anna spoke to him, they retracted from the woman with a soft slicking sound and gathered swiftly deep in the boy's throat.

'We haven't decided about her,' she said, keeping her tone reasonable. He had never shown the care and restraint of the true Kin, his half-breed self being a serious risk on Anna's part.

'She's not important,' Ozzie said. 'No one will miss her.'

'Her son will—'

'His memories are easy to change. Like Billy's, and Johan's, and Carl's . . .'

'Kevin has deep memories of his mother. He loves her, despite appearances. He would notice our interference.'

'You make me like this, and then complain at what I have become. I have a need, Anna!'

'And I have a purpose! Don't fight me, Ozzie. You'll lose . . .'

As she said this, Anna gave him a picture of her power; an unsheathing so monstrous that he gasped and shrank back into the attic's shadowy corner. He knew he could never fight that, and what was left of his human heart grew terrified.

But then she was back, silkily beautiful and smiling at him in the warm, fetid gloom.

'All of this will be worthwhile, Ozzie,' Anna said. 'It won't be long now. And then you'll be free.'

He nodded, dumb with love, stepped over to her and placed his hands on her belly.

'How long, Anna?'

'Soon now. Very soon.'

The only compensation for McAuliffe's weariness was the factless knowledge that he had done the right thing. Something told him that Christine had passed this way, and that he would find her a few miles ahead in the village of Leadmoor. In her fear and confusion, she had done what any normal person would do: she'd come home.

The train had carried McAuliffe as far as Dumfries; from there he'd hitched lifts, lying his way easily through half a dozen different identities during the casual conversations he'd had with his hosts. He looked respectable enough, though unshaven and red-eyed; but his story about the search for his daughter who'd run away with a boyfriend had been readily accepted.

But hitches had become increasingly difficult the deeper he penetrated into this unpopulated countryside: McAuliffe was finally forced to walk this last stretch, or wait interminably for transport. He could not afford that. The police would soon find out who had hired the car found on the wasteground, and equally quickly discover that Christine was renting the house on Western Road. Consequently, only an idiot would not come north to Galloway in search of them: either that, or alert the local police, who would arrive on the scene even quicker.

Ahead, the narrow roadway curved elegantly through the groin of the hills, pale and ghostly in the morning's earliest offering of light. The last signpost had said Leadmoor, three miles. McAuliffe would reach his goal in less than an hour.

The village, McAuliffe and sunrise formed a conjunction

that lifted his heart. A dozen yards farther back and Lead-moor was not visible at all. Now, around this final down-sloping bend, he was able to see a semicircular gathering of trees acting as a windbreak to the ribbonlike cluster of houses, and a few farms, that were the only buildings in this valley.

He increased his pace, shivering with apprehension and the cold.

Ironically, the dwindling distance between himself and others served to increase McAuliffe's sense of the deso-lation of the area. He could cope with the thought of an entirely uninhabited wilderness; but the presence of this small place surrounded by the hugeness of hills and sky brought a sadness to his heart; a kind of cold wistfulness that felt like dying. He had never been here: had not even known of the village's existence till recently: and yet some-how he shared the sense of past life and greatness to which the untidy spoil heaps all around him testified. Perhaps because of Christine – certainly because of her – some part of him identified with the heart of Leadmoor and its people.

Dawn followed him down off the moor.

The single main street was deserted, the pale greyish-gold stone of its houses looking cleansed by the sunlight – seeming both new for this, and yet incredibly old in the same glance.

McAuliffe stood in the road and listened. Birdsong came invisibly down from the sky. Sheep bleated, feeble with distance, among brown bracken. But nothing human stir-red; not a milkfloat, not a mailman on a bicycle; not a radio through an open kitchen window. Just the sounds of the natural world, and a chilly wind buffeting around McAuliffe's ears.

He walked on, the length of Leadmoor and then back

to the village's only hotel, Highview, which, together with the church perhaps, formed the focal point of the village's social life.

He had every expectation that the place would be closed; and indeed the main double doors were locked. They were painted an ancient maroon, sun-faded to the shade of dried blood, with matching bargeboards and pipework. Heydays were long gone here, McAuliffe thought: the Highview might well be empty and abandoned.

He walked around the side, through a low gateway, and came upon a door that he found he could open. He stepped into a small and dowdy bar-room, its air still heavy with smells of old cigarette smoke and beer fumes. But at least it was warm! A big cast-iron radiator set against one wall must have been belting out the heat . . .

The room was incredibly drab; floored with brown linoleum, much torn, and walled with cheap wood panelling whose only achievement was tastelessness. Three beertaps lined the countertop – bitter, lager and mild; all keg – but behind was a shelf display containing at least fifty malt whiskies, many of which were unknown to McAuliffe. Any of which he would accept with gratitude.

He leaned across at the end of the bar and rang the 'last-orders' bell. Rang it again a minute later.

After another two minutes, as McAuliffe was about to turn and leave, the landlord appeared. A gaunt man, mid-fifties, and as run-down as the establishment he managed. His hair was grey and scraggy, his skin pale. He wore grimy jeans and a grey sleeveless cardigan over a light green shirt. McAuliffe was instantly disturbed by the depth of his eyes. They looked, he thought, like the beaten eyes of the last blue whale as the factory ship broke the horizon and drew closer. McAuliffe's father had died of cancer six years back, and his eyes held the same heartbreaking expression during those final days.

Maybe this old boy was ill too, McAuliffe reflected. But he smiled affably enough and nodded when McAuliffe enquired after a room.

'Do you have a bathroom *en suite*?'

'Ah, no, we don't, sir,' came the reply, gently vowelled. 'But you can have a bathroom attached, if you like.'

'Fine.' McAuliffe wondered whether the landlord had a sense of humour or just a sheltered upbringing. 'I'll be staying for a week, maybe two. Can I get a breakfast here?'

'Yes, sir. Fried breakfast, do you?'

'Great.' The thought of hot food set McAuliffe's mouth watering. Hot food and a hot bath. He handed over cash and the landlord issued a receipt scribbled on a sheet of notepad paper. Oddly, there was no register to sign but, on the other hand, no questions were asked about the guest's lack of luggage.

'My name's Grigson,' the thin man offered, extending his hand.

'McAuliffe, Peter McAuliffe.'

'Nice to have you here, sir. I hope you enjoy your stay in Leadmoor ... But your hands are cold ...'

Grigson turned and poured a tumblerful of Scotch.

'Warm yourself. On the house.'

'Well – thanks ...' He craned forward and found himself unable to pronounce the name on the bottle. 'Well – cheers ... Mmm. Slightly peaty ...'

'Actually, light with a little sweetness,' Grigson corrected with no note of criticism. 'Auchentoshan, distilled in Duntocher. It's eighteen years old.'

'Ah.' The warm burn of the whisky smothered

McAuliffe's awkwardness. He tossed back the dram and felt better.

'Can I buy one for you, Mr Grigson?'

'No, thank you. I've your breakfast to cook – but I'll show you to your room first.'

McAuliffe followed Grigson out, noting that the landlord was a good three inches taller than McAuliffe's own five-feet-eleven.

They walked down a large gloomy hallway and came out into the main lobby at the end of which stood the double doors McAuliffe had been unable to enter. A wide red-carpeted stairway led to the upper floors.

Grigson took him to the first floor, first room along, which had a view out across the main road and the two terraces of streets opposite. Beyond these, the hills lifted high and round, scabbed with bracken and dead heather. The sky was an absolutely pure blue.

'There are towels.' Grigson indicated the bathroom. 'And a robe, Mr McAuliffe.'

'Thank you.'

'All part of the service. Shall I bring your breakfast up, sir?'

'No, I'll . . .' McAuliffe paused. He'd intended to eat in the dining room with the other guests. But something changed his mind: maybe a suspicion that there were no other guests. 'I'll eat here, please.'

'As you will.'

Grigson left, closing the door behind him.

Alone, McAuliffe stood in the centre of the room. It was large and square, with a high ceiling and ornate plasterwork coving. The wide bed and the oak wardrobe and dresser were bulky and functional, Victorian and depressing. The carpet's colours had long since been worn away to threadbare browns.

So, Christine had her origins in this dreary nowhere, but found enough remaining here to return. Was she here now, he wondered—

—and turned, uneasily, the skin of his back crawling as he felt himself watched, as though by a thousand eyes embedded in the wall.

The bath was everything it needed to be: long, deep, the water so hot that McAuliffe's body throbbed for an hour after drying. He topped up the water twice, as it cooled around him, smiling at the big antiquated taps that squeaked and shuddered as they delivered their load. The wall to his right was white-tiled up to the ceiling; the other walls decorated with striped wipeable paper. There was an off-white pull-around shower curtain on a rail, a vast square washbasin, a thin rectangular window whose sill was covered with flies, dead since the summer, a ceramic towel rail . . . Weird. All of it, just strange . . .

But not unpleasant. Despite its isolated location and the hollow sense of emptiness, McAuliffe quite liked Leadmoor. He could not say precisely why . . . It reminded him of holidays he'd taken with his parents, years ago now, in their banged-up caravan to a spot on the Welsh coast. McAuliffe visualized the name but knew he had no chance of pronouncing it.

Back in those days, that whole stretch of coastline had been unspoiled; kind of seedy and run down – which gave it the charm, of course, that was lost when the developers moved in with their burger bars and holiday flatlets.

McAuliffe remembered very clearly the beach, long and flat and lonely; the dunes spiked with marram grass; cliffs in the distance; huge mountainscapes of stormcloud sometimes . . . When his dad gave him a handful of change, he would run the mile down the sandy path to the newsagent's store – which was a salt-blasted shed also selling ice-cream and beach toys – and spend the lot on Superman comics. Then, find a spot among the dunes leeward of the wind, and dream of heroes and magic. And he had believed it all, too, before the world came along to kick the enchantment and the shit right out of him.

His greatest moment arrived one deep night when he woke, for no reason that he'd ever worked out. He just rose out of sleep into the warm dark of the caravan that smelt faintly of bottle-gas and chips and saltsand. His parents were asleep, breathing quietly together beyond the partition.

He'd wondered what the time was; how close to morning, so reached up to pull aside the small curtain that covered the window.

Without moving even to turn his head, that little boy had witnessed the starry heavens; the brightest and most spectacular view he'd ever seen. He felt as though he could put his hand up among them and pull down a fistful of fire. Still and untwinkling, the stars had blazed with a light that time failed to dim. And before too long, the light blurred and rippled with the tears that came unbidden, then and now, to McAuliffe's eyes. He'd drifted asleep staring at starlight, and decades on, when Superman was reduced to marketing and merchandising in his mind, McAuliffe fell back on his belief that he was meant to see that brilliant sky, and its significance would one day be known to him.

It was, he concluded, how he felt about Leadmoor. It too was deserted and poor, but somehow rich with potential just around the corner.

Either that, or the Auchentoshan was stronger than he'd thought.

He dried himself with the rough towels and put on the

blue robe that Grigson had provided. No more than a minute later there was a soft knock at his door and the man came in with McAuliffe's breakfast – a great oval platter filled with more than he could really eat. Also there was a tall silver coffee pot with a curl of steam at its spout, and a toast rack holding half-a-dozen golden slices.

'And it's all in the price?' McAuliffe wondered, an oblique compliment, but well-intended. Grigson smiled as he put down the tray.

'Aye. When you're our only guest, sir, you've got to be well looked after . . .'

And with a widening of that smile, he left.

McAuliffe decided his mood could take him two ways. There was something here that was unusual – he sensed it; some deep and ancient instinct assured him. And it was tied up – whatever it was – with Christine and the obscenity he'd found at her house, and the Clayton killer. It struck him again that he'd committed a murder yesterday; had run from his home and the police on a wild chase after some young girl half his age . . .

He could either sink down into panic and fear of where he was and what he'd done, or else simply enjoy the feeling that an immense weight had been lifted from him. His freedom here was complete. He could walk out into the hills and never come back. For once, maybe for the first time since those days in the dunes, he was in control of himself and his life, and able to believe in its magic.

Maybe too, he thought as he tackled his meal, I might glance up soon and see the stormclouds coming.

After breakfast McAuliffe took a short sleep, then went back downstairs in search of Grigson, or Mrs Grigson, or the cook, or one of the maids. Not a single bloody soul was around. A little annoyed, a little unnerved, he borrowed an overcoat that was hanging on a row of ornate hooks in the lobby, and stepped outside.

Apart from the sun being higher, nothing had changed. McAuliffe stared up and down the street, casting his eye along the short ribbon-rows of houses that reached like truncated steps, going nowhere, up the hill. He noted smoke rising from a few chimney-tops, but at this time of year, in this aching wind, shouldn't there be fires in all the houses?

He took a stroll, picking up other details as well. For instance, where the hell were the cars? He found not a single one parked along the main or any side roads; and the few garages that he dared to snoop inside were empty. Likewise telephone-lines. Normally they just escaped notice; were just part of the invisible background of any cluttered street. Now their absence was glaring: Christine could not even have phoned home.

As McAuliffe walked, it became clear to him that the road he'd followed here was the only road – there were no others cutting deeper into the valley or mounting through the moors in any direction. Maybe once it was different . . .

His spirits lifted slightly to discover a single-pump garage at the top end of Leadmoor, but it was unattended. A glance into the dark, oily-smelling cavern of the workshop did however reveal a battered Sherpa van with its rear wheels off and a calendar sporting a picture of a naked girl that had been sent with compliments by a motor trader in Dumfries.

So at least I'm in the here-and-now, McAuliffe thought gladly. This is no timeslip . . .

He found a sell-all shop, too, with a bell above the door that clanked flatly as he entered. A very old lady came through from a tiny living room that appeared large enough to accommodate only a huge coal fire and the armchair from which she had risen: the heat from the fire wafted over McAuliffe as he stood there.

She stood similarly, unsmiling, the countertop between them. McAuliffe asked for a packet of peppermints, abandoning his initial impulse of seeking information. He picked up a couple of postcards also.

'For the folks back home.'

The old woman took his money, gave him his change, and returned to her chair in front of the flames.

McAuliffe went out frowning. It was all so bloody odd, like the opening to a spook-film he might watch at midnight on Fridays with a pint inside him and Judith upstairs, already asleep. What did people do here for a living? God Almighty – where were the people anyway? He had met two of them: Grigson and the crone. Surely they could not be . . .

McAuliffe laughed it off.

Shortly afterwards he came to the church.

He had a thing about churches. They affected him powerfully and always had done. He'd been inside a number of them, less frequently since they'd failed to impress him with the presence of God. Increasingly they struck him as big cold empty buildings that did not exude reverence, but rather places out of which any remnants of faith or warmth had drained. I'm still looking for miracles, since I saw the stars all those years ago.

This church stood by the roadside atop a low grassy bank held back by a wall. McAuliffe approached with the east face of the church square-on: it looked like a vast headstone patterned with slit-like windows, beyond which lay gloom.

He walked right up to it, determined not to give way

to his dislike of such places – his unease of this one.

Unusually, the leaded windows were not covered with protective mesh. Nor were the facets of glass in them stained. No pictures of angels or saints here, no biblical scenes, no icons . . . McAuliffe decided to peer through the lowest window, and found that his hands were shaking.

By standing on tiptoe and pulling himself up to the window ledge, he could just about see over it.

Something cold burst inside him.

Weak sunlight cut through slabs of the inner darkness, enough to show him collapsed rows of worm-eaten pews, crosses fallen and tarnished, altar cloths reduced to cobweb and lace by time and insects. He guessed no one had been there for a century, maybe more, so that the last echoes of prayer and confession had long since faded from the stones.

McAuliffe lowered himself carefully, feeling for a second time since his arrival that somehow his actions were being watched, and tolerated.

He moved on.

Beyond the church, virtually the last building before the moors began, ran a narrow track that McAuliffe decided to take. Evidently it had once been wider, but now was shrunk down to a thin ghost of a path through the bracken.

After a mile, it levelled out among ruins. McAuliffe stared across a desolation of spoil heaps, many grassed over, and the remains of small square buildings reduced to crumbled piles of mossy stones. Here a much broader track swept away in a long slow curve that echoed the shape of the land; what was left of the narrow-gauge railway that used to haul the galena trucks off the moortops to the factory towns of the south and the east. The rails were still down, rusted orange by now and broken in many places. A hundred yards downline stood the skeleton of a signal shed, a few bleached boards still beating listlessly against their sagging verticals in the unending pressure of the wind that blew across.

McAuliffe walked on, past the shed, coming at last to the point where the rail petered out, though its shadow continued along the ground.

He was in a landscape of low lunar hills, utterly alone, cold now and increasingly less inclined to go on. I could die here, he thought, and never be found. No one would know where to come to remember me . . .

Even so he continued a short way until he reached the far point of the railway's curve, where the ground fell away, opening out into a fine panorama of the surrounding moors. Outcrops of grey slaty rock protruded roundly, like knucklebones out of the hills' feminine swell. Expanses of scabby heather were cut by fast thin streams the colour of scored lead, like sawblades in the the earth. It was beautiful and desolate, lonely – and yet . . .

A gust lifted the lapels of his coat, and small scree clattered down a slope nearby. Once again McAuliffe experienced a sense of company – of multitudinous company that he was unable to see in return.

The time is not right, it occurred to him to think. Soon I will be allowed in. But not yet. Not now.

He turned and made his way home.

Only one small but puzzling event marred the journey. On bypassing the church, McAuliffe noticed that the headstones in the patch of ground on its western flank bore no epitaphs. His first conclusion was that they were all positioned away from him, but he checked: every stone was blank and empty of goodbyes . . .

Back in his room, he washed and towelled the cold out of his flesh. His face had been numbed on the moortop; his hands felt like lumps of sausage meat.

McAuliffe lay on his bed and dozed and dreamed. His thoughts unfolded on many levels, sometimes under his conscious direction, but at other times he was lost in a maze of his mind's making and was helpless within it. He destroyed the Clayton killer a dozen times, jolting on every occasion as the wheels bumped over the body. Then forwards, then back . . .

He longed for Christine so badly between murders, and she came to him, a wraith of memory, and seemed to tell him things that he'd never known; wonderful things, terrible things. But each time he struggled awake the wisdom was lost to him and everything was a paradox.

He woke finally in the late afternoon, opened heavy eyes and listened to the clanking of the pipework as the heating was turned up. It had been warm enough before, but now the air grew hot and oppressive and sweat appeared on McAuliffe's skin.

He heard a door close deep in the building – above or below he couldn't say. Someone walked by in the corridor outside.

He stretched, checked his watch and decided he'd go down to dinner . . .

It was not strictly dinner, however. Grigson informed him that at this time of day, all he could get was a high tea.

'Do I eat it on the hill?' McAuliffe wanted to know, which produced no response whatever from the landlord and a certain embarrassment in McAuliffe: too many years of classroom humour, he chided himself.

But if there was any difference between high tea and

dinner, McAuliffe never found out what it was. He was served, and he ate, a splendid three-course meal, alone in the Highview's dark and formal dining room – a place of huge mirrors with oak frames, and crystal chandeliers, and a vast marble fireplace blocked up by a panel made gorgeous with marquetry.

And, as before, Grigson himself brought the food after a delay that caused McAuliffe to think that his host had prepared the meal as well. But for all that, it was beautifully cooked and set before him with elegance and precision. He ate to repletion.

'Will you join me in a brandy, Mr Grigson? You refused the malt this morning – but surely it's late enough now . . .'

'Well,' Grigson said, hesitating as his eyes grew distant. 'Perhaps I will.'

'Then sit, sir. Let a waitress bring the bottle.'

'It's no trouble at all, Mr McAuliffe. Part of my job.'

He vanished into the kitchen, returning shortly with a decanter and brandy balloons on a tray.

'And if I wanted a cigar, would you fetch that for me too, Grigson? Or if I needed to be ferried into town – would *you* drive me there?'

McAuliffe smiled thinly as he spoke. His day had been quiet and leisurely, but twisted with a strange tension that was now, he knew, finding release. After the house on Western Road, nothing would be the same again. This crazy scenario – of himself, Grigson, and no one else – had evidently been prepared as carefully as his meal: as though he was special for some reason. As though – but no, it could not possibly be true! As though his coming here was anticipated.

Grigson poured out the liquor. McAuliffe noted the

onion-skin smoothness and speckling on the man's hands; the blue veins protruding.

'How long have you run the Highview?' he asked conversationally.

'More years than I can remember. May yer lum ne'er reek, Mr McAuliffe.'

'Thanks, I think... Cheers, Mr Grigson.' They both drank deeply. 'But it's a wonder you make ends meet. I mean, I know it's out of season. But Leadmoor sure is off the beaten track... I bet you're wondering why I'm here?'

'Are you enjoying your brandy?'

'Brandy's fine. Food's fine. Your evasiveness sucks.'

'Explanations can be difficult, Mr McAuliffe...'

'I'm a patient man...'

'Difficult for you, I mean.'

'Try me. For instance, where have all the people gone, Grigson? Where are they?'

'They're dying.'

McAuliffe waited, as though for more, not believing the answer anyway. Grigson, sitting opposite, finished his brandy and held up the bottle to McAuliffe, who offered his glass. He knew that his host would not break the silence.

'Of what?'

'Simple old age. Look at me...'

'Mid-fifties.' That had been McAuliffe's earlier assessment, but then he remembered the man's hands. They were the hands of an octogenarian. Both men looked at them. Grigson's smile was ghastly.

'We are out of time, Mr McAuliffe. All our energy has gone, the last of it spent on our young.'

'There are no names on the gravestones—'

'None of us matters—'

'Not a single damned name, Grigson! Now, come on, man – what's happening here!'

McAuliffe's temper rose unexpectedly, flaring as it had tended to do these past few years, but subsided again as quickly. Loudness, passion, were out of place here in this room – in this village of the dead.

'You know why I'm here?'

'Aye.' Grigson nodded.

'Where is she?'

'Soon, Mr McAuliffe, she will come to you.'

'But where is she now?'

'Sir, please. She is nowhere you would want to be. She must be sure of you.'

'I don't understand.'

'But you will. We must prepare for your understanding . . .'

Maybe it was the brandy, but McAuliffe's head was spinning, his concentration drifting off-focus as the landlord's tired face swirled before him.

And then, the voices: like an echo of this fine dining room in the days when it was prosperous and bustling.

'More brandy, Mr McAuliffe?'

'I'm not sure I sh – shit!'

He'd looked around the room with semi-sober eyes, intrigued anew by the glitters in the chandelier crystal; marvelling again at the craftsmanship of the marquetry fire-cover. His gaze drifted past Grigson, across the room, to the lobby doorway.

And there they stood, Leadmoor's decaying population.

There were not many of them, to be sure, but a few were too many as far as McAuliffe was concerned. They approached slowly, carefully; wary perhaps of this intrusive stranger who had brought the scent of the outer world with him when he came.

McAuliffe's eyes flicked back to Grigson's, and were struck by their sadness.

'We are not here to harm you, Mr McAuliffe,' he said wearily. 'And we do not wish to hide anything from you. Please believe us. You will know everything eventually, but allow us the wisdom to judge how much, and when.'

'I – Grigson – I – ' McAuliffe wanted to articulate his agreement. They both understood that horror and longing in equal part had brought him north, and that he must have expected to find some trace of it here. But these pathetic figures . . . McAuliffe struggled for meaning. He stared at them again, recognizing the woman in the sell-all shop instantly. Perhaps twenty others were gathered with her; whether short or tall, lean, plump – all displayed a certain similarity that was probably inbred across the generations.

But there was more, a perception that cut through the brandy-haze. These people were of all ages – though children and adolescents were absent – and yet all looked worn: burnt out: brought incredibly to the ends of their lives as though the vigour of the blood had been drawn off in one draining. They had all been emptied . . .

I'm sitting with the dead. McAuliffe wanted to laugh. Wanted to cry.

He lifted his glass to accept more of Grigson's brandy.

Much later, he stumbled from the stuffy bar-room, having shared another few drams with the locals. The brighter and more revealing lighting there had enhanced the grotesqueries of these men and women. They looked like walking cadavers as they smoked, drank, talked among themselves in syllables that flowed like the running-by of a quiet stream. And as the hours passed, McAuliffe had come to accept them: they were Christine's people, her blood and kin. Her Community. Patiently he waited for her until tiredness almost caused him to topple out of his chair.

Grigson must have given some sort of sign – not the ringing of the bell – for a man at the nearest table to McAuliffe's ground out his cigarette, drained his tot-glass and rose. The rest followed, walking in quiet disorder out through the side door and into the sparsely lit street. They had not acknowledged the stranger, nor shown any sign that he was there.

McAuliffe was soon left, desperately drowsy, amid the stale fumes of the room and the clink of Grigson's perfunctory glass clearing.

'I'm going up, Grigson.'

The landlord nodded. 'Do you want any supper afore you do?'

'Too bloody tired. But thank you. Thanks for everything . . .' McAuliffe wasn't sure why he said it, and felt embarrassed.

Grigson replied with a smile. 'Sleep well, sir. I hope, now, you understand a little of our ways.'

'Yeah. I hope so too.'

McAuliffe climbed the stairs and staggered into his room without putting on the light. He'd decided earlier that if Christine didn't show by mid-morning tomorrow, then he'd move on: maybe back home, maybe not. Now he reaffirmed this decision as he tugged at his clothing – the damned heating was still firing on all cylinders.

Naked, but still too warm, McAuliffe went to the

window and pulled aside the drape. One or two streetlights were visible from this perspective, but no houselights. And yet there were gleams in the dark – shifting, flaring and dimming – torchlights, a couple of dozen of them, as the last inhabitants of Leadmoor streamed away from the husk of their village and out on to the hills.

Another puzzle to add to the headful of puzzles already tangled there, and he was too dead-beat to attempt a solution.

McAuliffe flopped down on the bed, dragging a sheet over him, out of habit rather than necessity.

He was asleep inside a minute, and that slumber was black and solid, going undisturbed until four a.m., when Christine came into his room and slid over him.

He could hear them calling far and wide: the voices of his fathers, his mothers; his brethren. His Kin. They knew – they knew he was not to be stopped. What they considered to be his weakness, his human side, was now a strength. Because of it he was independent of the Community and could swim against the tide. His thoughts were his own, the cliffs against which their heedless pleas could crash until it was far too late; for their ocean no longer held any fear for him, its depths now meaningless.

As he scrubbed down the stainless steel autopsy slab, Davies thought about life and death. Because now, it seemed, the distinction was not quite so clear . . .

Doctor Marius had been busy all day, sometimes in the lab, picking over fragments he'd examined often before, but for most of the time out on site with Scobie. He'd heard about the gas explosion down near the railway yards; the usual canteen gossip of near-escape and extent-of-damage. Usually in such cases there was a horror story or two – like the one where a housewife gets blasted in half, and the top half lives for two days before shock closes down the system. Or the one where a guy's burns are so severe he looks like something brought out of a tarpit, and every time he moves the carbonized skin cracks open and oozes blood . . .

Davies often supplied such gory fare himself. He'd seen it all, almost every urban injury imaginable, and then some. But his were tales of death, not of life or the boundary between. And he'd always thought of that boundary as being clear-cut and straightforward and permanent, one of the benchmarks by which the universe was measured.

Chesley Davies was twenty-eight years old. He'd come through medical school and then gone on to join the force in his present capacity as butcher's dogsbody; an observer and cleaver of those departed, rather than a minister to the living. He found the work interesting in the same way that a mechanic might seek satisfaction among the intricacies of an auto's engine. The pieces, united, functioned. Their design was ingenious but crude, grossly inefficient; fragile, vulnerable, ephemeral. Same with bodies – but jerry-building this time through natural evolution across geological ages. Fully understanding this clockwork was not impossible. There were no great mysteries left. There was no God. The watchmaker had been blind from the outset . . .

Davies finished his final sluicing and stripped off his disposable rubber gloves like a discarded skin. He snapped each glove and dropped it into the wastebin. Everywhere sparkled: all the instruments autoclaved, not a drop of stray blood to be seen: the organs that Marius had wanted preserving now hung motionlessly in their formalin-filled vessels. All done, ready for the next day's inevitable batch of corpses.

But Davies was pleased because he knew Marius would be pleased, would appreciate this effort; he didn't want to be an assistant for ever, and his promotion prospects would certainly be boosted if he pandered to the cranky old fart.

He sent his plastic apron the way of the gloves, then hung his labcoat up on its hook. He had been looking forward to the end of this day, because tonight he had a date out with Sharon. Davies whistled softly through his teeth at the thought of her. Jeez, you could cream yourself just doing that! The girl was built for sex, no doubt about it. She was one of the 'if-you've-got-it-flaunt-it' brigade, and they'd been going steady for three months. There might even be a relationship in there somewhere, Davies reflected. If my backbone can stand it.

He turned out the fluorescents – turned them on again upon hearing the sound. A weight shifting carefully; the scrape of a bone or a cuticle of nail over metal. Rats maybe. Or – the blood dropped from Davies's face – Jesus! They surely couldn't have made a mistake with one of the John Doe's!

He walked over to the ranks of cadaver drawers set along one wall. Hell's filing cabinet, he called it . . . Now his hearing was scalpel sharp, his whole battery of senses attuned to detect the impossible.

And now there could be no doubt. Someone that Davies himself had toe-tagged yesterday or today was still alive in there, and moving about.

He giggled nervously. Half a dozen other technicians were working within fifty feet of him. There was no need to be frightened. Just some little administrative slip-up, right? Even so, heads would roll ... Don't talk like that, Davies, he told himself sharply. You stupid bastard. Just get it sorted out before Marius returns.

He pressed his ear to one drawer, a second. A third. And backed off ... In there. It was the hit-and-run. The one they'd found on the gas explosion call-out. Mash-and-run more likely, so mangled up with the motor that there was no way that car could be driven away.

The body had been brought to the morgue in bags ...

Davies wanted to laugh again, but not nervously this time. This time the emotion came from somewhere rather deeper, and it was not mirth.

He wondered if it was a set-up. Those fucking techs were always at it. Once, they'd slipped a human hand on to his plate of chicken curry in the canteen. And the woman on the till, used to such pranks, had wanted to charge him extra for it. Lots of yuks on that occasion. A real pissing bellylaugh all round.

But not this time. Nobody could have a sense of humour so moronic. Or cruel.

Maybe ... Davies knew a lot about the process of post-mortem changes; the mechanics of decay. Gases given off by bacterial activity often caused cadavers to fart and belch, and groan sometimes too, which even put the wind up the veterans at the game. Must be something of that sort. Sure to be. All those busy little microbes getting down to the feast.

So, with a façade of indifference, Davies grabbed hold of the drawer's chromium handle and hauled it out on its rollers.

He had no time even to shriek.

Chesley Davies had not placed in that drawer what was dancing in there now. Some red and writhing thing whose eyes burned like a lunatic's; whose mouth gashed a sudden vast smile as the beast lunged up . . . A hand like a bony flipper webbed with skin clamped over Davies's mouth and nose, covering his entire face . . . And from somewhere the monster had found a machete. Davies heard it go in, come out again, enter once more.

Then he died, with the killer already right over him, smothering him like a shroud.

Johan Larson worked for an estate agency, and tonight had been grafting late. Why the shit anyone would want to buy a property in Clayton, he could not for the life of him imagine. But some people did, even though ultimately they might take a good deal of persuading. He had, of course, memorized the thesaurus of estate agent's euphemistic jargon – euphemistic my arse! It was all bull – but he still needed to embellish such decorative phraseology with his own personal touches. 'Yeah, my parents live in a house like this. Solid as a rock – they were built to last in those days – and, y'know, there's no way you'd get my folks to leave . . .'

That was a good one. And how about: 'Well, I know we're on the downside of the spending boom, but it's all cyclical, you realize. Look, buy now while prices are low. It's an investment. This place will double its value inside three years. You can't lose.'

That always got them, that little irresistible phrase. You can't lose.

Johan sighed, thinking of all the people he'd sold to who'd lost.

He tidied up his desk, checked his planner for tomorrow's appointments, glanced across for the fiftieth time that day at Carol's magnificent legs, then stretched and stood up stiffly. He was tired of the office now, tired of the suit and tie the job demanded.

He laughed low in his throat. Times he'd been barred from Clayton pubs for his black leather and denim. Those same ale houses had treated him gushingly when he turned up in his work-day clothes. Such is life. But he liked the contrast, enjoyed the release of loud music and the anarchy of its lyrics. Conforming was so confining.

'Fancy a drink, Carol?'

Johan asked her most nights, and most nights she said no. She said no again. It had used to irk him immeasurably. What the hell did she want in a man? Johan knew he was good-looking, knew how to talk to women, was never pushy; was intelligent enough to tackle most subjects on more than a superficial level. And he was well equipped in the meat department. None of his other dates had ever complained, anyway . . .

That's how the record used to run. Now Johan knew the answer. Carol's current – and maybe ultimate – boy-friend was called William. He was an accountant. He had a flat and a Mercedes. He went to France on wine-safari holidays.

Also, he was a dick-head.

Even so, it was an immutable law of the universe that salesmen called Johan could not compete with accountants called William. Despite the shape of their heads.

'I'll go for a drink by myself, then,' Johan added, just to spite. Carol gave him a friendly fuck-off smile.

Another cold evening. The rush-hour bustle was over: it was that limbo-time after the shops had shut and before the pubs opened their doors. Maybe he wouldn't go straight in for a drink. His armpits quietly stank and the suit he wore felt like a Terylene strait-jacket, itchy and tight. Besides, how could he possibly show his face at the usual haunts dressed like this? The guys would take him round the back and kick his face in, just to make a point!

Johan chose the quickest route home, flicked up his coat collar and hurried along the pavement. He much preferred being the crazy headbanger anyway. Making the transformation was worth delaying his pint by half an hour.

It was great, really. The squares at work just wouldn't believe his alter-ego, while the night gang – Ozzie, Billy – had only just got used to the nature of his day job. They'd ribbed him to begin with. 'Well, I'll see you all at the Nostradamus gig . . . You *have* got tickets, haven't you?' he'd say.

That shut them up good. As far as Johan knew, Ozzie was unemployed, Billy went to Tech and Carl made his thin living doing shady deals with ripped-off incar stereo systems . . .

Johan supposed he was the odd-one-out; the one among them with the best education, the most income, the one with the greatest stability in his life.

Apart from Anna, of course. Now she was the odd-one-out for sure, and not because of her sex. Johan thought about Anna Fuller more than he fantasized over Carol, who was only a face in a general fantasy, the name of the girl gasping and squirming as he bent her over the office desk. Carol was just cock fodder. If she ever left to marry Willie the dick, Johan knew he'd have forgotten her inside a week, and the new girl at her desk would be the one he waltzed with in his dreams.

But Anna – she was almost too lovely to abuse the vision of her with thoughts of lust. Her mind was sharp and deep, her opinions subtle and sincere, but thought-out even so. And more than that, she carried mystery with her like a shawl. Anna was an enigma, coming and going like the moon and with as much fragility. Johan reckoned he could love Anna in every sense of the word he could conceive. It would be ... Yes, it would be an honour to share the years with someone like her.

Johan's route took him towards the outskirts of town, along a deserted pavement that bounded the 'new' industrial estate: new in comparison with the gutted shells of the old factories closer to the centre. These more recent units had been built in the seventies as phase two of a county council four-phase project that reached phase one-and-a-half before the funding ran out. Mainly light engineering, although some of the sites were occupied by mail-order companies, knitwear firms, and a few were used for warehousing. It was envisaged that a loop-line would run from Clayton railway station to the complex, then hook back in to the mainline for the Midlands and the big ports on the East coast. The ground was defined, perimeter fences erected. But not a shovelful of soil had been dug out. Bloody typical.

Johan hurried on past the last of the security lighting, came to the no-man's-land marking the end of the construction work and the line of the non-existent railway, turned left and began picking his way across the wasteground. It was a bitch if you stumbled, and on a wet day was impassable, but it cut a mile off your journey and saved forty minutes waiting for the bus.

As he walked, he reflected. His current scenario was that Anna Fuller was some kind of eccentric millionairess; the daughter of an earl or a count, or maybe of a prominent public figure. And true to stereotype, she was bored with garden parties and a load of big balls. So she dropped out – though retaining her hotline to the cash – and came to the seediest, grimiest hole she could find. It was her playing place, her toy. There, her real self would be unknown, and she could be anybody and do anything. Johan imagined she loved heavy rock for the same reasons as he: it was uncompromising and direct, screaming in the face of a fucked-up and uncaring world. It disdained the bureaucratic labyrinth of modern society that was really no more than a mechanism for keeping common folks under the thumb. It was an anthem of love and death and high hopes and low desires. It was proud of its hard and simple truths.

Wouldn't it be great, then, if this was the face of reality? And in true fairytale fashion, when Johan won her heart and offered her marriage, she'd accept and then tell him her secrets. They'd buy a big place far away from Clayton – far, far away – and he could tell Carol where she could get off, and where his boss could stick his job. Then Johan would ceremonially burn his two suits and three ties; build his mum and dad a little cottage in the grounds of the Larson estate; buy a Ferrari and all the CDs he could want. Then they'd settle down to a life of total happiness.

But, of course, they'd both still play rock 'n' roll . . .

Johan came out of his fantasy smiling. He felt good, and only slowly came back down as he assessed more realistically the chances of someone like Anna Fuller going for someone like him . . . She seemed closer to Ozzie anyway; though for the life of him Johan couldn't think why.

He was almost across the wasteland now: instead of stumbling in near-total darkness he had the lights of the estate to guide him over some of the pitfalls.

The land rose gently two hundred yards ahead, a terracing of houses and quiet suburban roads. Between, ran the mainline embankment, a high bar of shadow with a tunnel access that stank of piss and was hazardous with broken glass. But a necessary evil, if he wanted this short-cut home.

Johan had never met any trouble here, but was always wary of the place: Clayton kind of seeped through the skin and made you alert for violence. He stopped, delved in his pocket, brought out the knife and small pencil torch he usually carried for just this kind of situation. Johan grinned. The bands he loved yelled their defiance and God help anybody who interfered; but the thought of risking or taking life was a terror he tried to put out of his mind. This was simply a precaution which hopefully he'd never need to use.

He approached the tunnel, entered. And stopped. Some-one was in there already; a figure swathed in shadow, outlined in faint light. OK, no hassle. Here was someone taking the same short-cut to get to the town. A girl, to judge by the way the stray gleams wreathed in her hair; and a tall girl too. Johan carried on with confidence, but with one hand around the hilt of the knife and the other on the torch.

Ten yards in, he slowed and stopped again. The figure was not moving, just standing there – probably scared witless by his appearance.

'It's all right,' Johan said quietly, 'I'm on my way home. Don't worry. There's no trouble . . .'

A moment's pause. Then:

'Johan?'

What? – It was Anna. Johan's heart surged. But why was she here? Looking for him perhaps . . . Wanting to talk to him privately . . .

His fantasies flared in a flurry of colour before him.

This was perfect: he the conquering knight, she the damsel in distress.

Johan turned cold. 'Anna – are you OK? You've haven't been – I mean—'

'I'm all right. Johan, I can hardly see you . . .'

Something was wrong. Even as he moved towards her, his senses recognized that. Her voice. Almost her voice. And the shape of the body. But no one could've known he would come through here at this time. And her hair – her outline. Anna.

'Anna,' Johan said, troubled, switching on the torch.

He screamed.

It was Anna dipped in acid: a raw and bloody thing. She was naked, but the awful rips and deformities concealed whatever Johan might have wished to see. Her hands, gloved in blood, reached out towards him. The finger-ends of her left hand were showing white and skeletal, but as he watched them the flesh flowed forward and covered over the bone.

His screaming went on and on, an insanity of echoes magnified by the wet walls of the tunnel's throat.

'Jo–han . . .'

Now the voice rotted into another's. There was no longer any pretence of femininity. This outrageous horror was a drag-queen caricature of Anna that half walked, half melted until his shuddering body was within the ambit of its arms. Amazingly, he kept the torch focused on that face – could never have switched it off and survived – and discovered again the knife he was clasping.

He drove it desperately, but powerfully, into the thing's chest. It didn't even flinch.

'Oh – Jo – haaa – nnn . . .'

It countered with a blade ten times larger, drawn from

within, that lifted now and dropped and severed Johan's limb with ease.

It bent forward to kiss him.

Johan's terror was complete. He felt his heart stumbling. The creature's body, sticky, hot, touched his own and wrapped about it. The lips, shapeless flanges around the hole of its mouth, suckered on his face and flooded him with dreams.

Oh, Holy Mother, let me die . . . let me die . . . sweet fuck, let me—

But it was not a rapid death nor, it must be said, an unpleasant one. Johan felt himself sinking, sinking. But into what? The being's flesh, or oblivion? They were the same. It took everything from him that he had to give; clothes, memories, blood, come, bones. So in a sense he never died, but fell like a jewelled drop of rain into a darker ocean.

Some minutes later, the Kin Slayer moved on, leaving in its wake a small heap of remains that the dogs and the rats that followed after took trouble to avoid.

For the first hour they spoke not a word between them: Christine, McAuliffe – like one being uncoupling its two separate halves with regret, and then only temporarily.

'I missed you,' McAuliffe said at last. The darkness was total. He sensed her only by her perfume and the warmth she gave off, and by her breathing, slowing now as their latest passion subsided.

'I was afraid I wouldn't see you again.'

'Pete. Forgive me. What happened – it was so awful. I was confused. I needed to think . . .'

'I understand.' He squeezed her hand. 'Of course I do. And so did I need to think – at least, I needed to reflect on the thoughts I had afterwards. I didn't phone the police,' he confessed. 'I just got out of there. They'll have traced the car by now, naturally: Judith will know all about it. And, Christine, they'll have found what was in your house; what's left of it, anyway . . .'

He waited for an answer out of the silence; any kind of explanation.

Her breathing had slackened to the easy curling of languid waves on a midnight shore.

'You remember I said I was sharing the house with someone else?'

'A friend of yours, yes.'

'It was him.'

He wanted to laugh at that. What else was there to do? She had said it so seriously, the very tone of her voice heightening the brittle hysteria that sparked in McAuliffe's chest. But if he did laugh, he'd not be able to stop it: on and on, laughter so intense he knew he would never emerge on the other side sane.

'Chris – Christine. Please . . .'

He wanted to be told that she loved him and that his foolish plan of running had succeeded, that now they'd be together. He wanted her to affirm that the old world was still there; hard, cold, a bitch of a place. But believable.

She started talking.

Sometimes, Christine Lamb used 'I', sometimes 'we'; singular and plural dissolving together in the sense of what she said. She talked about Leadmoor as a special place, somewhere inhabited by her family for a vast span of time. They – it – had been here long before the Celtic tribes had come, even before the last glaciation when the land was desolate and empty of humanity. Earlier than that, her kin (no, he thought; her 'Kin', she said it with a special emphasis) dwelt far to the south in what was now southern Spain. They had crossed the land bridge between Europe and Britain prior to the antepenultimate ice age, some 450,000 years ago ... They had crossed it as mammoths and whoolly rhinos and bison, the protohorses, the big cats ...

'With them, you mean ... ?'

'McAuliffe, I know what I mean ...'

And when early man followed after, it was an easy matter for the Kin to nest in humanity's shadow; to breed under its skin.

Centuries passed. Millennia swept by. Human lifespans marked brief seasons in the cycle of the Kin. They, too, lived and died, but each at its ending returned to the heart of the Community; the Whole wherein was kept and treasured the contribution of every life.

'Nothing truly dies, you see,' she explained in the quiet voice he knew and loved so well. 'Everything has its time and its purpose. Without the existence of each single blade of grass, there would be no Grass. If no human being walked in the world, there would be no Humanity.'

'You are saying', he spoke to the dark, 'that you, that the other people who live here – are not human?'

'We are as human as you, McAuliffe. But humanity is as lightly worn as a summer coat. Can't you hear the ocean sometimes, in your mind? It is the ocean of life itself, the complex interplay of creative fields sweeping through the universe. You, on this world, are like sandgrains cast up on the beach. We *choose* our beach: and to us, there is no difference between the sand and the water around it ...'

He recognized that her metaphor, for his benefit, had simplified her reality. She was talking about life that took

another form – or rather, many forms; never having special-
ized in a single shape set within a solitary world. Her life
was more generalized, purer, driven by consciousness
rather than blind evolutionary forces. It was a kind of life
whose wonder and beauty, its utter difference, he could
barely comprehend.

'But the people here . . .' It was a vague and woolly
objection. The inhabitants of Leadmoor were as ramshackle
as their houses, as dour as the hills they lived among. How
could he equate them with the incredible being she was
describing?

'The people here are dying, Pete. Because the Flesh is
dying. It too reaches an ending.'

'And you?'

'I, and a few others, are its last energy, a final effort of
continuance.'

'But why are you – like this? I mean, why Christine
Lamb?' McAuliffe felt her shrug beside him.

'Youth and beauty are effective weapons for survival,'
she said. He smiled wryly. 'Would you have befriended a
middle-aged man like Grigson? The old woman in the
shop? Besides, a healthy and vigorous body was needed to
care for Bruce – he was the one you found in the house,
Pete. He was not able to complete the transformation.'

'Into what?' He dreaded to ask. He had to ask.

'Into a form capable of sustaining itself here, and one
able to give rise to the Kin as any number of separate
individuals.'

He realized then that she hadn't been born; not of a
mother and father, anyway. Her genesis was out of some
indefinable mass of flesh, a matrix that bound bones around
an idea, and then clothed those bones with meat. She and
the rest of her Kin were one creature. And when It died,
she died also.

'Where is the old flesh, Christine? Where is your heart?'

'Originally we dwelt in caves. Then, when people came to the valley and started the mines, we lived in the worked-out shafts and galleries under the hills.'

'The people must have known: you could not go undiscovered.'

'The families here were uneducated, ignorant, inbred. They were easy to dominate.'

'You destroyed them—'

'We enhanced them. We lived on the borderline of the human world; we played in its corners. The folk here never suffered because of us. We shared each other, and each benefited from the communion.'

His head was spinning now. He found himself caught in the wonder of it, but it was too much; like too much drink or mountain air; like a glut of beautiful paintings, a flood of symphonic music. McAuliffe felt himself saturated.

'Two more questions, Christine: why Clayton, and why the killings?'

'We need somewhere lost and forgotten, Pete; somewhere whose people are low of spirit, defenceless; susceptible to the thought that there can be more to life than rain and empty hours. Human consciousness makes our melding harder. Superstition and despair make our magic easier to work . . .'

Christine stirred next to him and made a sound like a sigh.

'Occasionally we mirror Man too precisely, and out of the Kin comes a human birth. The killer is one of these – not a man, not Kin. Un-Kin. He harbours a terrible hatred for us, perhaps because he has lived too long with humans. He has been tainted by Mankind's madness and its drive to destroy anything not like itself. He knows that the Flesh here is exhausted, and that the Kin at Leadmoor are too weak now to stop him. His one aim is to destroy those of us sent south, before we can accomplish the enseeding . . .'

'How many more of you are there?'

'I don't know. My knowledge could be his knowledge.'

'But why—?'

'You said two questions, McAuliffe. I've already answered three. The night isn't over yet.'

'I've only seen carnage', he told her. 'And no proof.'

She answered with a touch, and his reply was wordless also. She was so soft and yielding, mounting him, riding him, she gave him the best he could imagine from any girl. What more human act could there be than this?

He came quickly, with a sigh, and weariness swept him up and carried him out to sea.

Christine smiled and laid a hand on his smooth belly – a hand that grew and spread until it covered him everywhere with its weight and heat. And he, asleep, dreamed of himself still inside her, and she in him. The perfect union.

I love you, McAuliffe, Christine said.

I'll help you all I can.

Grigson looked at McAuliffe anew, but stared as though with a hint of disapproval at Christine sitting opposite him at the breakfast table. The sun had been rinsed by early rains and shone a clean, bright light into the otherwise empty dining room.

Both the man and the girl were silent. Their talk, now, was instantaneous and in a form far more efficient and less ambiguous than words.

McAuliffe discovered – it was like a soft rush of under-standing in his head and his heart – that the Community had passed through thirty generations since its arrival on this earth. It spread quickly into a diversity of forms; life hidden within life, each helping the other to adapt to changing conditions and problems.

With the arrival of modern humanity, there arose a dilemma: for, while the Community wished to coexist with this resourceful and tenacious species, and learn from it and teach it in turn, it realized that human beings would never tolerate its presence. *Homo sapiens* had survived through destruction and domination, built its whole philo-sophy of life around those principles which now threatened even its own existence – or as Christine expressed it: Those whom the gods wish to destroy, they first make Man.

Caught in this one form, humanity grew away from the idea of transformations. The old legends of shape-shifting sank ever more deeply into the collective unconscious until they lost all weight of belief, though a taint of the fear remained, which they had once inspired. Civilization advanced by fighting what was natural and good. The Community shaped itself to the land: Mankind changed the land to fit. It succeeded by slaughter, its creed an insanity of mutilation.

How can you hope to survive, then? McAuliffe wondered.

And the reply came back in the same fraction of a second . . . Perhaps it is better, after all, if the last of the Kin died here with the old heart of the Community, leaving Man to determine the fate of the planet. The alternatives are war, or perhaps eventually some kind of bonding between the two intelligences.

I don't know, McAuliffe. I begin to doubt we can con-tinue even with human help . . .

McAuliffe finished up his coffee. He took Christine's hand and they set off to walk out of Leadmoor and into the hills.

His instinct took them both to the site of the abandoned narrow-gauge railway, along its trackbed to the spoil heaps where the lead-bearing nuggets of ore had been sorted. Yesterday McAuliffe had been frightened to venture further – warned off, he now recognized, because he had not been adequately prepared. Today there was no such hesitation in his heart. They continued to a tunnel entrance cut in the hillside, around which lay the discarded firebrands of those Kin who had come this way the night before.

Proof now, McAuliffe, Christine told him.

They walked together down into the wet gullet of rock.

He had thought to bring an electric torch, but knew even so that he would not be allowed to lose his balance and fall in this place: whatever lived here lived in Christine, and both wished only to protect him.

They continued for fifteen or twenty minutes, at which point the chill of the passage gave way to a rising moist heat. The tunnel branched. Christine took the right fork and her lover followed, his torch picking out among the flaring shadows streaks of minerals deposited by water filtering down from the moortop.

They came to a shaft which they descended by means of an iron ladder whose rungs were slick with slime: this they had to do blind, the torch stuffed into the pocket of McAuliffe's overcoat. He took the coat off when they reached bottom. He was sweating now, and the darkness stank like a byre, an unholy mixture of meat and excrement . . .

A death-ward smells like this, McAuliffe thought. The man in the bed next to mine in the hospital smelt like this . . . And his breathing sounded the same . . .

But whatever was sharing the darkness as they stood there must have been a hundred times bigger. A thousand. Its inhalations brought a great draught of air down the tunnel, enough to make McAuliffe stagger in the force of the wind: the exhalation was softer, a dank miasmic breeze from the depths of the abandoned workings.

'Christine—'

'Here, McAuliffe. Don't worry. You're safe. You've never been safer.'

He believed her. Perhaps it was the intimacy they'd shared, or the trust that the Kin had put in him to bring him this far. Maybe it was something altogether deeper. But McAuliffe knew that no harm would come to him. He was among family now.

At Christine's word, McAuliffe switched on the torch again, and what he saw almost broke his heart.

The creature occupied a vast pit in the rock, from which it hung with an impossible complexity of webs and drapes and threads of itself. It filled the amphitheatre and the tunnels radiating from it: indeed, McAuliffe realized that he was not so much looking down at the Community, as standing within it. His torch could, of course, illuminate only the smallest fraction of this spectacle: most of the details – and the sheer scale of the being – reached him through Christine's mental landscaping of it for his benefit.

They moved closer, to a place where he was able to see the nature of the beast in a purer form.

This was a narrower tunnel; hotter; the walls skimmed over with fine peritoneum carrying nerves and capillaries.

The slow rumble of the creature's colossal metabolism shuddered through McAuliffe's chest. The presence of this formless, fathomless body was almost overwhelming.

Christine touched McAuliffe's hand and moved her fingers to switch off the torch.

He could still see. Something in the chamber, a by-product of the life down here, gave off the light of a full moon. The thing in the chamber seethed like a cauldron – something totally alien to McAuliffe's eyes: protoplasm in a constant state of becoming and unbecoming: latent life: a million possibilities only waiting for the will to make them true.

His heart raced at the sight. Once, when he was young, McAuliffe had lifted a back-garden stone and seen a hundred crawling things scurrying out of the sunlight. He had been both disgusted and thrilled by the squirming diversity; this multitude of fragments that looked so bizarre, yet with whom he shared a common ancestry, far-distant but undeniable.

As he looked now upon the featureless source of the Community, upon the Arcanum, he recognized a greater gap than the one separating him from the worms and the ants. This was life of a fundamentally different kind with an utterly alien perspective. Its offspring sported arms and legs, tears and smiles by its own design, and not by the hand of God. Did God, indeed, feature at all in its universe? Beside him, the girl he loved was nothing more than an appendage, to be discarded at will to decay should the need arise; a sloughing-off of skin when the purpose of the Community required her no longer. Did she possess any function or meaning beyond that conferred by the Self-Existent?

'Christine . . .'

Still he mouthed her name, too quietly to be heard. Yet in this world, thought was shared and spread like bread broken for the crowd; each tiny gift of it was sustenance for all.

'Help us, McAuliffe. Please.'

They would all have vanished within a few weeks. That much he knew, somehow. Whatever assistance he might offer might not save them – but it might save him and salvage something from the one who stood beside him.

Please, McAuliffe . . .

He realized that Christine was not speaking to him: her eyes were fixed upon the leviathan in the pit. He followed her gaze to where a face had formed in the skeins of loose flesh, pleading for the salvation of the Whole.

It was McAuliffe's own face that begged.

He was never sure afterwards if his pledge was insanity or the most clear-sighted thing he'd ever done. Whatever, the relief he felt at being away from that place was an exaltation. He was reminded, as they left, of a grave. And like the unnecessary tombstones of Leadmoor, this one also bore no message of remembered friends.

They had spent several hours underground. The afternoon was ageing and the sun cast a low but brilliant light across the moors, making the heather glow bronze.

'We must get back to Clayton,' he told Christine firmly. McAuliffe had no plan in mind, but felt impelled by the sense of urgency infecting him.

'But we must make Leadmoor safe first . . .' She pointed.

He noticed, half a mile away, two figures talking beside the car parked at the front of the Highview Hotel.

They moved closer.

Now, McAuliffe saw, one of the figures was Grigson. The other belonged to a stranger.

Scobie was scared. He'd admitted it to Marius: but words were easy. More importantly, he'd admitted it to himself. And there was no lying about the way he felt, no denial of the black oily swell in his guts as he'd made the five-hour drive up the M6 from Clayton to Dumfries.

Peterson, at the Divisional Office here, had prepared the ground efficiently. As far as he was concerned, D.I. Paul Scobie was following-up a couple of leads in the Clayton Killer enquiry: the least Peterson felt he could contribute was to do the dogwork of checking out the archives as he'd been requested . . . But Scobie was asking for some pretty obscure information; odd stuff about Lead-moor and its parish records, census returns for the area, a history of the mines . . .

Peterson wondered what Scobie was on to. Something. A cop learns to listen to his intuition. In this case, absence of data whispered to him of a basis for Scobie's suspicion. No local hospital, for instance, could supply him with the name of any Leadmoor inhabitant who'd been admitted, for any reason, since records began. And, as he'd previously discovered and passed on, there had been no murders in that valley, ever (or none that had been reported – was there a difference?). As an overlay to this rather odd statistical glitch, the Leadmoor villagers rarely ventured beyond the confines of their hills; and they displayed a quiet but penetrating antipathy towards incomers . . . Actually, that was another fragment Peterson had learned, which he pieced together to make nothing: whoever had moved into Leadmoor had stayed, generation upon generation, as though whatever emotional contagion lay at the heart of the place tainted the newcomers also.

The village was part of Peterson's patch, but he had to admit that there'd never been a reason to take him there. Good God, he had enough to cope with as crime increased elsewhere in his territory: why go looking for trouble where there was none ... ?

Nevertheless, since Scobie's telephoned request, he'd been tempted to make the ninety-minute journey, just to see for himself. Got as far as sitting in his car with the engine idling, before something warned him away. Call it what you like, but he'd found a dozen excuses to keep him in the office that morning ...

Peterson himself called it superstition.

Scobie struck him as a good cop who worked too hard; a man burned-out by the brightness of his integrity and the unrelenting effort he put into the job. It made Peterson feel slightly guilty. However bad things got here in the Lowlands, it couldn't look anything like the industrial South, where the ghost of past prosperity came back to haunt in the form of bankrupt businesses and bitter dole queues. Peterson had attended some courses that way, once. He still preferred hills to towerblocks, and the clean purity of lochside air to the greasy stink of chip shops.

Who would blame him then, he concluded, for maintaining a professional politeness in the face of this man's questions; a distance he insisted upon to keep him from the air of desperation Scobie radiated?

They talked for an hour in Peterson's office; an intense and quite uncomfortable hour as far as the Scot was concerned. Part of the problem was that Scobie failed to reciprocate any information. It was obvious that he was piecing something together, maybe something serious, to judge from his mood: but it struck Peterson that the man had turned it into a personal thing – crusade, vendetta; he couldn't say. Whatever, it was eating away at Scobie to the point where doubts rose in Peterson's mind as to his competence in the matter ... But then, raising that issue would lead to endless internal stresses in the system, and was not likely to do his own career any good, to say nothing of Scobie's. Let sleeping dogs lie, he thought at the end. Especially potentially rabid ones.

However, he did go so far as to ask:

'What I can't figure, Detective Inspector, is why inhabitants of Leadmoor should be murdered once they've left the area ... Johnson, the Vines girl ...'

'I didn't tell you about those!' Scobie came back, looking more alarmed than Peterson thought the revelation warranted.

'Your requests for information pricked my curiosity: first a phone call, now a personal visit. These people are my responsibility, you know, even more so when some of them end up dead.'

Peterson held Scobie's gaze until Scobie himself broke it and looked away.

'I'm sorry. But the leads are pretty tenuous at this stage. Any theory I might come up with now is likely to be changed in the light of further evidence.'

'I understand,' Peterson said, and he did. There had been occasions when he too had been chasing the tail of a big case; although each time there was the added factor of personal aggrandisement if it was sewn up – and the lack of it if someone else elbowed in on the act. In this instance, though, he judged that glory was not Scobie's prime motive, and maybe not a motive at all.

He flipped over some sheets in a thin file he'd built up over the past few days.

'You asked about another person from Leadmoor – this girl, ah, Christine Lamb ... A suspect?'

'Possible future victim', Scobie replied briefly.

'Right . . . And she's living in Clayton now?'

'Was. Her house was destroyed in a gas-blast yesterday. No trace of her body, but I've a suspicion she's returned home; probably frightened and confused, although she may not know about the incident at all.'

'I see,' Peterson said, and there was something in his eyes that put Scobie even more on edge – and angry. The man was holding back on him, he was sure.

'Did you dig up anything?'

Peterson shrugged. 'Have you met this girl? Or people who know her?'

'She was a pupil at the local comprehensive school a couple of years ago', Scobie explained. 'Studying at university now, but returned to the school as part of her undergraduate studies. I checked and that's true; she's listed at Lancaster.' Almost reluctantly, Scobie took a card from his pocket. 'Also, we have a picture – bit grainy: it's a blow-up from a year-group photograph.'

Peterson looked surprised. 'Her I.D. checks out?'

'All the way back to Leadmoor,' Scobie said. 'I'm hoping you can add to her file from your end.'

Peterson stared again at the picture and shook his head.

'What's the problem?'

'Only that no girl with her name was born in Leadmoor during the year that you say Christine Lamb was born. In fact, only one Christine Lamb has ever lived there.'

Peterson lifted his eyes, from the photo to Scobie.

'She died in 1925, age seventy-three.'

Both Scobie and Peterson decided to leave it at that. The meeting ended ten minutes later. Scobie knew that he was being cut adrift to wrestle with this thing himself. He surmised that Peterson thought the case might go bad suddenly, and he wanted no part of it: he was too set in his soft and quiet ways, and looking forward to his retirement too much, to have his paradigm shifted – or his mental stability questioned.

Scobie thanked the man and left. He drove straight round to the town's main library and was pleased to find it contained a fine collection of local history books, including many rare volumes bequeathed from a private collection.

He sat alone in the small and stuffy research room and started scanning for references. The place smelt of new carpet, of the coffee he was drinking at the rate of four cupfuls an hour and, eventually, of himself. He'd been wearing this shirt for rather too long, and would not now describe himself as pleasant company. He decided to give it another half hour then call it a day; book in at a hotel and treat himself to the luxury of a bath and a late lunch.

Five minutes from his deadline, Scobie came across what he had secretly hoped he would never find.

It was a photograph, an ancient daguerreotype, taken in the 1880s and showing a cluster of dour-faced individuals grouped against a background of grey smudged hills – the villagers of Leadmoor.

The first thing Scobie noticed was the odd similarity between the faces; inbreeding maybe, a common genetic thread. Or perhaps something else.

He let his eyes move slowly from face to face: old, young, male, female. Until he found Christine Lamb. Here, she was somewhat older than the university student from Western Road: mid-thirties, with another forty years to live. And what happened then? Did some indescribable process repeat itself? Did another individual with an identical set of chromosomes appear on the surface of the earth? Or did the same girl regenerate and live her span through again?

Pointless questions, Scobie decided.

A minute later, he found the likeness of the salesman, Johnson. And he had no doubt that here also among the crowd would be Tracy Vines and whoever else the Clayton killer had slaughtered, or would attempt to slaughter in the coming days.

The hills too had not changed. Scobie turned off the main A76 and found himself alone within a rounded landscape, patchy with dying heather and bracken the colour of rust. Maybe in the summer the scenery was picturesque and welcoming, but today the slight haze of cloud, and a lower sun, cut it in a different light. Shadows were already pooling here, and the roadway had turned to the colour of steel. Great scoops of rock and soil had been taken out of the slopes by the weather, wounds in the flesh of the ground. Scobie looked but could see no animals – no sheep or cattle or birdlife – and not another car passed him during the entire journey to the place where he hoped he would find some answers.

'Ghost town' was an inappropriate description of Lead-moor, and Scobie revised this initial impression within a few minutes. A ghost town implied occupancy of sorts, of the dead; but this village went beyond that into another kind of emptiness. No one was on the streets. Smoke did not rise from the chimney of a single house. There weren't any cats or dogs to be seen. No litter. Scobie slowed and stopped his car and wound down the window. Silence, except for the sound of his idling engine.

He laughed, wishing Carter, or even Peterson, had come

with him. Then he slammed the tape nearest to hand into his cassette player and turned the volume up full. The Carpenters sang with him as he drove on, loud to the point of distortion.

The sight of someone standing on the pavement unnerved him even more than the emptiness had done. Scobie felt the irrational but extremely powerful impulse to put his foot to the floor and keep going. But then, he argued ruefully, how could I possibly live with myself afterwards?

So he pulled in opposite the Highview Hotel and stepped out of the car, gazing around as though he was just a passing stranger, a little road-weary and wanting a drink.

'Good day to you! Fine weather we're having.'

'Looks as though it'll cloud over, to me,' Grigson said. The man, McAuliffe, had mentioned that other outsiders might appear in his wake, chasing anomalies. This was obviously one of them; his feigned innocence was pathetically shallow. Besides, McAuliffe's mind spoke its still small voice to the Kin now that they had touched him: he was watching, and knew the face of the stranger. A policeman. Dangerous.

Grigson turned his pale green eyes upward and gazed at the greying-over of the sky. It was not as bright as it had been, right enough . . .

'Maybe rain tonight . . .'

He failed to notice Scobie's close scrutiny, and subsequent expression of horror. For it was not the light but Grigson's eyes that were failing, misting over with the cataracts of senility minute by minute.

'Is the hotel open?' Scobie wondered. It would be the natural place for McAuliffe to stay; either here or at the home of Christine Lamb's family. And yet the question, the entire encounter, assumed an air of dark absurdity as the years seemed to pour out of Grigson like subtle blood from a sudden wound.

'It's open, and I'm the landlord . . . Would you come in, perhaps? The bar's closed but, ah, I daresay I could get away with offering you a dram on this occasion. I don't see any police driving by, do you?'

He gave a wink and a laugh, following the rural pub-owner stereotype which had been his function here since his beginning. Scobie laughed with him, a strained and throaty sound. He watched the man's eyelid crack like rotten leather: and the inside of his mouth – it was red and seemed to be filled with wet meat, the words twisted by the very machinery that made them.

'It's very good of you, sir. I'll bet your other guests appreciate your generosity also!'

'No other visitors at the moment.' Grigson shook his head and Scobie took a half-step backward. 'Well, out of season—'

'Actually, I'm just passing through. I stopped, um, to ask if this was the best road to Cumnock?'

'Ach, you're way off!'

'I am?' Scobie pretended disappointment, annoyance. There were further signs of the other's deterioration now. The man's body was starting to smell, and scarlet-brown liver stains were appearing silently beneath the skin. One of his eyes, the left one, had turned milky-white, like a dove's egg buried in the socket. The other glittered, either cheerfully, or with an intensity signifying something else that Scobie failed to understand. And the skin had thinned out and pulled away across the bridge of the man's nose, displaying yellow gristle.

Scobie felt his stomach turn, sluggishly.

'You should've stayed on the main road out of Dumfries,' Grigson explained. 'Takes you straight to Cumnock via Kirkonnel.'

'I see.'

Grigson started to lift his right hand to point the way back, but thought better of it. He slid it into his trouser pocket instead, where he felt the fingers loosen and drop.

'Aye. Coming down this road to Leadmoor is no shortcut. It's not a shortcut to anywhere at all ...'

He stumbled, but managed to regain a precarious balance, understanding now, at last, what was happening to him. The Kin were calling, their songs so varied and so beautiful, but melting into harmony even so. This stranger, he could never understand. And now Grigson wanted him to go. His time had come: the tides were high and roaring: he had but to relinquish his fragile hold on this flesh to be rid of it. And then, well, maybe the Community would welcome him into their throng, and he would awaken again in a different place, at another time ... Or there would be merely oblivion, which held no terror for one who had seen so many centuries come and go ...

The policeman was moving away, getting into his car.

'Back the wuh – ww – w—'

Grigson's mouth filled and he spat, red and solid, into the gutter. He could feel the cartilages between his spinal bones starting to give, a progressive crumbling away that threatened to pitch him forward on to the stranger's bonnet.

Scobie twisted the ignition key and gunned the engine. He'd learned enough. Learned too damned much, in fact.

Have a nice day, Grigson thought, as Scobie whirled the wheel and swung the car round and sped away. Only thought it, because now his bottom jaw, freed of flesh, hung slackly as though in huge surprise. His other eye gave out. The sunshine turned off. And he existed for a moment like a lone passenger aboard a dark and derelict hulk, run aground on the rocks of extreme age. With what was left of his dissolving mind, he expressed his love of the Kin and his final wish to be among them.

And they granted it.

Grigson's body stood upright for a second or two after its essence had departed. Then it fell, its coloured fluids running out, across the worn flagstones, to the gutters, to the drains.

McAuliffe watched it all happening in a bizarre overlay of vision and mental impression. Somehow Christine was conveying to his head what she and Grigson experienced: he thought of it as *sheGrigson*, because for those instants there was no difference or distance between them.

And Scobie had witnessed it too, of course. The speed with which he'd high-tailed it was eloquent proof of his terror and his understanding.

So what now? Would he alert the regional police, the armed forces? If the Government were told, would they react with swift effectiveness once the barrier of incredulity had been broken down? With enough manpower and high-technology, the Kin were doomed in their every hiding place.

'My God, Christine.' McAuliffe's voice was shaking. 'What do we do now? Where the hell do we *go*?'

'Back to Clayton.' She said it firmly, using the advantage of her confidence before her man could panic further. 'It's the right place for us, Pete. It's emotionally right to give us the best chance to start again—'

'It'll be swarming with cops.'

'Maybe. And perhaps they will find a nest. But we have prepared the ground carefully. No matter how thoroughly they search, they won't root out the Kin completely. And it will take but a few days for our next integration to be accomplished.'

'I don't know. It sounds so risky.'

'Risky for whom?' she demanded. 'Those they take are never lost to us. Grigson's body lies cooling down there, but he is already one with the Many. He is a part of us still, McAuliffe. If you could listen carefully enough, you'd hear him ...'

She said it with utter sincerity, but McAuliffe's belief struggled and died as he leant upon it.

'I need to listen more carefully, Christine.'

'It means you'll cross the boundary – do you realize that? By touching us, we share you. By losing yourself, you gain the heart of the Community.'

McAuliffe looked out across the soft panorama of the hills, wondering what differences he'd see in them afterwards. This was a sacrifice and a commitment more profound than any he'd ever made, or been called upon to make. It was his utter dissolution as an individual he was contemplating now; an invasion by outsiders of the most pervasive and intimate kind.

'I've heard it said,' he answered quietly, 'that to gain everything, you must first lose what you have ... It's at the heart of the great religions.'

'Believe it, McAuliffe.'

And after a silence – his last private reflection – he said, 'I want it. I want to become Kin.'

Christine gave a smile and stood up, offering her hand.

'Soon then. Come on, let's prepare to leave ...'

They hurried into the hotel. Christine told McAuliffe

that there was no point in burying the sad corpse of the landlord. Grigson was still here with them; what he'd left wasn't of any consequence.

'The other villagers, though—'

'They returned to the One, it's true. But the mystery of a deserted village would cause less of a stir among humankind than a hundred bodies, dead, of no cause.'

They packed a meagre suitcase with food from the kitchen. McAuliffe, on an impulse, took down the bottle of Auchentoshan from the shelf in the bar and added it to their provisions, together with the money from the till.

He had a rendezvous with Christine in the lobby.

'OK, then. I reckon that's it.'

'Grigson kept a car in the garage round the back.' She held up some keys. And laughed. 'If we hung around for a lift outside, we'd be waiting till doomsday.'

Her smile softened. She put down the small case and stepped up to him.

'I'm happy you're with me, Pete. With all of us.'

'It keeps me from growing bored in my spare time . . .'

He bent to kiss her. Christine's hands went round him and moved up his back, a caress that tightened as his kiss deepened. It altered, too, as her hands unsheathed a new shape, a bristling of stick-insect legs that pricked the skin of his scalp and drove down painlessly into his mind.

McAuliffe shuddered under her grasp. She seemed to tower over him. He was nothing in comparison; a fragment of flesh whose significance was so slight the universe failed to register its presence. He was only one man.

Until she released him and gazed at the agony in his eyes.

They drove away in the deepening dusk without looking back. McAuliffe was at the wheel of Grigson's ten-year-old Cortina. He was fully aware of the swing and dip of the road, and of the pretty girl beside him. Perhaps he felt a little tired after the events of the day, but they could always stop on the way down for a coffee and some supper. No problem. No problem at all . . .

But behind those surface thoughts and feelings were others that he had never before experienced. His mind, he felt, was brushing by the fringes of ideas so great they seemed to go on forever. As he took a corner, the moon slid out from the side of a hill, and there was a sprinkling of stars. Yet inside himself, the cosmos opened and world upon world rolled by in the night: and stars streamed past like sparks plucked from a vast bonfire and scattered away downwind.

McAuliffe turned on his headlights.

A mile away in the hills, Scobie watched the twin gleams appear. He started up his own car and set off to follow his quarry back home.

'Johan's dead.'

Anna said it quite matter-of-factly, as she and Ozzie, Billy, Carl and Kevin Steiger sat in the poky living room of Steiger's council house. A pile of oily newspapers and chip bags had been thrown down on the carpet; the cheap coffee table supported a mess of beer cans, and the sticky rings of dozens more. The TV was on, sound turned low, rolling out its unrealities as the group came to terms with this new truth.

'*He* did it?' Ozzie asked, and they all knew who was meant by that. They knew enough so that Anna had no need even to answer. She had spoken to them plenty during the past few days, always quietly and calmly; but they all sensed the urgency in what she was saying. They understood more about the killer now, and were glad of that because they realized that they were his targets. But it was only Ozzie among them who knew the killer's motive. His little angel had stayed with him through the night and without saying a word – by some wonderful osmosis – had made him understand it all. These others, they were nothing set against the purpose of the Kin. Let the killer have them if it granted Anna a few more hours in which to complete the cycle of the Community . . . In fact, Ozzie wished that they would go away and leave the two of them alone. He was still human enough to respond to the sex of Anna Fuller: he desired her all the more strongly, in fact, when he contemplated her power. He wanted to be a part of it, a part of her . . . He wanted to kiss her lips, while they were still lips to be kissed.

'I want to destroy him,' Ozzie said, imagining this might impress. Anna shrugged lightly.

'He is hard to kill. He will come at us with fire, and that is the way we must defend ourselves . . .'

Steiger, mightily frightened by the turn of events, stumbled out his question: 'Do you think – he – knows where we are?'

'He knows everything that Johan knew. So he will recognize your faces. But, Kevin, you never revealed to Johan where you lived. And the killer's mind is hot and seething with confused thoughts. At Home, the Old Flesh is dying, using up the last of its vitality to screen us from harm. We must work quickly to finish our purpose, at the same time leading him away on a false trail . . .'

'Give us the chance, Anna.' That from Carl: young, handsome – worshipping, as they all did, what they believed Anna Fuller to be.

She nodded.

'Tonight he will be abroad once more. While I prepare myself in this place, you, my friends, will go out to meet him.'

Anna smiled. She had them, had them all, held in utter silence and hanging on her every word. How long the Kin had debated among themselves the use of human beings for the furtherance of the Community; how many years had the tides of morality ebbed to and fro to no avail! Once, it had been considered taboo to taint men in any way, even down to stealing the shape they wore for the purpose of meeting them on the common ground of having a head, two arms, two legs, a smile, a voice . . .

That backward thinking could never last. Survival on this planet was easy enough; it burgeoned with life. But to evolve, to become something more than One had been, was a different matter. Human intelligence was able to flourish because of hands and mouths – the vehicles of manipulation of ideas and the physical world. The Kin were formless and could evolve only by using the templates of life where they found it. And here, they found people.

It was ironic that the Community's reticence drove It to take the mask of ignorant peasantry, and just of individuals who had died. Only then was it considered proper – deferential to the dead! – to assume the form that they no longer needed. And so the Kin grew poor in wisdom and health; trapped in a high valley, with the Source Of All That Was, living out Its span in the dark and the cold, imprisoned by memories.

But morality was in any case a human invention. And now the One was eking out its last hours in an agony of indecision – life, yes. But life at any price . . . ?

The Community had chosen Anna to be its representative, one of them anyway: had invested her with vigour and a high degree of independence. Rarely was anything produced that was so powerful, and then only in the direst circumstances. The Kin wanted her to master the tides of life on this world; let the morphogenetic fields of energy pour through her, so that in her abandonment of what she was, new multitudes would arise which would disperse, settle in a hundred far places and, when the time and place were right, leave the limited shapes they had copied; they would become one with all life – a part of the pulse of existence itself.

This had been the way through a thousand centuries. And during this time the Community had been safe, hidden, content to live in the undercurrents of a planet's progress.

Well, no more! Anna Fuller had tasted a freedom beyond the thoughts of the Community. Flesh was a fine and easily moulded clay: its sensations were exquisite – its pains and its pleasures a joy she would not abandon for the dull abstractions of her breed's antiquity. Even the basic act of copulation – a meaningless ritual to the Kin – assumed a new horizon in Anna's mind as she felt the weight and form, the length and breadth of her human self.

Now, on this night or the next, was the chance to change for ever the ways that had been followed through the long tunnel of time since the Community first arrived.

There were dangers, of course: the Slayer was near and would close off every opportunity if he could, with his blades and his flames. But even that danger was alive with excitement! A vital and necessary thing blazing beside the dull fearfulness that epitomized what the Kin had become.

Anna could feel him now – his thoughts sharp and vibrant in the telepathic landscape where, in part, she dwelt.

He was there, but he did not know yet which direction to take. Another had arrived in this town – Kin like herself – and the imminent transformation of that one was sure to distract him in his search for Anna and her small, close band of acolytes.

Thinking all of these things, she stood and stretched languidly. Her eyes had assumed a new bloom of darkness, and her voice was husky.

'Carl. Turn on the music. I want to dance.'

He obeyed at once; and although the slow, rich guitaring throbbed through Steiger's big Technics speakers so that the boys could barely hear themselves speak, a deep anticipatory silence grew in the room as Anna lifted her arms and ground her hips, lowering her head so that her fall of gold hair swung heavily in time to the rhythms.

The boys watched spellbound, desire like hot liquor in their throats.

Ozzie's control broke first. He made a grab for her, but Anna spun away out of reach. Her arms came down, she shrugged and let her leather jacket slide off her shoulders to the ground. Her breasts pushed tight against the cotton of her T-shirt. The music began gearing-up to faster riffs, chords piled on chords to a background of palpable basswork and a clatter of hard crisp drumming.

'Take it off, Anna.' Carl mouthed the words with sweat gleaming on his top lip, which he wiped with the back of his hand. 'Take it all off . . .'

She was moving more quickly, her gyrations mimicking sex. Her fingers worked at her belt and zip, hooked in the top of her jeans and dragged them down over her hips. Ozzie groaned softly. Steiger's mouth hung slackly open, close to dribbling.

As the guitaring splintered up to new heights of desperation, Anna whipped off her T-shirt and flung it in Billy's face. She stepped out of her jeans, reached round and snapped the hook of her bra.

Ozzie started clapping and yelling, his previous thoughts of monopolizing her company all gone now as this amazing experience unfolded. He realized distantly that someone was banging on the wall next door. Well, let the fuckers go to hell. This was now and it was red hot. This was what they'd all wanted since the beginning. Nothing was going to stop it.

There was just the final flimsy garment, white lace mistily covering curves and shadows. Ozzie jabbed his finger at her pants.

Come on, then – come on, boys . . . Her lips curved around the syllables. Then she was smiling, inviting them with her beckoning hands and her feet placed well apart on the old carpet. She was cream and gold and bright blue eyes, and all four boys were rocking to the music, but never taking their gaze from her for an instant, their erections rockhard and painful in their jeans.

Come on . . . Anna took a step back, found the far chair and eased herself against it.

Come on then, you mean muthafuckers!

With a wild yell, they scrambled forward together, tumbling and jostling to reach her, to be the first to lay rough hands on her pale smoothness.

Steiger struggled with the rest, and against them, as though carried by a surge of the tide that he had never planned. He felt as if he would be washed up against her, then dragged back by undercurrents he couldn't control: taken away from her unless he did something about it soon.

This was great – this was electric. But ultimately he

wanted Anna Fuller for himself, and would do anything to get her.

Carl's hand reached and pulled. Other hands joined his and ripped the filmy underwear away.

Oh Jesus, Steiger thought, I can smell her! He believed he would faint from sheer lust.

But by unspoken agreement, Ozzie took her first, from the front, slamming her back into the chair and pumping with a rictus grin on his face. And he didn't take long; barely time for the others to struggle themselves out of their flies. Billy. Carl. She gasped for each of them and kissed each as tenderly so that they loved her with all of their soul.

Anna's hands were as gentle with Steiger, caressing him, then urging him on with nails dragged jaggedly down his back.

I love you, Anna. I love you.

Did he think it or speak it? There was no knowing, but he burned with it.

And she spoke back to him, above the blitzing rock music and in spite of the others watching this act of animal coupling: I love you too, Kevin Steiger. My heart is yours. Whatever happens. It beats for you.

He spat himself into her so that she arched up, accepting him fully; then slumped back and curled herself on the chair, hiding what she had just so eagerly shown: her eyes closing, her hair wisping across to cover her face. She became childlike, her lips a little parted in sleep.

Ozzie came over and gently covered her with his jacket. They all did, one by one; it was a kind of prayer.

Billy walked over and turned down the stereo. The wall-banging continued for a few seconds, then stopped. Let the bastard knock on the front door, that's all! Something had put him in the mood to tear the neighbour's liver out!

He went and slumped down on the sofa and cracked open a can of Stella. Ozzie joined him. Carl dropped into the other chair and started to snore.

Steiger turned up the gas fire, then walked across to draw closed the curtains against the dull afternoon.

The sky was growing dark already, this early on. The wind lifted suddenly and flicked water against the window. The rain had set in for the night.

'What have you made me?' McAuliffe stared at his hand as though wishing for a knife with which to sever it. 'What have I turned into?'

'Do you feel ill? Frightened?'

'Different.'

'How else would you expect to feel?'

Christine snuggled up to him in the Cortina's warm cab. At last, after long hours, they had achieved the double aim of losing the car that had pursued them from Leadmoor, and arriving safely home. Almost. McAuliffe had swung unexpectedly on to a rutted country track and taken the motor down to an old and deserted farmhouse that over-looked the town. They were parked in the lee of the hill: curtains of grey rain all but smudged out the tiny lights of Clayton; it looked like a loose spillage of jewellery, chains and sparks of glitter in the growing gloom.

But here they were out of the wind and the wet. Grass rippled and flashed before them on the downslope; clouds poured across. Somehow they both knew that this was perhaps the last night they'd share: one of the last anyway. McAuliffe wanted this poignancy and quietness before they came to the parting. In the heat of what they both had to face, he knew they would have no time for promises or goodbyes.

'You know well enough what you are, Pete. You're still a man . . .' Christine planed her hand along his thigh, to his crotch. McAuliffe smiled, too damned tired to react. But he appreciated the gesture.

'But what else?'

'Anything you want to be . . .'

She showed him, moving her face, her fingers, to new appearances that awed rather than disgusted him. It reminded him of a swirl of oils – a magic trick from one form to the next. He saw it being done, but couldn't spot the transition in between.

Finally she was back as herself, her smile for him as he'd remembered it and not a chimera that could take the head off a dog or a man.

'How is it possible?'

'Reality is just a thin covering over what's true,' Christine said. 'Impossibility is just the way you look at things. Isn't it the case that your science always looks for boundaries?'

'We're always extending them.'

'Yes, but really there aren't any. Right down the ages, sorcery has existed not to give access to wonders, but to put limitations upon them; to stop them running out of control. Out of sorcery grew science.'

'OK.' He shrugged, admitting defeat. 'I know better than to argue. You've had considerably more time to work out your philosophies than I have. Besides, you're in my head – you know what I'll say before I say it.'

'Saves time and ambiguity.'

'But it takes the pleasure out of talking, Christine. The same as being Kin robs loneliness of its piquancy . . .'

He chuckled self-consciously. Although he was not the same as he had been, he was not Kin. A hybrid, rather; a Frankenstein with human dreams and the flesh to make them happen . . .

But not for a while. He couldn't yet face the prospect of watching his body slide into new shapes. That would be the final proof that his view of the universe had been wrong all along.

'Yet we have to disguise ourselves,' Christine said, picking out his thought. 'The police are obviously trailing us. We can abandon the car together with our likenesses. We can evade them for long enough.'

'Are you close?'

'Tonight, perhaps. Or tomorrow. After that, the Community will be dead.'

'And you—'

'Like Grigson.'

'Oh, no . . .'

McAuliffe held her tightly.

'Don't be frightened of it, Pete. We have the means to prevent that finality. Down there, we must find somewhere safe, somewhere hidden. While I am immobile, you will serve my needs and protect me.'

'From the killer.'

'Now you can meet him on equal terms.'

He sighed. The rain had closed in around them and drummed with a random monotony on the car roof. McAuliffe flipped a switch and the wiper blades licked at the windscreen glass, clearing a momentary view of the valley.

'Why not here? No one ever visits this farmhouse.'

Christine shook her head.

'*We* visited it. Anyway, we're vulnerable. In the town

there are a million corners; abandoned places underground. And I can sink my mind in the wash of thoughts of fifty thousand people. Up here, my mind would shine like a beacon light for him to see.'

'Are you sure . . .' He hated to ask, because he feared the answer. 'Are you sure I didn't kill him?'

'Listen with your mind, McAuliffe. He's there.'

McAuliffe closed his eyes and relaxed. And yes, there were the songs of the Kin like the calls of distant whales in a desolate ocean: and human songs, chaotic and small. But beneath both, a sharp and clear note of bitterness, was the Slayer's mind – that McAuliffe could not bring himself to approach, for there was no greater darkness.

Shortly thereafter, they made their preparations. Christine dragged an old coat from the back of the car – one of Grigson's that hung loosely on McAuliffe's shorter frame. She pulled on a couple of heavy jerseys over her cotton shirt, and over those put on a bulky anorak.

'You look like an Eskimo,' McAuliffe laughed.

'Better than looking like a frozen leg of chicken.'

He did not find the comparison amusing.

'Now,' she told him gently. 'Ourselves.'

As Christine spoke, a wave of lightness ran down the strands of her hair, changing each to a pale honey-blonde. The rich brown of her eyes bleached out to a light blue; her nose thinned, her lips altered subtly; her chin grew rounder; her cheekbones lifted half an inch beneath the swirling milk of her skin . . . McAuliffe held the dreadful suspicion that he could paddle his fingers in her face like a liquid; that her flesh would close over them instantly.

He shuddered, unable to contemplate similar manifestations in himself.

'Christine, I can't.'

She was finished now, a different girl; an altered prettiness. Her smile tantalized him anew.

'Of course you can. I'll help you.'

She did nothing as crude as touch him. Her mind worked his changes, and upon her command, his muscles and bones came adrift and shifted and realigned. There was no pain: actually, there was very little sensation of any kind. Doing it came down finally to a *perception* that it was possible.

I think, therefore I am anything I want to be.

McAuliffe laughed with another man's mouth.

Five minutes later, two figures clambered out of the car into the brunt of the wind. Together they hurried, hand in hand, down the hill towards the outskirts of the town. They paused once for McAuliffe to throw away his keys.

Sergeant Carter had seen some rare sights in his time: most of them horrible, a few of them just plain strange. One of them sat before him now; he smiled, but, all the same, a kind of horror broke gently inside him. As he walked into Scobie's office, he found the man there at his desk, crying softly. And worse, he made no effort to cover up his hurt. A glass tumbler was overturned between Scobie's hands as they lay limply on the blotter. No liquid had spilled out. The D.I. had drunk it all, and the air held the sweet scent of whisky.

'Sir? Are you – OK?'

Scobie's eyes lifted, webbed red with weariness, glazed with too much seeing.

'OK? Yes, Carter, I've just won the pools . . .'

Luckily Carter caught himself before offering congratulations.

'Marius has been on the line . . .'

'Ah . . .'

'Yes, ah.' Now Scobie dragged a handkerchief from his trouser pocket, wiped his face and blew his nose.

'Goddam it, Dennis, I'm tired – I know, before you say it – I'm always tired. It's what gives me that distinctive leathery look.'

'Like an elephant's arse – sir.' Carter's uncertain smile broke out into a grin. Scobie dredged up a little humour from somewhere and joined him.

'What has Doctor Marius said to you?'

'He was vague,' Carter replied, truthfully. 'Told me there'd been another killing – he thought. That was the odd bit. He thought.'

'Yeah. Well, maybe he's not sure judging by what he found . . . But, we've got a couple of missing persons also.'

'What?' Carter could barely believe what he was hearing. If this was the case, it had been kept under the lid so tightly that not a whisper had gotten out. 'Shall I—'

'No point winding up the machinery.' Scobie paused. However this tortuous trail ended, it would end here in Clayton. Pointless keeping someone as useful as Carter in the dark.

'One of the m.p.'s is Davies, the path. assistant. The other is the hit-and-run victim—'

Carter's burst of laughter erupted, then stopped as quickly.

'Holy shit. But who'd – I mean, this is necrophilia on a grand scale!'

Scobie stayed silent, remembering his brief hour in Leadmoor, where disappearance seemed to be woven into the fabric of the valley's reality: and he remembered Grigson – had he remembered it right? That strange sense of the man standing there, caught on the borderline of life and death. His dreadful disintegration...

'Anything else to tell me?' he asked at last. 'Anything on Peter McAuliffe or the Lamb girl?'

'Nothing, sir. Did your trail go cold?'

'I'll give you the background later... I think they came back to Clayton. Actually, I'm pretty sure of it. Why the girl went to Leadmoor for only a couple of days, then returned, is anybody's guess.' Scobie could hazard several guesses in fact: they would take the place of his nightmares in the early hours.

'But I think now we've got to consolidate what we know, estimate what we don't know, and prepare for what we fear.'

'There's still no support from upstairs, sir.'

'The Chief Inspector has my permission to use his anus as a pencil sharpener.'

'Even so...'

'If we take the time to try for official support, Carter, it'll all be over, bar the shouting. There's something monstrous happening here – but beneath the surface. The killings are simply a symptom of a greater illness affecting the body of Clayton. And I don't want the town killed by a plague before the C.I. realizes it's running a temperature... If you follow my analogy...'

Carter shrugged.

'Whatever you think's best. Do we see Doctor Marius now?'

'Go and warm up the car for me, Dennis. I've a phone-call to make first.'

Carter left. Scobie dialled Peterson's office himself and barged through the secretary's smooth evasions that Peterson was unavailable right now. When the man took the call, Scobie spoke with a quiet firmness for approximately three minutes. He told – *told*, not asked – him to take a ride out to Leadmoor, where he would find one dead body and several hundred others missing. Scobie stated his belief that the villagers had gone up into the hills. He advised Peterson to follow up with some uniformed officers, who should be armed ... Something made Scobie add that maybe they should arm themselves with fire, petrol, paraffin – flame-throwers if there was any chance of requisitioning them.

Peterson began to laugh. Scobie told him to shut-the-fuck-up and do what he knew was necessary.

Then he put the receiver down with exaggerated care and followed Carter to the basement garage.

Marius was glad to see Scobie again – having thought at least a few times that he wouldn't have the chance. He noted the weary look of fear in the policeman's eyes and knew it to be justified.

'Where's the SAS, eh, Paul?'

'When you need them, they're out to lunch ... What's the news?'

'This way.'

The pathologist led Scobie and Carter through to the post-mortem room, where two heaps of what looked like offal lay side by side on the slab. Carter groaned softly. Scobie made an expression of disgust.

'You're not going to tell me ... ?'

'I don't know what I'm going to tell you!' Marius came back sharply, then apologized. 'I guess we're all feeling the strain. Sorry, Paul.'

The other acknowledged with a nod.

'The object on the left was reported to us by a member

of the public, some guy working the late shift who was on his way down to Cooper Engineering. He found it in the tunnel where the railway bridges the wasteground.'

'I know the place,' Scobie said. 'And this one?'

'I found it myself in one of the drawers. The hit-and-run Joe Doe.'

'Is it him?'

'I don't know what it is. Under the microscope the tissue from both of these objects looks amorphous, featureless: it has no structure . . .'

'But, it's flesh?'

'Yes, it's flesh. Or was, at one time.'

'Ideas, John?'

'What we talked about before . . .' Marius began, then glanced across at Carter.

'It's OK,' Scobie said, 'he knows more or less what there is to know.'

'Well. We have discussed a kind of life that can suit itself to any pattern, and with a speed we would regard as impossible. Paranormal at the very least.'

'Go on.'

'Here we have a once-living substance that is patternless . . .'

'As though it failed to develop?'

'Or somehow had its pattern removed: a complete and utter disruption, a rendering-down of the cells to this mess.'

'Is it the same as the stuff we found at Western Road?' Scobie wanted to know.

'No.' Marius was definite on this point. 'I had that carcass burned after taking some samples. Like the remains of Tracy Vines and Vicki Bell, the Western Road tissue continued to grow, but randomly. It had the potential to become anything – bone, blood, muscle – but without direction it simply ceased functioning after a short while.'

'I want it destroyed,' Scobie said. 'Burn everything you've got that shows this propensity for abnormal growth, John.'

'But the scientific value—'

'I want whatever's causing it – whatever force is behind it – isolated. It might already be too late, in which case you'll have all the samples you need. They'll be coming out of your ears.'

Scobie's grin showed that he'd caught the pun, but that he wasn't joking. He turned to Carter.

'Arrange for the lads on patrol to look out for anything unusual – they'll know it when they see it,' he added grimly. 'Also, I want an APB out on Peter McAuliffe and Christine Lamb. You've got the details on file. They were travelling in a mark four Cortina, but it's likely they've abandoned that now. My guess is they'll be hiding up somewhere, or, if they've got some nerve, staying with friends. You might contact the pneumatic Mrs Adams and get a list of who Christine Lamb hung around with at school.'

Carter nodded. 'Where will you be, sir?'

'I'll stay on with Doctor Marius for a while and try to put together enough evidence to convince the unbelievers, such as the rest of the human race. I'll follow you later.'

'Right.'

Carter left. Scobie looked at Marius and searched around for something confident to say. He could think of nothing.

'We can't torch the whole town . . . Can we?'

'My guess is,' Marius said, 'that this stuff is intelligent. Maybe it's open to reason.'

'So we sit round the table and talk terms!'

'Perhaps,' Marius said, quite seriously, 'we could pray to it?'

It was time. Anna, Steiger, Ozzie, Billy, Carl sat in a silent circle listening to their music, their eyes closed, their minds open. Anna was talking to them, explaining what had to be done, what sacrifices needed to be made. She told them that death was not the end; as long as one of them remained alive, they would all live in the hearts of those who loved them. And the rain poured on, and the sky darkened towards chaotic black.

At last, as one, they stood up and Anna kissed each of them in turn, fondly, with tears in her eyes and theirs. Ozzie turned away and could not look at her any more. He put on his jacket: its back-patch showed angels and demons, beneath which was written the words: Sex 'n' Drugs 'n' Rock 'n' Roll . . . And My Mum.

'Cheers, Oz,' Steiger said, his voice low and broken.

'See you in Hell, man.'

Carl and Billy left with him. The door slammed shut.

Steiger felt suddenly alone, despite what he'd been told. He knew that Anna was looking at him, judging his response.

'He's coming for us, isn't he?'

'Are you frightened of it?' she asked. Steiger shrugged.

'Dunno . . . No. Just sad, I think, that it's nearly over. This is a shit-hole of a town, but it's better than nothing, right?'

Anna smiled. 'You won't die, Kevin. If you trust me, then believe me when I tell you that. The slayer will try to wipe us out, but we're clever . . .'

'I don't feel clever. What have I got to do?'

'Soon, when this is over and you are settled, you will

go to work as usual; explain to your boss that you've not been well. Just carry on with your life.'

'Will you be here?'

A touch of her mind cowed him, reassured him also. But Steiger could feel that she was trying not to interfere with his thoughts. For what was to come, he had to be himself, untainted by dreams of the Community. He must contain nothing that the killer could trace.

Anna went out, returning a few moments later with a bundle wrapped in sacking and tied with twine.

'At work, Kevin, I want you to go into your meat fridge and hide this. Can you do that – is there a place?'

'Easy. I rotate the stock; I can just keep this at the bottom, out of sight.' He took the package. 'But – why?'

'Trust, Kevin. Just trust.'

'Just lust,' he echoed, and with his heart beating quickly he touched her breast. The lightning jagged through him once again.

'It's no wonder you have survived so well,' Anna chuckled, allowing him to caress her. He asked with his eyes.

'Yes,' she affirmed softly. 'Now, while there's time.'

Black marble moonlight, and the temperature was down towards zero. But at least the rain had finally stopped. Something of the balm in McAuliffe's body kept the cold at bay, but he was not sure whether he or Christine could survive the night. And what about food, and what about sleep for godssake! She said she'd need somewhere warm and hidden for the process to occur: and occur it must – and would, imminently. Already she was shivering, her teeth clenched tight against the changes that would wrack her body and erupt it out into a kaleidoscope of new life.

But it couldn't happen here on the street. This thaumaturgy was not meant for human eyes to witness or human ignorance to destroy.

After searching out likely places that McAuliffe knew, they found some boarded-up houses in a run-down street; tall, Edwardian structures with ornate stonework and long, overgrown gardens.

'Not here . . .' The clear thought came with stuttered words.

'Just for an hour. I'll get some blankets and food.'

'I know another place – I've searched . . . in the railway yards—'

'That's a couple of miles away. And it's early yet, too many people about. Listen to me, Christine!' he pleaded. 'You've trusted me so far. Look! I'm a changed person because of it!'

She barely managed a smile.

'So trust me now. An hour, and I'll be back. We'll rest, then go on.'

After a pause, she acquiesced, and it pleased him that she looked to him for strength, when she had enough of her own to claw down this slum and beat it flat into the earth.

They broke in through a back window. He left her in the musty-smelling cavern of what was once a lounge, with Grigson's voluminous coat draped over her. He hoped she would still be there – and recognizable – when he returned.

He had enough money in his pocket to buy them a feast, and many takeaways were open still. But first there was something to be done, a final pilgrimage McAuliffe had to make for his own peace of mind.

He had selected this semi-occupied street for another

reason: it lay on the western edge of Clayton, and not even three miles across the fields was Melsham, where McAuliffe used to have his home.

He clambered over the roadside fence and set off at a run towards the distant glitter of lights.

A half moon hung in a clearing sky like a weathered lump of crystal dropped to the bottom of a pond; a smudge of its own light. At first McAuliffe used this pale illumination to see his way across the ploughed ground, but he found that very swiftly he did not need it. His body accommodated to the environment of its own accord – or, more likely, prompted by the stirrings and commands of deeper levels of his mind. His eyes changed and grew and adjusted to the lack of brightness, and his face inflated around these new orbits. Again there was no pain, no effort; it felt like shifting up through the gears of a powerful car.

He began to understand something of how the Kin lived. Left alone, their bodies would simply mask themselves according to whatever other living things were around: the Community sinking down into whatever ecosystem existed nearby. Perhaps, ultimately, the Creature had no native intelligence of its own, but merely mimicked the consciousness of other lifeforms ... But its holographic power of tenaciously clinging to life in its every shred and fragment was what made it wonderful. Monstrous. Dangerous.

McAuliffe understood, suddenly, the motives of the Slayer in wishing to rid the world of this epidemic of germplasm. Once it established a foot-hold, it would be here forever ...

And yet, Christine had told him that the current generation of Kin had survived intact and self-contained for hundreds of years; and that the original being arrived many hundreds of millenia ago. And mankind was still around, eagerly looking for ways to exterminate itself. Was it even feasible that, apart from isolated instances of cross-contact, the Kin had become absorbed into human geno-types? Were Man and Kin in any way brothers across these vast spans of time?

McAuliffe didn't think so. The Community had kept itself sacrosanct, uncontaminated; using Man only as camouflage. And while each regeneration had presented its own special problems, the current cycle was the first to occur in the technological age, with communications well-established and with a deep awareness in civilization of its own fears and shortcomings. That's what made this transformation so vulnerable. That, and the Slayer who would see the Kin finished for ever, by his own hand.

The same adaptations that gave McAuliffe his eyes put new legs under his body, so that he loped along at twice, at three times, human speed, reaching his goal in a matter of minutes.

The village, typically, was quiet, its only activity being in and around the pub on the green. The houses along the main street and the loop of the West Road were marked by the colours of their curtains glowing out into the dark. McAuliffe could hear scraps of TV-talk, a raised voice, a laugh, love being made in a bedroom as he passed like a grey ghost . . .

He reached his home, noticing at once the unfamiliar cars parked on the macadam driveway. He told himself he'd half expected it, that Judith would carry on with her life after he'd gone, as though he'd never been a part of it. But it hurt him anyway.

He moved closer.

He gazed through the window into the lounge, which was busy with a dozen or so people, all smartly dressed, standing in little clusters with tulip glasses of wine and plates of vol-au-vents; contacts making contacts making contacts. McAuliffe had lost all track of time, but recognized suddenly that this was Judith's dinner party which she'd planned before he'd gone to Leadmoor, a million years ago. Watching the tableau of human ordinariness drove a pang of regret right through him. Although he'd hated his life and its meaningless tedium, it called to him now, and he needed what was left of his will to resist it.

Judith herself, dressed in the pale blue that suited her so well, was laughing with a tall, dark-haired man whom McAuliffe didn't recognize. He was paying his wife the closest attention – leering in fact. It would not take long, he decided, before this intruder suggested and Judith relented ... And that hurt the most; that she should go ahead with this gathering when he, these past days, might have been lying dead in some ditch.

Then came a new emotion as Judith's partner leaned close and whispered in her ear, and together they left the room.

There was a power now in McAuliffe to make his fury manifest. He slid around to the side of the house, then to the back that was hidden in moonshadow. He willed himself upwards over the sheer bricks, climbing like a grotesque leech to the lip of the back-bedroom window.

McAuliffe could not contain his anger – literally. Whereas in the past he would have clenched a fist in his rage, now his hand sucked loose from the brick and twisted anew, to a horrible stinging barb, an insect blade capable of inflicting instant and fatal damage ...

An oceanic swell washed over the land and crashed

upon the house and through the village, almost dragging McAuliffe from the wall. The songs of the Kin came, high and desperate, to his ears: and Christine's voice was among them, laced with doubt of his return. The Community's voices spoke a million meanings in the space of a human second, but it was human intercourse in which McAuliffe was interested, that pinned him to the wall around the bedroom window like a billow of black skin bristling with knives.

Judith sat before the mirror at her make-up table, not seeing him, preoccupied with the details of her years. She applied powder and lipstick with experienced care, tilted her head this way and that; pushed her fingers through her hair and shook out the night's curls in a looser spill.

The door opened and the dark-haired man stepped in.

McAuliffe, all weaponry and hatred, gathered beyond the glass.

Then, he saw Judith's mouth turn down in anger: she said something sharp and final. The man shrugged and slipped an oily smile on to his face. He stepped forward and she stood up, gesturing. He got the message then and apologized, trying to mend his mistake. Judith was still snapping insults after him as he turned and left smartly.

McAuliffe relaxed, drawing in his killing shape. The air was rich with flows and currents. He released himself from his grip on the house and blew down in the wind, as though his fathers had done the same since the morning days. In his mind, he gave Judith the last of his love and felt happier, now, that she would be seeing him no more.

The transformation left him elated but weakened. He reached the town on shaking legs that were woefully his own, and human. The man in the fast-food shop stared aghast at his rags and his ragged complexion. McAuliffe threw down some money, scooped up his wrappings of food, and hurried out.

The chip man had obviously thought McAuliffe was a down-and-out, a drunk. He wondered if he was: his head was spinning with sounds, a great darkness of terror like a stampede of animals caught in a storm which they could never outrun.

But Christine's voice came clearer now, her imperative his only light. He hurried on through backstreets and filthy alleys, trembling, sensing the presence of the Other – an undersound; the berserk roar of the Kin Slayer.

She was awake when he reached the house, huddled in her blanket like a chrysalis. McAuliffe unwrapped the oily food he'd bought and they gorged on it, her hand pale and so thin, his fingers rippling on the brink of change.

She glanced at him with sharp caution in her over-bright eyes.

'Your job is just to protect, McAuliffe. These powers bind you to us – you do not have independence with them. Remember?'

'I realize that. Don't worry. But I have to know what I can do . . .'

'Your body knows. Trust in us. We'll guide you.'

'You sound', he admitted hesitantly, 'like a wailing of old women—'

'Because you aren't attuned to us. You still try to understand with your conscious mind, logically, what we tell you.'

'What's the quote . . . ?' McAuliffe struggled for it. 'Yes – "Logic is the art of thinking and reasoning in strict accordance with the limitations and incapacities of human misunderstanding." ' He grinned.

'You got it,' she told him.

The mood was lighter. McAuliffe held her close.

'Just one thing . . .'

'Anything – '

He gazed at her. 'Why do you use my surname when you're pissed off with me?'

Later, when the silence had deepened further on the streets, McAuliffe and Christine picked over the waste-ground beyond the houses, wary of many things. The voices of the Kin continued to sound their distant alarms and terrors: the heart-wrenching humpback-whale songs of alien seas. And there was the fear of the police and capture in this town where murder had been done and where folk were afraid.

They walked for the best part of an hour, a tortuous route through nowhere, until they came to the old railway yards which Christine and her kind had long ago selected as the site of the Community's rebirth.

'It's poorer than a stable,' McAuliffe muttered sullenly.

'God plays in a million places,' Christine said.

Her words reminded him to ask about the Kin's religious beliefs, when and if the opportunity ever arose . . .

Across the way, in a pale wash of streetlight, they could see Western Road, still roped off, and the wreckage of Christine's old house.

'It's too close,' McAuliffe said. 'The cops haven't finished here.'

'We're safe enough. There'll be plenty happening in Clayton to draw them off . . . I only need a night, Pete. Once we've gone in, the process can begin quickly.'

'Gone in where?'

She pointed to shadows among shadows.

'There's a place below ground, just over there. Only one
entrance. I went down once – it's just an empty space in
the earth.'

'Home sweet home.'

Christine caught the bitterness in his voice; the fear. She
held his hand and squeezed.

'By this time tomorrow, Pete, we'll be walking free. A
new life together. Isn't it worth waiting for?'

'Of course,' he said, trying to mean it. But the dread
that stalked the Kin had infected him also. Life again was
such a slim hope, when all you could see was cold and
dark and fragile vows.

Doctor Marius sat in the tiny office that was glassed-off
from the rest of the lab. His table beneath its cone of
lamplight glittered with microscope slides and precise
instruments of dissection. And there was a heavy glass jar
filled with saline solution, in which floated the last fragments of flesh belonging to those who were not human.
Tracy Vines, the Bell child, the hit-and-run John Doe, the
monster from the wrecked house on Western Road –
threads of fibre and substance still alive, when every other
part of them had been burned.

Marius knew he should have burned it all, as Scobie
demanded. What he was doing was madness. He asked
himself: would you preserve the last phial of a plague of
appalling virulence, just to see how it worked?

Bloody stupidity. He said it aloud. But a corner of his
mind whispered yes, I'd keep it and tease out its every
secret. Just to know. Just to see for myself . . .

Besides, there was still plenty more where this came
from, of that Marius was sure. The hit-and-run was obviously one of them, quietly regenerating in its coffin until

it was whole enough to escape. And poor Davies had been in the way as the creature revived, its path direct through the bones of the living. Why, it was out there now; growing, changing, ready to take over the world!

Marius giggled, an unsteady sound. He shook his head. These meagre threads of meat would not make any difference at all to what tomorrow was going to bring.

And they were – fascinating. He had experimented already: placing some of the alien fibre on a slide with a pinprick drop of his own blood. Within minutes the obsolete muscle tissue had vanished, becoming instead more blood. Then, from a freshly-killed laboratory mouse, some bone. And the blood had turned quickly, in precise imitation, to bone . . .

Now . . . Marius picked over the body of the mouse, a spreadeagled scrap of fur-wrapped red. Shall it be intestinal tissue, liver, heart? Nerve tissue perhaps. Brain substance!

He lifted his scalpel and probe to the eggshell skull.

And paused, a wave of coldness freezing his movements.

In his post mortem of the hit-and-run corpse, Marius had removed and weighed the major organs, looking for pathological anomalies. As a matter of course, he had replaced them in the body cavity (no point in half a funeral). Also as a matter of course, he had kept the brain for further analysis, hoping to use it as part of some research in which he was currently engaged: links between cerebral structure and psychotic tendencies. It was in a canopic jar now, hanging there in fluid. He fancied he could almost hear it, knocking on the glass to get out . . .

Very carefully, as though this slight movement might upset the equilibrium of the whole universe, Marius put down his instruments and rose slowly from his seat. Suddenly the lamplight was glaringly bright, dazzling and nauseous: but the gloom beyond was far too dark; it could hide anything.

The pathologist's hand took hold of a larger scalpel, good for chin-to-crotch incisions; his reason told him this weapon was useless but the fingers stubbornly refused to let go.

He walked up to the glass door, opened it with a cat-burglar's care, and snapped on the light switches to the lab.

For a few seconds the scene strobed confusingly as the striplights flickered on. Then, beneath their sub-audible buzz, Marius saw that nothing had changed. The tension within him subsided a fraction.

He crossed the floor to the cold-room and wrenched at the door. It sucked against its seals and swung open. A lick of frost unfurled against him.

Marius switched on the internal light, a single high-wattage yellow bulb within a wire guard. Organs in their jars loomed out at him, grotesque pinks and purples dulled by time. The specimen he was after stood at the far end on a high shelf. He hurried up to it, his eyes alert for any changes in the grey convolutions of matter. There did not seem to be any.

But that was not all, of course. Now he had to turn the jar around. Which meant putting down his weapon.

With a little chuckle at the exquisite fear running through him, Marius laid down the scalpel and eased the jar round an inch at a time, its heavy base gritting against the shelf.

Another inch. One more. A final turn.

Marius jumped away and crashed against the opposite wall.

Holy Mother of Jesus – it was alive. It had grown!

He felt his heart stutter, clutched it and wondered if this was the end of him . . . Bloody good place to drop dead, anyway, a crazy singsong voice from within opined.

The lobed hemispheres he had first seen now formed the humped back of some kind of animal; greyish, obscene; it looked as if it had been skinned a week ago and thrown in a canal to fall apart . . .

A face suggested itself in the loose and sloppy flesh. And hands like the unformed limbs of a foetus waved feebly, clenching and unclenching claws or fingers, making little baby fists.

Marius was disgusted, a healthier emotion maybe than the pure stark terror which had pierced through him, but which was ebbing now with the slowing of his pulse. He allowed a minute to pass without doing anything. His thoughts raced . . . The being was weak, stirring listlessly against the weight of liquid in which it was immersed: and there was no chance, of course, that those pathetic proto-limbs could exert sufficient pressure against the five-mill glass to shatter it. He was safe – and mentally so as well, most probably. The creature had not infected him with any foul telepathies, nor had the sight of it tipped his sanity . . .

Marius took a deep breath of chill, sterile air. I'm going to be all right. Thank God. Thank *God*. I'm OK. There might even be scope here for some further – and highly original – research.

A shadow grew along the cold-room floor.

Marius turned.

A man. Bedraggled. Ill. For a second it looked like Davies, until the resemblance slid away into a more hand-some, more boyish face.

'Hi,' Johan's borrowed voice said, a little shrilly. 'I wondered if I could have my brain back, please?'

They made a fire out of scraps of wood around a core of screwed newspaper, doused in a little paraffin. And there was one of those AA special offer multipurpose lamps, to keep away the darkness. The air smelled of damp and dog shit, of dead rats and decayed vegetables: but the boys had plenty of cans to while away the time; and each had brought along his Walkman so that music might keep the fear at bay.

Only Ozzie was bothering to rock right now. He sat away from the other two on an army surplus blanket, headbanging like there was no tomorrow; his dark hair flying, his face twisted, his eyes focused on elsewhere. He stopped momentarily now and then to swig at his beer, then resumed the heavy metal mantra.

Carl glanced across at him, then looked at Billy over the variable glow of the smoky fire.

'It keeps him from crapping his jeans,' Carl said with a wide grin. It looked to Billy just as though that smile was Sellotaped up at the sides.

'Yeah, right. I think I'll join him in a couple of minutes.' He belched richly. 'After this can.'

Carl gave a brief and brittle laugh and decided he was not helping his own nervousness by homing in on Ozzie's.

'What I can't understand is, why keep Steiger back? What the fuck's he got that we haven't?'

'A safe house,' Billy offered. 'Maybe he pumps better than we do, too.'

Carl shook his head with not-quite-sober vehemence.

'It wasn't like that with us and Anna – you know that.

She's no whore, man – she's . . . Well, I know we all did it to her but, well, it was an honour, man. It was an honour to be with her. She wanted it to be that way. We wouldn't have taken her if we'd decided. She wouldn't have let us . . .'

Billy nodded. 'I know all of that. You ain't talking to no piehead, Carl! Anna is always in control. She knows what's best. That's why we're here: that's why Steiger's back at the house with her.'

'Do you suppose they're on the job now, Billy?'

Billy looked at the other's face and sneered. 'Does that matter? Listen, what happened was the closest to heaven I ever been. Same for you. She took us to the top, Carl. Better than any song, right? Live fast, die fast. Don't you believe it all of a sudden?'

That made Carl pause; time in which to grow sick and regretful. Anna's enchantment was in him now, like a tune he couldn't shake out of his head. It buzzed like a fly about his brain. But it was weak, her concentration absorbed elsewhere. He could defy her, if he chose . . .

Billy finished his drink and delved into the big rucksack he'd packed earlier that day, after Anna explained what had to be done. He took out his personal stereo with a cassette already clipped in, and fitted the tiny earphones. Then he searched again and pulled out something else, an object wrapped in oiled cloth, which he removed lovingly.

'Christ . . .' Carl whispered at the sight of the sawn-off shotgun.

'Christmas present from my Auntie Sheila,' Billy quipped with a thin smile. He broke open the weapon and pushed in two cartridges with his thumb; snapped the gun whole again.

'Just to make sure Anna's plans go like clockwork.'

'Cheers to that, man!' Carl swigged his beer and dribbled some down the front of his leather jacket. 'Oh shit—'

'Carl . . .' Billy put down the gun and stared at his friend with an intensity of concern. 'Carl, why don't you look around outside? Take a breath of air. Calm down. Come back and give me the news, OK?'

Carl was fiercely grateful for that, but he realized too that it was a test; that maybe Billy would be watching him do the rounds in the empty mall, waiting for him to run. Just waiting, so he could—

'Carl?'

'OK, Billy. I'll look around.'

Billy smiled. 'Head up, man, it'll soon be morning.'

Carl pulled another can off his six-pack, hefted its weight a couple of times, then stood and cracked the stiffness out of his knees. He went across to the boarded-up front façade, eased a warped panel aside a little and stared out into the blackness. He could see that the sky was completely clear of cloud; a cleansing north-westerly wind had left only stars in its wake, and a three-quarters moon like a worn white pebble that seemed to perch on the roof of the opposite building. No need for the fancy torch. It wasn't so dark once your eyes were sensitized to it.

He looked back into the hideaway, at Billy's cross-legged buddha shape silhouetted against the fire.

'Back in ten minutes.'

'Take care, Carl . . .'

He slid outside through the boards, then stood and blinked away sudden tears, brought on by the air's frosty sting. The grey bulky angles and surfaces of the mall had an icing-sugar coating of crystals that were too small to see, but which glittered back every stray beam of starlight: for once the place was oddly beautiful, and he was the only one here to see it.

Carl put his beer can down on the nearest ledge. Better than a fridge, this! By the time he'd had a little walk round, the stuff would be cooled to the ideal temperature. He flipped up his collar and set off . . .

Not that he knew what he was looking for. Anna had made the link between the Clayton killer and her 'mission', but even then it wasn't in so many words: most often, what Anna said came as feelings deep in your guts; a kind of intuition of rightness. That's why they all loved her so, Carl realized now – because her language was a syntax of emotion. She said it all with her eyes.

Dreaming of her eased his nerves a shade. What had she said? That each of them would live in her heart for ever: that no matter what happened, they would all be together again one day, and that nothing could pull them apart . . .

It wasn't so bad then that Steiger had stayed with her back at the house. Physical distance meant nothing set against the unity she'd promised. Soon – tomorrow – they'd all be back, the gang assembled . . .

But what about Johan? He'd been missing for two days and it was pretty obvious the killer had taken him out. How could *he* come back? How could *he* live on, except as a sad memory?

Carl was on the return now. The paved levels and stairways of the shopping centre were empty; not even a copper on the beat bothered to come here after dark. There was nothing to steal, and all that could be vandalized had been, long ago.

He came round the final corner and saw Johan.

Carl stopped, and for a second his time-sense would not mesh, so that it seemed like Johan had never left them. There he was, grinning back at his friend. But—

'Whatcha doin' up there, ya mutha!' Carl meant it to be loud and confident, full of bluff camaraderie. But his voice failed him and the words came out hgh and heavy with puzzlement.

It was Johan all right. Johan's head. Stuck fifteen feet up on the sheer shadowed surface of a wall. He looked strange; still looked dead. Carl began to fear the worst.

'Oh – oh soddit Johan – the b-bastard's hung your h-head u-up there . . .' Carl felt bile and panic rising in a double tide. He gathered his voice to yell for Billy.

Johan spoke to him.

'Hey, Carl, howya doin'?'

A throat couldn't speak, buried in brick. Carl's locked tight also. What madness was this, that a disembodied head should attempt to hold a conversation and get away with it?

'F – f,' Carl almost said. 'F – uh – kk—'

'Oh, come on . . . Carrrlll. Let's be friends. Heyyy – shake hands.'

The white lump of skin and hair and bone that was Johan's head wobbled on its perch. Now Carl could see that this was not the end of the creature. The whole wall was alive with rippling green skin, and things like great coiling ropes were dropping down from the roof and the other walls . . . How big was this sonofabitch?

Carl had no time to scream. Inside a second, a tendril tip touched his face with a lover's tenderness: another twenty more wove a net around his body.

Then the whole huge canopy of flesh pulled away from the wall and kited down to enfold its prey, like a vast octopus hunting in a deep and lonely sea.

A half hour went by. Ozzie's cassette ended. He sat on, listening to the static hiss of empty tape, the click of the machine, then silence.

'Welcome back,' Billy said, his smile lit by flames.

'Some fuckin' great tracks on there!' Ozzie lifted his fist. He felt good, felt bursting with optimism. The music had melded with Anna's thoughts to reassure him that everything was going to be OK. There was danger, sure, and maybe death: but there were more things in heaven and earth than he'd ever dreamed of. It was a universe of wonders, and he was tapped into it now!

'I think Carl's buggered off, Oz,' Billy said.

'He wouldn't do that.' Ozzie sounded sure, and guessed inside himself that Carl was dead by now. It was time. This was the hour that Anna had prophesied.

'Go look for him,' Ozzie suggested. 'I'll be OK.'

'Well, if you're sure.' Billy picked up the shotgun, perhaps guiltily, since he'd be leaving Ozzie without it.

'Go. I'll see you soon.'

Billy went out with a final wave and Ozzie waited for what was going to happen. He was not scared any more now, because the proof that Anna had given him was more complete and more profound than any she'd shown to the others ... Sure, their cures by her hand were wonderful enough; Billy had his fractured skull mended, Johan his gashed artery healed: Carl's arms were broken, and Anna had made them whole again, and strong. That should've been enough evidence for any man, magic enough for a messiah. Ozzie's mind had been fuzzed about what she'd done for him; it was a muddle, confused. Then one night Anna had reminded him and the others swore to the truth of it ...

The concert had been brilliant, the crowd responsive to the band's every move and melody. A great atmosphere, until the end when trouble flared amongst a knot of people; angry violence that grew like a whirlpool in the streams of rock fans leaving the hall. Ozzie remembered some little weaselly kid getting drawn in, pitched against a punk who was twice his size and just itching for a fight with anyone and everyone.

Ozzie had known that his heroic gesture would be futile, mere theatricality, but he couldn't stand to see folks standing idly by while this little squirt got his face kicked in.

He stepped between predator and prey, trying to look tough and confident even though his knees were buckling.

Ozzie never quite knew how it happened, but suddenly before he could react, pain like fire had burned up from his belly, a red flower of agony blooming throughout his body. He watched his own blood gush out over his jeans and put his hands there as though to cup it in. He fell and thought then that somebody was hitting him with a cricket bat over and over and over ... But it was only the pain of the stabbing, each piercing hurt a beat of his heart, another rush of blood pumped out steaming into the evening air.

Screams and confusion, the peripheral accoutrements of his dying. He saw, hazily, faces looking down at him in horror and pity ... He felt like he was sinking through his own body, growing distant from it. Down and down towards darkness.

This is the highway to hell, Ozzie thought as the red sun dimmed inside him and set. And I'm walking it all the way.

He died.

There was no denial of that simple truth. Plenty said he just couldn't have, but Ozzie knew that whatever happens after a life is over, had happened to him. He'd died. There had been no dreams, and no awareness. Maybe in the timelessness of death, he might have reached some other state beyond the ultimate limbo of darkness that spanned the space between his last heartbeat—

—and the next.

The ambulance wasn't here yet. The crowd had thinned and the uniformed security men who hadn't done their job that night were milling around snapping instructions to the morbidly curious, telling them roughly to push off.

Ozzie surfaced once more into his brain, stepped back into life and opened his eyes. Nearby, a kid whose name he later learned was Carl, was arguing with the security guys that it was the injured boy's girlfriend and they couldn't send her away . . .

Ozzie turned his head and saw Anna. Her hands were pressed to the rips in his stomach. For a crazy second he thought maybe she was inside him, mending him from within.

The pain ebbed anyway, though he was still weak from blood loss and he needed a transfusion and two days in a hospital bed to get well. The doctors there treated him for shock: they could not explain his low blood count, for there was not a mark on him. Anna and the boys came to see him twice a day during his stay, and, by the end of that time, she was his girlfriend as much as she was Johan's and Billy's and Carl's.

I'd die for you any time, Ozzie said later. Now, he was being called upon to do that very thing.

He heard the killer enter the building. A thin creaking sound somewhere above alerted him to a skylight being forced. Ozzie wondered if Billy was dead now, or if the killer would deal with him afterwards?

He tossed some more paper and sticks on the fire, which blazed up to show the mould-riddled ceiling crawling with black monsters.

They were beyond description – a multitude of heads and jaws and flailing arms, all sprouting from an evil, crawling matrix of flesh that was somehow suspended against gravity. It was just one creature, mimicking many.

Ozzie dragged out a firebrand he had under his blanket, dipped it in flame and hurled it at the moving mass.

A long red arm looped out and caught it, brought it close to a face that was a caricature of Carl's.

'You're going to diieee – Ozzie!' The tone held a pit viper's venom.

'Fuck you, asshole,' Ozzie replied without passion.

'You'll die – because she has tainted you. In you lies a fragment of her – and so – the whole – of the Comm – unity. Inside every – atom – there exists the – template – of the entire – universe.'

'Then you can't kill me. You can't wipe out every atom!'

'Oh yesss – I can. The Kin are weak. Now. At the start – of the – new cycle – I can obliterate our – curse.'

'Eat shit,' Ozzie said. A hundred misshapen mouths opened up to laugh at him.

Ozzie fitted his earphones, turned up the volume to full and pressed the switch to Play.

The Kin Slayer, with a whim, sent a part of itself down to destroy him.

Billy heard the scream and ran back, kicked in the boards and fired both barrels into the darkness. By the dual momentary flash he saw – something. A crowd of demons gathered around the dismembered remains of Ozzie. He thought it was Ozzie, at least.

In an ecstasy of fumbling he broke the gun and searched in his pockets for more shells.

Johan walked up and gently took it away from him. Billy saw that his friend was joined by a fleshy tube to the seething mass that filled the floorspace and extended upwards to the roof. He shrieked like a terrified child.

High up, a light came on. It was the AA special offer multi-purpose lamp, held by a raven's talon.

It cast a sidelight on Ozzie's face. A face that was as big as a car, and melting as it moved.

'*Fuck you, Asshole!*' The face yelled in booming cathedral tones.

And dropped down to feed.

Anna felt them die, every one of these poor human boys who, each in his own way, was lonely and had needed her. She doubted if they could have survived according to their own parameters, among their own kind, let alone with her help. Ah, well, she had conferred a sort of immortality upon each, according to the way of the Kin. That way said: whatever the Community touches, it keeps as part of itself. For, as well as flowing liquid-like along the tidal flood of a planet's life-fields, the Kin remembered every form they had ever encountered and copied. Nothing was lost. Only when the very last molecule of the Beast was destroyed were the massed souls of the Kin obliterated, and that creature ended.

And that was something she was determined would not happen. The Slayer was strong, of flesh and of purpose, but the irony of its being was that while it lived, it too carried the data to create a million species: Noah's Ark in bone and blood. Only by annihilating itself also, having swept the Earth clean of brethren, could it achieve the purity of its aim.

Anna waited for the last echoes of Billy's screaming to die in her mind. Their deaths had been terrible, but swift at least. And there would be a rebirth. Oh, yes. And a reckoning before the night was over.

For a moment, and incredibly, waves of sorrow and of rage crashed across Anna Fuller's being. She smiled, knowing she had inherited more from humankind than their cumbersome anatomy. It helped to explain the driving force of her enemy as it cut its way through flesh towards her: the Slayer too was motivated by more than the Community's urge to survive – or was it, in the end, by less?

Whatever, her nemesis would be here soon. She must make haste to prepare.

Anna walked to the stairs and listened.

Above, she could hear breathing, which paused for long moments between times, as though Steiger also was trying to catch some faint sound.

'Kevin? Are you there . . . ?'

She needed to call twice more before Steiger appeared on the landing and came slowly down, although his gaze kept drifting back.

'Strange.'

'What is it?'

'I thought I heard crying. In the attic. But I don't see how . . . I can't – quite – remember . . .'

She had hated to deceive him, but the presence of Steiger's mother would merely have added a further complication to the plan. Apart from that, in readying Oz for the part he had to play, Anna was required to infuse him with something of herself; an ability to change when it became necessary, a strength of will to make that possible, a hunger equal to the needs of his new body . . . It would take the Slayer time to set the fire in the shop and burn out every last fragment of what it had found there. Ozzie lived complete in a billion cells, and all of them had to be destroyed.

'Don't worry about it, Kevin.' Anna took his head in

her hands, turned it gently and kissed him, so camouflaging an utterly non-human act with the most familiarly human of gestures.

'Now?' He said it for her.

'Yes,' she agreed softly. 'It's time. You have everything?'

'Money, my papers, your bundle . . .'

'Lie low, Kevin. And when you go back to your work – remember.'

'I know what to do.'

'Then goodbye, and take care.'

He did not linger, but opened the front door quickly and walked away without looking back, carrying as he did the future of the Community under his arm.

In the quietness of the house, Anna breathed a sigh of relief. Another human trait she had inherited from her time among them.

She climbed the stairs and went into the back bedroom, leaving all the houselights burning below. She sat on the bed, swung her legs up and lay there, acquiescing to the nature of her breed.

It happened swiftly. She felt the need grow within her and press for release. A final cry, a closing of eyes . . .

And Anna Fuller gave birth from every pore.

Midnight came and went without incident. The time was well past one o'clock when the killer turned the corner and walked along the empty pavement to the Steiger household. Beyond the rooftops the air glowed pink from a distant fire. No one nearby was awakened by the wailing of fire engines.

Lights blazed from one house along the terraced row. Here, the killer paused, checked his bag, and hurried down the side path to the backyard. Anna would recognize him, he knew: his features held a little of Carl, a little of Billy; he had Ozzie's mop of hair and Johan's handsome smile. Had their memories too, and knew the layout of the house and that the son, Steiger, would probably be in there and waiting.

The killer was not troubled. He had come through too much to be thwarted in this, his final night's work. There was this one to take care of, and one more – he could feel her echoes in his head, not far away; close to the Western Road, in fact, the site of his recent 'accident'. Well, no matter. He would destroy her human companion at the same time and thus be doubly avenged.

He stared up at the wall, stained green and black by a spillage from broken guttering. Fifteen feet up was the window he sought. An easy matter to lift himself that distance and peer inside . . .

For once in his long and eventful life, the killer was taken by surprise. Keven Steiger, with a fury, lunged at him in a blade-shower of glass. A bar of metal followed, slamming deep into the Slayer's head and almost knocking him back into darkness.

His nervous system, based ephemerally on human patterns, registered the agony. The Slayer roared and exploded outwards in a rage of shapes. Steiger staggered back, tried to swing the bar a second time: it was snatched by a nightmare claw, twisted into an abstract and flung away.

The killer retaliated with horn and tooth, melting itself around deep racial memories of satanic dread. Hell came in through the shattered window, ignored the feeble flames that Steiger was attempting to fan, took him up in a crowd of wetly glinting limbs, and ripped him apart like a message that no longer had any meaning.

220

Across the landing in the next room, Anna sensed the passing of the part of herself that she'd sacrificed, to make the killer think that Kevin Steiger was now destroyed. With luck, and in his haste to obliterate Anna's sister and his own, he would not spot the deception. She braced herself, easing back into the euphoria of creation that was the point around which the universe pivoted.

The Slayer, human-seeming again but bristling with the urge to transform, kicked open the door and stood naked on the threshold. The skin of his shoulders and chest lapped across with changing colours; his ribcage bones heaved under their muscle. He had never felt as powerful as this. And yet, watching Anna's act of birthing, was never so powerless as now.

Bizarre beyond human understanding, yet beautiful in the killer's eyes; he watched the emergence of creatures out of the matrix. Butterflies in a delicate spectrum rose from the wreckage of Anna's mouth. A cupped hand, disembodied and lying on the worn carpet, held a mouse in its palm, the tiny animal formed with a clockmaker's precision. The stump of the arm oozed a black and yellow snake, which licked its tongue at the killer's proximity and spat with a venom that was surely Anna's own.

The mass on the sagging bed quivered, and a human head appeared, wet-haired in its first moment of being.

The killer realized he had waited long enough, mesmerized by the wonder of what he was seeing. This was the clean and pure reason for the Kin's existence: it had seeded a thousand worlds this way, and lived hidden on a million others. It was, perhaps, ultimately the most successful form ever to evolve – by the very nature of its formlessness. It could, and would, spread everywhere throughout the cosmos; a living network of uncountable creatures that all belonged to the One. It was the most beautiful, the most terrifying of visions.

The killer hurried back for his bag, returned with its contents and began sloshing petrol over floorboards and walls.

Home felt a million miles away to McAuliffe. He had never been so wretched. Despite all of the promises made to him, despite all of the reassurances, his mortal side thought only of death and its imminence. His head, like a clifftop castle, was besieged by visions. He saw once again the curvaceous hills of Leadmoor blotched with October bracken; the empty skeleton of the village itself like an abandoned scatter of shells on a forgotten beach. The great beast beneath the ground had gathered in its children in readiness for oblivion. It lay, waiting, using the last of its strength to live long enough to witness the outcome of Christine's bid for new life . . .

She leant against McAuliffe, shivering a little. A yard from where they sat, a pile of oily rags burnt and smoked with a greasy light, barely illuminating the black mud that formed the floor. Certainly the light failed to reach the brick boundaries of this underground place; some kind of chamber where generators were once housed, perhaps, or where fuel was once stored.

It was deafeningly quiet here apart from the fitful snap and hiss of the smouldering cloth; quiet enough for McAuliffe's concentration to catch glimpses of cars and men arriving at Leadmoor. He thought of the policeman who had trailed them, and guessed it was his word that had led to this betrayal.

McAuliffe smiled. No betrayal as far as the cop was concerned. His job was to root out the filth of evil as he saw it, to catch the serial killer while making sense of the monstrosities he left behind. The policeman imagined he was engaged in a struggle with death: McAuliffe knew there was more of life in the telling of the story.

'Pe – ter . . .' Christine's whisper lay flat and listless on the dank air. There's still her, McAuliffe realized. And we're together. I have brought her to a place where we have at least a chance of a tomorrow . . .

She held his thought as it passed by, and huddled up to him. McAuliffe turned in the gloom and kissed her cold lips, from which the Community broke in all its frightened singing.

A heart attack. Clean and simple and swift. Doctor Marius's body did not have a mark on it when the night guard found him, slumped against the wall of the cold-room with his eyes still open. There were no signs of struggle, or of forced entry into the building. He had died, so the phrasing went, of natural causes. The only mystery, if such it was, lay in the fact that one of the big specimen jars was empty. But then, Marius must have had a reason for that absence. The guard didn't bother to mention it in his report.

Scobie sat in his office at the station, his clothes and hair rumpled and smelling of stale cigarette smoke. Somewhere else in the building, Carter was busy overseeing the search of Clayton for – Scobie knew not what. Not any more. His quarry had become ghostlike as well as elusive. A few days ago – but it seemed like for ever! – Scobie had believed he was chasing the dragon's tail. Now, that beast had vanished into dark mythology, taking all common sense with it. Clayton was being used for something that Scobie couldn't fathom even now: the killings, these monstrous appearances, the fires . . . perhaps even Marius's gentle passing – must all be linked. But how? And why? Could it have been as Scobie believed, some kind of infiltration by beings not human – beings vast and cool and unsympathetic?

Scobie rubbed at itchy, red eyes, not allowing himself to weep for his old friend. He'd had enough, though knew that more was to come. His hunger had been for information, for leads; but this week had brought a glut of blood and slaughter in its ugliest clothes. Now he wanted sleep and a drink and a good meal . . . On second thoughts, never mind the good meal – and he could hit the sack when this was over.

He switched off his desk lamp, left the office and walked down to the ground floor room that housed the R & R facilities of the Division. A couple of years ago there'd been a dartboard and a scatter of steel-framed, formica-topped tables. Then someone had the bright idea of bringing in a fruit machine. Within three days, it was jammed – not malfunctioned: the tech who came out to repair it said it was crammed full of money. The profits from that one machine had over the months brought the R & R room new wallpaper and carpets, a full-size snooker table, some video games, a colour TV and stereo . . . Scobie chuckled. It sounded like the haul of a game show winner. And it did provide something of a home from home . . .

There was also an honesty bar tucked away in a corner cupboard. Nobody was that honest that the contents of the tin moneybox ever paid for the drinks that were bought in, but everyone, Scobie included, made a token gesture for conscience's sake.

He opened the cupboard doors, dropped a couple of quid into the box and took out two cans of bitter and the whisky bottle. He snapped the ringpull of one can, half-filled a plastic tumbler with Scotch, and walked through into the washroom to top-up with tap water.

He went and sat at a table by a window. It gave him a view of the nice upsloping lawns of the station grounds, with some bushes beyond bordering the road: a kind of green oasis in the middle of Clayton's bricks and grime.

Scobie tipped back half of his whisky-and-water, relishing the warmth down to his stomach. He swigged from the can, fizzed the beer around his mouth and swallowed.

He'd been alone in the room, but now someone else was there.

Scobie turned and saw a kid standing by the door: late teens, scruffy, looking kind of wasted. He jolted, thinking for a second it was Davies . . . There was something about him . . . But the fleeting similarity was gone even as he noticed it.

The kid was carrying a dirty holdall, which he put down at his feet.

'Hi, I want to help you,' he told Scobie. 'My name's Ozzie.'

McAuliffe drank. Then a little more – but not so much that he was unable to articulate his desires and then fulfil them. It was absurd, of course, that in this drear hole in the earth, beneath the abandoned railyards, with a being beside him whose girl-shape was one facet of a complex crystal, he should want her with such heat. But now he put down the much-travelled bottle of Auchentoshan, asked and then reached for her.

Christine smiled, oddly, as many passions within her contended. If he was about to witness what few of his breed had ever seen, then he deserved what he wanted of her. She stripped herself, and then him, as McAuliffe's mouth hung slackly open. She was still perfect in his eyes, the whole world to him. And so they made love quickly and urgently in the chill and dark, with her leading and him following, obedient in her hands like the clay that all men were in truth.

Soon afterwards, as McAuliffe drifted in a half-doze, he heard a sound that startled him out of sleep. He shrugged off his blanket and turned in the gloom to see.

The fire had dimmed to little more than the faintest of glows wreathed in greasy smoke. Having been hot inside her an hour ago, he was cold again now and frightened.

'Christine?' He whispered the name, not so much to avoid waking her, but afraid in case that identity had long since been outgrown.

She stirred. Her arm flopped across him like a heavy timber, much larger and more powerful than it had been before. It's happening, he thought, and believed that he might cope with this horror and accept it for the wonder it was . . . But then came the crash of minds not his own, the haunting telepathy of the Kin as they contemplated their destruction and a new life, in the same moments.

McAuliffe's inner eye swam with impressions of Leadmoor. He was unsure through whose eyes he watched. Midnight swarmed with fireflies, jiggling playfully in the huge darkness, flaring and guttering like sparks, but all moving relentlessly closer . . .

Many men, armed with ignorance and fire, were climbing out of the valley.

Christine's concentration now was intense. She was following the old wisdoms of the Community and of the personality she had formed as this individual. Unlike poor Bruce, she would not become a Pandora's Box flung wide, powerless against the Slayer. Her control would be rigid – and also, she had McAuliffe as her defence.

How can I help you? he asked her now with a blade of thought stabbed desperately into her head. Tears were running down his face. The cold air was rank with the stink of the guttering fire. She wanted warmth, she wanted light; but these were beyond his resources. At the very least, for the next few minutes, she wanted his company.

I will not leave you, she reassured him, pinning the centre of her attention on the memory of his face. We are safe, McAuliffe: there is just one way into this chamber, and the soil above is rich in nourishment. I can survive. I can return to you . . .

He understood what she was promising: that her transformed flesh could spawn another Christine Lamb, complete and intact. There would be no difference; McAuliffe could have the girl and the glory both.

It happened in all the best fairytales, he told himself cynically.

Her thought-voice wavered. She groaned aloud. There was a snapping sound, a bursting.

Protect me. Guard me until my flesh brings me back again. Ah! Yes! Together always. Life anew!

You know I'll stay with you! His mouth was redundant: words anyway could never capture the depth of his feeling. You know I'll stay! But he debated how much of a lie he was telling.

He put out his hand as he heard the ripping of cloth. It was futile to seek her now. Something very large and wet and muscular bumped against him.

McAuliffe backed off.

Scobie felt quite calm, but mildly annoyed that this kid's

appearance, and what he had to say, sobered him up so
bloody effectively. Suddenly the pieces of the crazy jigsaw
had fallen together to make a picture from Dante: the
compass needle swung away from Peter McAuliffe –
the schoolteacher was incidental – towards this flint-eyed
weirdo with his bag of tools and the story he told. It
rambled, it was filled with hate and dark and confusion –
but enough substance to make it the truth. And so, while
what Scobie wanted to do was run, cowering into the
night, what he actually did was follow procedure and call
a constable to escort this boy down into the cells.

He made a couple of phone calls. One, internal, to
Sergeant Carter to call in the biggest patrol cops he could
think of; then, to break out enough small arms for each
cop, and never mind the damned red tape. Next, get in
touch with the fire brigade and have them stand by ... If
Scobie was right, then this kid's presence was always followed by fire. He might yet see Clayton gutted before the
morning.

Scobie's second call was to Brian Haskins, Deputy
Assistant Commissioner of the Regional Force, whom he
reached after twenty minutes and some complicated patch-
ing-through by the switchboard staff. Haskins was the
highest rung of the ladder that Scobie could hope to reach
in the time he felt he had left. While the contact was being
arranged, he sifted what 'Ozzie' had told him – and what
he'd garnered himself since the start of this nightmare –
sharpened it up into some kind of coherence and appended
a brief list of suggestions for action. These suggestions
started with a request to fence Clayton off from the rest
of the world using military means, but stopped short of
alerting and alarming the Government over what was happening here. But they didn't stop far short, so that even as

he spoke, Scobie knew what kind of impression he was creating, and what Haskins' response was likely to be.

He wasn't disappointed.

When Carter arrived at the office, Scobie took him down to see Ozzie. The cell was guarded by the largest policeman Scobie had ever seen, looking pretty fearsome with his night-stick and pistol, but more so because of the shit duty he'd been handed as an extra towards the end of his shift. He stood smartly as Scobie appeared, but gave him a look that, if it were translated into physical action, would end in Scobie's swift castration.

Scobie ignored the glare and stared through the door-hatch into Ozzie's bare cell.

The kid was sitting on the bench against the far wall, talking to something. It might have been his hands. They were lying in the folds of the loose overcoat the boy wore – and had been wearing since his arrival. Scobie had removed the toolbag, but not bothered with Ozzie's clothes . . . Tiredness, that belter of Scotch, or just plain slipshod work . . . What the hell, the mistake had been made and God knows what the boy had concealed in those pockets.

'Stay here,' Scobie told his sergeant, and indicated for the guard to unlock the door.

He stepped inside, with Carter a pace behind him; and was profoundly glad of the man's company.

The mental blow of flame flung McAuliffe to the ground. Black semi-liquid filth filled his mouth and nostrils: he turned with a gasp and strained to see in the utter darkness, while, close by, the brute that was bigger than a house thrashed and yelled with a hundred voices.

Beyond the physical nearness of Christine's horror,

McAuliffe's mind smelt the Solway air, felt stiff moorgrass beneath skin that was not his own. A thousand new eyes opened to show him seagulls and stars, a moon blurred by draperies of smoke and rising fires. Human silhouettes with their machinery poured petrol into every throat in the hill, and charred further anything that tried to come out. Eyes closed and shrivelled: more eyes came fluidly into being so that these agonies could be known and remembered.

McAuliffe floundered away, mortified. This was no momentous meeting of great races or minds over gulfs of space, as his juvenile dreams would have wished. All his boyhood long he had rehearsed what it would be like for mankind to make first contact with an intelligent universe ... And never once had it stunk of scorching flesh.

He felt the shame of it, and the rage against his own: but other emotions also tore into him; echoes from what remained of Christine and her Kin, a teribble sorrow mingling with hope and desire and feelings too fine to name.

Something fell close by with a thump. Warm wetness spurted at McAuliffe's face and chest ...

A new pain flared over all, blocking the image of Leadmoor's hills. It was the Community's heart staggering to a stop at last, withering in a fire that was too much to bear. Christine, vulnerable in her embroidery of creation, was suddenly unable to direct the force.

There was great activity nearby, and McAuliffe inched away, step by invisible step, until he felt slimy brick press against his back. The blackness grew full of twitterings and scurrying things: small specks of life flittered at his face: heavier organisms splashed in the cellar mud. A mouth laughed, low, unhinged. Another voice was speaking what was not quite language. Children with glass in their mouths were crying, their sobs driven by the same lungs.

A weight slid its length over McAuliffe's foot.

If Scobie didn't know better, he'd have sworn the kid was tripping on something strong and fast-acting. He spoke and behaved as though his eyes were seeing some other drama, hardly seeming aware of the D.I.'s presence at all. Ozzie kept mumbling about voices and the sea of drowning, of burning. But wasn't this better than the slow indignity of decay, he wondered in a whisper. The angels have fallen at last into ashes . . .

'Ozzie—' McAuliffe touched the boy's arm, and drew back. Even through the thick serge material he felt the heat. But was the kid ill? He was burning up, feverish – hallucinating, quite probably.

'The rivers and ways have carried us here: we have learned barbarism and selfishness and want . . . The perversity of this failed breed is beneath us—'

'Hey, come on, snap out of—'

'What I did was right,' Ozzie said, fixing Scobie with a look of manic conviction. 'Everything, all of it, was right.'

Scobie smiled. It was a double smile, outwardly reassuring and calming, but fierce inside with triumph. This kid was going to confess. Whether he was the killer or not (but he had the look of one, and his head was full of devils), he was about to admit to murder. Then the matter of what was found on the Western Road would be somebody else's problem. Let the high-ups grow ulcers puzzling over it; that's what they got paid for.

'OK, Ozzie. You were right.' Scobie said it gently and touched that hot sleeve once more. Did the kid have ferrets in his coat, or something? What had moved under the soft pressure of Scobie's palm?

'Of course you don't believe me,' Ozzie said, looking down on the other from his great height of madness. 'Because you don't understand. Anyway, what are words? Policemen need proof.'

Scobie was on the brink of yelling for the duty cop to get his gun out and hurry the fuck up about it – Ozzie was unbuttoning his coat, lifting its tails aside. He pushed his hands to his chest and brought out—

'Jesus Christ . . .' Carter walked over to the corner and threw up tidily in the slops bucket. Scobie felt himself losing it, made a huge effort of self control and managed to stay where he was; his eyes squinted up with disgust at the thing in Ozzie's lap.

Some kind of animal – what was left of one. Greyish. Hairless. It must have been skinned. It was ridged and featureless – but no. No. As Ozzie turned it over a face came into view in the centre of the torso. A baby's limbs waved above the eyes and below the mouth. An ugly sprouting of bristles showed beneath the bottom, yellowish lip. For a second, just for a single chaotic instant, Scobie was reminded of Doctor Marius . . . But then common sense reasserted itself and the resemblance faded away.

'Is this what they really look like?' Scobie thought he knew enough to ask the right question.

'They look like anything they want,' Ozzie said. 'This has nothing to form around. It's out of context.'

'I don't understand that.'

'No.'

There was a silence. Then Ozzie told about the hatching-place which was – he thought about it – which was down in the railway-yards somewhere. That was much bigger. It was an infestation that needed to be destroyed.

'How, Ozzie?'

'Burn it. Burn it down to the core. And this – I want to see it fried also . . .'

It seemed a fair request. Scobie and Carter took the risk of escorting Ozzie out to the neat yard round the back of the station. Carter used some loose bricks there to build up a pit in which to pile papers and burnable rubbish. Ozzie laid the creature down. Immediately it tried to make a mouth with which to plead. Its little flailing limbs moved more quickly as it lay in its cradle, in its pyre, which Scobie doused in spirit and then set light to with a dropped match.

He turned to the boy.

'There's another, you say, down on the wasteland?'

'On the East side, I think—'

'You think! Jesus wept, kid, this is no time—'

'Sir.' Carter intervened. 'It's no problem. We can get plenty of men down there and do a sweep search; cordon off the place. Maybe Ozzie, if he came with us, could remember more clearly when he saw the thing . . .'

Scobie smiled through clenched teeth.

'Are you after my job or what, Sergeant?'

'Pardon me sir, but – not on your fucking life!'

The long legend was almost over. Ozzie closed his eyes in the speeding police car and watched visions more vivid than anything this mundane and pastel planet could ever offer. In its death, the Community was reiterating its life; releasing this last gift of memory to whatever fragment of itself still lived to receive it. Well, this time there would be no phoenix: the Kin's ashes would be buried for ever, dead and staying dead.

Scobie had brought with him Sergeant Carter, his usual driver McNab (who was either fearless or psychotic at the wheel, Scobie had never decided), and the bulky cop who'd guarded Ozzie's cell. His name was Wilton. Every officer on foot or with wheels had been alerted. Scobie meant the alarm he raised to *be* just that. Let Haskins fire him tomorrow and pick up the pieces himself . . .

McNab swung the car round the Fairway and sent it bulleting through the middle of the town. And then there were more flickering blue lights, ululating sirens. A fire-engine pulled out of a side-street and joined the patrol cars in their panic rush to the south.

'We'll be in time,' Ozzie muttered with furious glee. 'I know we will . . .'

Nobody bothered to answer him.

The police Escort slewed around the junction of Western Road and Cairncross Road, its lights clawing across the weathered red-brick of the abandoned BR shunting yards and repair sheds. Skeletal girders looked rib-like set against the low-slung city neon cast upon the clouds. Scobie got pressed against Ozzie by the force of the car's controlled skidding – and beneath the loose overcoat he felt the rippling of flesh growing eager to break free from its bonds.

McNab, despite his driving years, almost wrote the motor off when Scobie screamed. As it was, the car mounted the kerb and had its offside front wing torn away in a spray of sparks against the wall . . .

Inside the cab, the damage was somewhat greater.

Ozzie rode the marvel of change for what he knew was the last time. The Animal was dead. He, and what he'd come to kill, were all that remained. The great heart at Leadmoor ceased and stilled blood filled the streams and the rivers. And even though he'd wanted it – made it his life's purpose – the Slayer understood briefly the meaning of Community, a sharing he had never comprehended before.

It made him smile . . .

That smile extended sideways to the left, and Ozzie used its momentum to wish for teeth with which he decapitated Scobie before any gun could be drawn.

His hands erupted into loose cords, whipping spray around the cab. A bone from his right forearm continued growing, straight through Carter's disbelieving eye. McNab went past fear. He sat in his own hot excrement while his mind, like a mouse under the shadow of the cat, scurried uselessly, wondering what to do . . .

The Slayer whipped something like red leather around the driver's neck and throttled him swiftly. Wilton was still struggling for his gun, then thought better of it and slammed open the passenger door.

It was easy now for the Slayer to slide his thoughts down into a forelimb that was hot and steaming with growth: the blades he wanted were instantaneous and scalpel sharp . . .

Wilton shrieked midway through his lunge for freedom, and half of him anyway reached the pavement and began to crawl – one yard, two, before all the blood spilled out of him and he died.

The killer heaved himself over the officer's divided remains towards the wasteland, dragging the bubbling mass of his body on like a sack of all his world's possessions . . .

The danger was close, McAuliffe sensed. The part of him that was Kin throbbed and pulsed in every cell, telling him this secret. He knew that if he had melded any more closely with the Community, then no splinter of his consciousness or flesh would have survived. Christine – he realized with a piercing loss – was beyond his help. Maybe within him enough information remained to recreate his dreams, someday, perhaps . . .

But there would be no other days unless he could escape and vanish, anywhere away from Man's meddling and the Slayer's fury.

McAuliffe felt for the chamber's one exit; found the way with its dank downward breeze; ran-crawled along it towards the light.

He emerged into a drizzly mist of rain that had come on in the last hour. The haze was soaked orange with sodium glow. The night was chilly and full of looming shadows—

One of which moved out into McAuliffe's line of sight.

I have come for you, Un-Man, the killer said softly; words rich with nuance that reached McAuliffe both through the air and as a tumble of thoughts.

He recognized the Slayer for what he was: McAuliffe's killer too, unless some action was taken quickly and intelligently. He wondered how much of the human inhabited the body that stood before him; a body that had gathered itself back into mobile form for this encounter. But McAuliffe guessed he was ready to come apart at the seams due to the dying of his Community at Leadmoor, and yards away in the clay under his feet. The killer's very thoughts were shaking.

And I am ready for you, Un-Kin, McAuliffe replied. He felt his rage rising. Christine was a dead echo: all he had ever been promised, this creature had ended. There was no future for McAuliffe now, unless he coud forge it himself from the destruction of his adversary.

The Slayer chuckled, trying out his ripper's menace on one who had, by now, seen far too much to be moved. McAuliffe laughed back, but then gasped at the changes billowing in the foggy air . . .

The killer's head bulged and grew hooded, a fungal eruption from his skull that split to show plates of armour and spikes like timbernails hammered up from beneath. He roared through a throat that boiled around his neck, flung out his weaponry of jaw and blade, and surged forward.

McAuliffe shrieked, but it was another making the sound – some distant relation watching from afar. The Kin-face he'd kept hidden rose to the surface and blew it asunder. New sets of reflexes forged a tough shield of flesh that fended the Slayer's first attack, and primaeval jawbones that bit in return.

This was how it must once have been, McAuliffe thought as the other backed off, hacked limb swinging. In the early days of the Kin's beginnings, pain and blood and the screams of the swamp-forests were the world's hallmarks. It had been so on Earth; could be so everywhere.

It was amusing to think that Man in all his arrogance believed he knew the universe from its germs to its galaxies. But the far corners were always hidden, weren't they? And some corners crept closer, bringing their shadows to frighten children in the night. So it was that the cosmos remained, not too vast to know, but too deep . . .

Yet here was simplicity indeed – high ideals reduced to severing necks and putting out eyes. The one left standing at the end made all of the laws.

The Slayer came again, bursting forward in a splay of eyes and teeth, its germplasm sliding even as it ran on tyrannosaur legs, as though selecting from a mental array of torture instruments. McAuliffe parried and blocked, then wrapped his impossible arms around the killer's muscular body. They both bellowed thunderously, each invading the other's boundaries.

McAuliffe took a last look at the sky before grey bat-wings arched across. He could not fathom their origin – his, or his enemy's?

Then he sought his foe's flesh and ate his way in.

Panic had woken in the town, shaking souls free of their apathy. Rumours and garbled eyewitness reports spread like the shockwave of an explosion. Fear detonated in every mind.

The word was going around the police station that there was chaos on Western Road. Scobie had left some brief note with the duty sergeant, but where the hell was he now to give further information? Why wasn't he responding on the RT?

The low-key night routine was now in shatters: men were hurrying, white-faced, going nowhere, as hearsay rampaged through. Haskins was brought out of bed again to the phone, where he listened for a couple of minutes to the duty sergeant's increasingly desperate babbling.

'Sergeant Delgado – it is Delgado, isn't it?'

'Yessir—'

'I want you to put out a general alert to all cars in the area to—'

'Sir, with respect, that's been done. I've got townsfolk clogging the streets on the southern side; I've got a report of men down at the railyards. There are several subsidiary accidents caused by some kind of panic measure to evacuate that part of Clayton—'

'Sergeant—'

'And there's fighting. Something appalling is ... Bakker's just brought me another flimsy on it. Bloody hell! These things must be—'

Haskins had had enough. He spoke sharply and briefly, using the kind of language a man in Delgado's state of tension was likely to respond to. The sergeant shut up.

In that minute, Haskins had felt his mental balance tip from scepticism to some kind of belief. What Scobie said must have had a core of truth. Delusion maybe, but if so it was contagious.

He told the sergeant he'd be driving directly to the site of the incident, and that – unofficially – he wanted Delgado to organize a defence: semi-automatic weapons, petrol – anything short of taking this beyond the town, for the time being.

Delgado reminded his superior that there'd be hell to pay afterwards.

Haskins said he was willing to pay it.

Defeat or victory were equally impossible. It was like the mythological battle of dragons, entwined for all eternity in a struggle when the outcome could only be further struggle.

They fought flesh with flesh, a kaleidoscope of transformation that brought dark memories out into the damp night air. Both McAuliffe and the Slayer understood this predicament but could not, now, withdraw. Indeed, the limits of what they were became blurred as the minutes passed. Rain streamed from powerful flanks that might have belonged to either creature. Teeth locked on teeth and bit down, claws raked an opponent's flesh, but both contenders felt the pain. They'd met as separate entities but now they were one being. And a million others joined them, voices articulating beneath the roars that the Community could not be ended by conflict among any of its Kin. The million were contained in the One. That was the nature of the beast, ad infinitum.

Nevertheless, McAuliffe's conscious mind remained whole as he delved and slashed in the maelstrom of living meat. He saw many humans thronging on the edge of his vision; and big vehicles – tankers – pumping liquid over the churned black mud of the wasteland. There were lights, dozens of them. Torchlights. Arc lamps. They showed him the entrance to the cavern within which Christine's spawn had erupted. Machine guns clattered flatly on the air. A team of men were drawing up a thick hose to the cavern mouth . . .

McAuliffe understood, yet could not fight the impulse to thrash and struggle away . . .

But the Slayer knew, too, and spent its whole strength delving itself deeper into McAuliffe's body.

Only half aware of his own danger, McAuliffe watched a solitary fireman hurry up to the tunnel entrance. They were going to do here what had been done at Leadmoor. Then, something tall and monstrous with abnormally long arms winged with green membranes leapt out. Its mouth was a man trap of bone. Its fingers impaled the officer – but the flare in his hand was fizzing.

He screamed, the very ground cried out, as he threw the flare and cascaded flames down the red and pulsing gullet in the earth.

Then there was much activity. With a kind of mass intuition, people knew what to do. They began flinging brands and curses. The land lit up in a curtain, with a roar.

The fire pained him unbearably, but McAuliffe knew it would soon be over, as the Slayer had wanted all along.

The dream of heaven had never gone sour: only his dreams had done that.

He let himself fall back in defeat, relishing the dancing firelight. The flame intensified, a vaporous agony. McAuliffe could smell his own burning.

With a last deliberate thought, he put forth new eyes and saw bulkily suited teams of men vanishing into the smoking tunnel for the final act of cleansing. He reached – he reached for Christine or his memory of her. They were both the same to him now ... Then it was over, and a darkness bloomed that was filled with neither spectres nor stars.

Months passed. What had happened in Clayton lost its razor-sharp focus, became blurred, became embroidered with confusion, as such things always are. The railyards were isolated by a new wall of prefab concrete slabs, topped with barbed wire. The ground was left alone, and sterile. Its burned-out, sour smell was gone by February.

April came by. One dawn brightened on a hazy space of scrub and mud. Spiderwebs glittered among the ungodly wreckage of girders and bricks. The wasteland seemed empty, but this was another of life's illusions. Nearby, a rabbit twitched its nose, unravelling the first smells of the day. A blackbird grew from the shadows of a hawthorn tree. A kestrel peered needle-eyed into the sunrise, caught on the hook of its hunger. It planed off into the chilly spring air, not finding anything of consequence in this strangely soiled ground.

A man stood unnoticed on the edge of the wasteland. He had arrived alone and would leave alone. Most days he came down here, just to look. Just to check for any unnatural changes coming up out of the earth.

Brian Haskins, it must be said, was a changed man. He'd

read enough of poor Scobie's notes, and read through a sufficient number of Doctor Marius's files to put the fear of God into him over what had happened here . . . No, not the fear of God. Haskins smiled. No, not that. It terrified him to think that if this thing broke loose again, or ever again arrived upon the face of the world . . .

He was fifty-three now. Retired in another seven years at most. Safely dead, perhaps, in another twenty after that. Maybe he could live out the rest of his life untroubled by demons.

Haskins spat into the mud then returned to his car.

On his way to the station he almost ran down a teenaged kid who was slouching along, hands in pockets, not looking the hell where he was going! Haskins stamped on the brakes and horn simultaneously. The kid – hair uncut, gold ring in his ear – Haskins knew the type – didn't even stop. He just lifted his finger and carried on walking.

Haskins saw red for a second and was tempted to get out of the car and give this shiftless bastard a mouthful. But then, what would it achieve? Louts like that, dead-end kids on a round trip from gutter to gutter, just had no purpose in life. Nothing you could ever say to them would make any difference.

So he drove on, while Kevin Steiger completed his daily journey to the supermarket.

He'd taken nearly six weeks off, sick-leave after returning to work just once, only for an hour. Goss, the meat department manager, had given him plenty of verbal when he'd got back. Steiger had listened, then wondered why Goss hadn't fired him and kept his replacement on instead?

'Because he was even stupider than you, Kevin! Now get to it, and don't lose any finger-ends in the sausage maker . . . !'

It was one of Goss's old jokes. Never had been funny.

Steiger went about his work. He felt pleased today, like he'd just woken up after a long sleep; or was well now after a difficult illness. He hadn't really been ill, of course: just a bit confused. Things had happened . . . Nightmare things . . . But all that was over now. It was spring and he felt great!

Since the autumn, Steiger had bought himself a flat and put plenty in the bank once the insurance had paid up on his Mum's house. Odd that: he could never remember her dying. Must've happened in the fire . . . Still, he was set up at last and even had a girlfriend . . .

Sharon was OK; went like a jackhammer in bed! But Steiger felt somehow that he dated her not for herself, but because she reminded him of someone else. Who . . . Who also was blonde, blue-eyed, with a smile that tilted just – so . . .

Anna's face came to him like a dream, as though she was standing right in front of him after months apart. Yes – he could even hear her speaking, such gentle and encouraging words.

He obeyed them, remembering the promises they'd both made.

No one was around. Steiger went to the walk-in meat freezer and delved among the crackling-cold bags and sacks in the corner.

He pulled out from under them a small bundle, wiped the sawdust off it and brought it out into the warm.

He let it thaw. Then, at lunchtime, instead of going down to the staff canteen, Steiger took the bundle home and unwrapped it, holding up its contents to the light, the better to see by.

It was miraculous. A little scary. But Steiger knew Anna

would always keep her word. She was like that. He thought to himself, how many other girls would promise you their heart?

And presently, on the sunny windowsill, it began to beat.

Freda Warrington
A Taste of Blood Wine £4.99

1923. Madeline Neville watches as her father fills Parkland Hall with guests for her 18th birthday party. Amongst them is his handsome new research assistant Karl – the man she has already decided will be her husband. Her sister Charlotte has generously agreed to stand aside. Until she sees Karl . . .

For Charlotte, it is the beginning of a deadly obsession. As their feverish passion grows, Karl faces the dilemma he fears the most. For Karl von Wultendorf is a vampire. And only by deserting Charlotte can his passion for her blood be conquered . . .

'Readers in search of the charms of supernatural terror should love it'
RAMSEY CAMPBELL
'Not merely one of the finest fantasy novels of recent years, but one of the finest ever'
BRIAN STABLEFORD
'Romance and dark shadows, lit with glamour and horror'
TANITH LEE
'A talent to watch'
BOOKSELLER

All Pan books are available at your local bookshop or newsagent, or can be ordered direct from the publisher. Indicate the number of copies required and fill in the form below.

Send to: Pan C. S. Dept
            Macmillan Distribution Ltd
            Houndmills Basingstoke RG21 2XS
or phone: 0256 29242, quoting title, author and Credit Card number.

Please enclose a remittance* to the value of the cover price plus: £1.00 for the first book plus 50p per copy for each additional book ordered.

*Payment may be made in sterling by UK personal cheque, postal order, sterling draft or international money order, made payable to Pan Books Ltd.

Alternatively by Barclaycard/Access/Amex/Diners

Card No. ☐☐☐☐☐☐☐☐☐☐☐☐☐☐☐☐☐☐

Expiry Date ☐☐☐☐☐☐

_____

Signature:

Applicable only in the UK and BFPO addresses

While every effort is made to keep prices low, it is sometimes necessary to increase prices at short notice. Pan Books reserve the right to show on covers and charge new retail prices which may differ from those advertised in the text or elsewhere.

NAME AND ADDRESS IN BLOCK LETTERS PLEASE:

....

Name _____

Address_____

_____

_____

_____

6/92